PZYCHE

PZYCHE

Amanda Hemingway

faber and faber

First published in 1982
by Faber and Faber Limited
3 Queen Square London WC1N 3AU
Printed in Great Britain by
Willmer Brothers Limited
Rock Ferry Merseyside

British Library Cataloguing in Publication Data

Hemingway, Amanda
Pzyche
I. Title
823'.914[F]   PR6058.E4918/

ISBN 0-571-11875-5

FOR MY PARENTS

PART I

1

They say that by the time you get to Hiboryn, civilization is running out. Since the invention of timespeed the farthest reaches of the galaxy can be attained within a few units of decelerated time, but the Hiboric Chain lies on the uttermost edge of the twenty-fifth circle, and not many travellers care to spend so long under the necessary controls. In any case, there is nothing very much when you get there. One theorist claimed that as you move farther out towards the edge of the galaxy everything is spread more thinly: the stars and the planets are too far apart, the landscapes are bare and swept by winds that seem to have come from the depths of the void, the airs are thin and the seas shallow, and the living things that survive there tend to be leafless, hairless, and pallid, with unlimited imaginations and indeterminate processes of thought. In the five sun-systems which make up the Hiboric Chain the natives seem to epitomize this idea, spending their time deploring progress and contemplating infinity, which lies incidentally a little too close for comfort, just beyond Ingellan, the Last Star. Although timespeed has brought teeming spaceports, towering skyblocks, and the advance guard of scientific ideology to Hiboryn itself, at the other end of the Chain, in the Outmost System, civilization moves at its own rate, frequently stopping altogether to let a century or two go by unremarked. The oldest traces of human habitation in the entire galaxy are supposed to exist there, and visitors to the Outmost System often have the feeling its Time has grown so ancient the old greybeard can hardly stagger forward from day to day. The natives live mostly on Fingstar and

Ifings (the main habitable planets), devoting themselves to painting masterpieces, writing quotations, and performing the traditional Seven Plays which (they claim) propound, allegorize, or imply the essence of all galactic philosophy. On the other three planets, Gnall, Tzorn and Krake, foreign investors own the mining concessions and finance the occasional archaeological excavation. The Ifingen peoples very rarely mine anything themselves, since they consider science and technology the main causes of progress, and in the Outmost System progress went out of fashion a thousand years ago. The spaceport at Camarest, planet capital of Fingstar, is usually empty but for the odd foreign traveller who got on the wrong spacetrain two systems ago. The people of Ifings and Fingstar all maintain that the only real reason for going away is in order to come back afterwards and talk about it.

Doctor Corazin did not come back. He left Fingstar two years after his marriage to the actress Tnar Meliander, and he did not come back at all. He was a psychospecialist, an acknowledged genius in his field (genius is always acknowledged on Fingstar, even when there is very little there), whose ideas were far beyond the range of scientific proof or practical application and could therefore be regarded as art instead. His theory of territorial violation made people look nervously at each other as they passed in the street, in case they had passed too close, and one enthusiast had even been known to commit suicide after her breast brushed a man's arm in a crowded autocar. Doctor Corazin himself was a solitary man, more interested in psychotypes than in people. He had a high forehead, a low brow, and concave temples, with scanty hair that grew scantier by the year and pale eyes webbed with tiny broken veins, like windows which had cracked but not yet disintegrated. His shoulders were rounded and his fingers thumbed, as though with a constant flicking through files, a kneading of knobs, a correcting of controls. He often wore spectacles. His wife Tnar Meliander was tall and slim and beautiful, with a small round face on the

[12]

end of a long supple neck, green serpentine eyes and dimples under her cheekbones. No one was surprised when he left her.

He went to Krake. The University of Thought on Fingstar awarded him an absentee fellowship, and he installed himself in splendid isolation among the wastelands of the oldest planet in the galaxy, with no other human life on planetface save a mining colony a few miles away. He had his own austracisor, his own (unused) communicator. His library of brainprints was the largest in the world. Whenever a new theory was formulated, he sent it out via the mining colony in a code no one could break. His house, Castle Kray, had smooth eyeless walls and steel towers reaching up towards the moon. He studied the human mind but he never saw a living soul. Except his daughter.

There were two daughters of the marriage. The younger, Tnoe, was not yet born when he left his beautiful wife, so he was only able to take the elder with him. No one knew whether Tnar cried. Her first child grew up never having seen another human being since she left Fingstar, and to all appearances Tnar gave her whole heart to the second. Perhaps she was merely realistic. Somewhere in one of the Seven Plays there was bound to be something about the folly of giving affection when you were not going to get anything in return.

Pzyche was less than two years old when she came to live on Krake. Her child impressions of Fingstar faded very quickly and although she studied galactic geography when she grew older and gazed, faintly unbelieving, at many pictures of green valleys and rainforests, mountains of snow and deserts of sand, the planetface of Krake alone remained real to her. It was an uninspiring place, with vegetation that stayed close to the ground and here and there outcrops of greystone breaking the scant soil and jutting like fractured ribs out of the plain. Beyond Castle Kray the land rose into a distant plateau, low under the sky. Certain impurities in the atmosphere affected the colour of O, the Ifingen sun, so that at dawn and dusk the horizon was rimmed with green and the occasional etiolated cloud formations typical of Krake looked dimly purple. There was no sea. Krake is a dry planet, dry as dust, watered only by a few shallow lakes scarcely deep enough to cover your knees, and rivers that never find the shore, trickling away into subterranean waterfalls and artesian reservoirs far underground. The extent of these reservoirs has never been measured, but it is from there that the moisture comes which makes Krake qualify (narrowly) as a habitable planet. Evaporation occurs through numerous fissures opening onto the reservoirs, and in the heat of the day pale vapours can often be seen rising from cracks in the ground. In the Cold Season, evaporation slows up, and the very earth becomes brittle. At such times Tnar's daughter often thought about the sea. There was a picture of a tidal wave on the computer at home and she would sit staring at it for hours, trying to visualize all that water, not merely lying limply against the rock, but climbing up towards the sky and rushing forward, growling, to envelop whole cities and kingdoms and colonies of men. It was beyond imagination. Eventually she would go off to the hydrant, make herself a drink, and wander through the library in search of an interesting brainprint, concentrating on something which she knew to be real.

She never had any toys. Far away, on Fingstar, little Tnoe played with a theatre of matchwood and gilt and ruined her teeth on sugarfruit and sicklysticks. Pzyche ate meat substitute and vegetables from the austracisor and learned that if you pushed certain buttons on the computer coloured lights went on or off and wiggly lines appeared on the screen. After many weeks of continual experiment she found she could even have a conversation with it, as far as it is possible to have a conversation with a computer. Such discussions were informative when she asked the right questions but where the machine was in ignorance it would lapse into monosyllables and it never inaugurated a new topic or used its imagination at all. There were even times when Pzyche suspected it had no sense of humour. She knew about humour from her reading but it was difficult for her to develop any of her own since her father never made jokes, not even small, dry, pedantic ones, and the computer, in response to her enquiries, merely rattled off a few lines of verse in its flat staccato voice and theorized about the psychology of laughter. Pzyche had a feeling she had missed something essential, a feeling which was not at all new to her, but as there was nothing she could do about it she dismissed the matter from her mind and grew up without laughing at all. Like her mother, she was a realist.

Her education was fairly comprehensive, but there was very little on Krake to which she could apply her learning. She could draw a section through a cyclamen and would watch, fascinated, speeded up film of uncurling tendrils and unfurling petals, but outside her back door there was just the scurvy grass, brown mosses, grey lichens. She was enchanted by the mystery of the bees, but on Krake there were only a few evil varieties of beetle, with horned wing-cases and claws as big as crabs'. If she had been able to study geology she might have done better, since there were rocks in abundance, but geology was not in the computer's repertoire. The Ifingen educational curriculum invariably comprised very little science. Biology, psychology, essential physics (a very narrow field), evolutionary theory, and universal law: that was all. Pzyche's growing mind, unformed and ill-fed, groped here and there like an irresolute amoeba, feeling its way towards the promise of daylight and finding in every direction only darkness. Her natural inclination was scientific rather than artistic, and although she enjoyed the literature of other systems that of her own she found rather hard to understand. Unfortunately, the computer knew very few external works. She watched the Seven Plays (a recording without her mother) and would have found them sterile if she had had any comprehension of artistic sterility. She studied interminable chefs d'oeuvre of Ifingen painters, and wondered if Other People really looked like that, and why so few artists could draw hands, and what was meant by parallelism, angular spherology and primordial

[15]

claristructure (even the computer did not seem able to explain). Her only hope of intellectual expansion seemed to lie in the doctor's library of brainprints. When she was eleven her father at last permitted her to use it, and from then on she channelled all her restlessness into a fever of psychoanalytical experiment, rising needlessly early and working needlessly late, as though her scant suppers and long midnights would make it all important, a part of the universal destiny and the world beyond. In the end, she even came to believe she knew something about people.

There was one other person at Castle Kray. Shortly after Pzyche's seventeenth birthday, an event which was celebrated by the computer sending her an official reminder while her father, who had not received one, entirely forgot, a space capsule from the Inmost System crashed about seven miles away. The computer gave warning of the impending accident and Pzyche saw it from a window: the swift trail of fire streaming earthwards and the blink of white dazzle among the rocks. She went on her own to investigate the wreck. It was the greatest day of her life, or so she thought at the time, stumbling across the plain shivering from head to foot and burning in the chill wind, terrified they would all be dead (she had never seen death), still more terrified they might just be alive. In the event, there was one survivor. It would have been suitably romantic, considering her age and situation, if he had been a good-looking young man with whom she could have fallen violently in love (and vice versa), but life is rarely so well planned. The castaway, though male, was a former waiter on a spaceliner teetering on the verge of retirement, and even Pzyche was conscious of a vague disappointment when she saw his greying temples and the tucks around his mouth. Brought up on the theory of territorial violation, she was reluctant to touch him, at least without his permission, but it was obvious he would have to be moved. Eventually she fetched the Ita Spear (a vintage mark of land-

[16]

movile) and managed to lift him into it. Afterwards, she had to sit down for a while, fighting nausea, but perhaps that was just excitement.

Back at Castle Kray the computer performed a rapid analysis and told her his burns would have to be tended, but Pzyche, doubtful about how her victim would react to having his face and arms handled so intimately, left him alone for a day or two. Presently, she began to fancy she could hear him moaning even in her sleep. One morning she rose in the green dawn feeling reckless and went to him. His flesh was flayed raw in places and leaked pus, and the touch of it filled her with horror, not only her own horror but the horror she imagined for him, the soul-detroying humiliation of having the very plasm of your blood exposed to another human being. However, on the rare occasions when he emerged from semi-consciousness he merely seemed grateful. Pzyche's treatment, as prescribed by the computer, was elementary but effective, and his burns gradually healed. She never spoke to him. For many years she had tried in vain to have a proper conversation with the computer, and now she had a human auditor the art of communicative speech failed her altogether. As for the man, he made odd, shapeless noises of comfort or discomfort, but he never uttered a word. Afterwards, the computer said the shock of the crash had affected his vocal chords. Perhaps if Pzyche had been able to talk to him this paralysis might have worn off, but even in later years, when he had become as much a part of the furniture at Castle Kray as the computer or the Ita Spear, she rarely addressed more than the briefest sentences to him. His name was Goloro; he wrote that down for her. Possibly out of courtesy she wrote down her response too, explaining that he could return to civilization via the mining colony if he wished; but he shook his head. His family were dead or scattered and only the fruitless leisure of retirement awaited him at home, whereas at Castle Kray he seemed to feel he could be of use. He cleaned

[17]

out corners that had never been cleaned out before and polished the Ita Spear with wetleather and attempted, not very successfully, to prepare appetizing meals from the output of the austracisor. Perhaps he thought Pzyche had saved his life, and was filled with due gratitude and devotion. His eyes followed her down the long corridors, warmly, unhappily, as an old man might look at his daughter if she were shut in a tower of glass, far out of reach of both princes and woodcutters, with no knowledge and only the vaguest curiosity about the world beyond her crystal walls.

The years passed, and the mirror in Pzyche's bedroom would have told her she was tall if she had had any conception of relative height. Her hair, which was a sort of dull greeny gold, the colour of old brassware, grew straight and silky and well down her back. Her eyes were her mother's, but colder. Sometimes she wondered if she was beautiful, and what "beautiful" meant. But in the absolute isolation of Castle Kray it did not seem to be very important. She never visited the mining colony. Miners were scientific, and outsiders (some even came from beyond the Hiboric Chain), and Doctor Corazin disapproved. Pzyche, programmed by her father, hardly thought of them as people at all. If she was restless, she did not know it. "The life we lead could conceivably be said to approach perfection," her father informed her once, in a rare moment of communication. "It is people who create suffering, both for themselves and for others. Human beings exist inevitably in disharmony. How could it be otherwise, with the inept compromise of so many different psychotypes, some of whom actively wish to live in discord and most of whom are too unintelligent to care? Only in total solitude can homo sapiens really thrive, his emotions untouched and therefore intact, his territory inviolate, his concentration unbroken. Curious that so few among men have followed in my footsteps, when there is so much room in the universe to be alone. People are cowardly and unimaginative at heart. Fortunately, my dear Pzyche" (as an afterthought he re-

[18]

membered he was talking to his daughter instead of the mono-tape by his bath), "fortunately, I am a great man." And Pzyche may well have believed him, if only because she had nothing else to believe.

2

There were two people standing by Departure Desk C at Spaceport Camarest. They were standing because there weren't any
seats. Desks A and B both had waiting bays with cushioned
benches, but they dealt with standard insystem and outsystem
flights; Desk C was for freightlift passengers, and there were no
seats. Except that it was smaller and not very busy, the spaceport was just like any other. The incoming corridors were lit in
blue, the outgoing ones in green. Neutral areas were pink. Behind Desks A and B, girls in rose-coloured tunics handed over
tickets and baggage cards with a flash of bright plastic teeth.
Behind Desk C, a man in grey overalls said: "Hang on a
minute", and began to look for something he could not find. On
the wall, there was a poster advertising Inter-Planetary Services
luxury spaceliners. The girl found herself looking at it and almost wishing she were there, sitting in the peach-bloom seats
among the sugar-plum cushions and drinking essence of pathé
out of very tall glasses with fluted straws. She had never been
further abroad than Ifings in her life. But Derec was very fond
of looking out at the night sky and pointing to some distant star,
saying: That is Iscys, or Fosces, or Axum, and if you get close
enough it is as bright as our sun and there are worlds turning
round it bigger than Fingstar and many times as populous.

The man in grey overalls found what he was looking for and
stamped a further authorization on her boarding card. There
were four stamps on it already. She also had a disembarkation
card, an exit visa, an entry visa, and an insystem pass card, each
with its proper quota of authorizations. Through a mixture of

sheer determination and influential connections she had managed to obtain them all within a fortnight, and every so often she started to wonder what she had forgotten, and whether it would be a relief when she could not go after all. Beside her, the other traveller at Desk C accepted his boarding card from the man in grey overalls, tucked it away in the front pocket of his shoulder-bag, and leaned back against the desk looking faintly bored, with all the assurance of someone who has looked faintly bored in spaceports all over the galaxy. He wore skins and a black leathertype which had not been made anywhere in the Hiboric Chain. The girl wore furs, mock anapuma, more expensive than the real thing and much more ecological. Cargoships, so she had been told, were never warm enough. The man did not look as though he felt the cold. He eyed the poster without interest and presently pulled out a pocket calculator and began to play push-button chess. He did not speak to the girl at all.

Tnoe Meliander glanced covertly at her travelling companion from time to time and decided he was not her type. His face was unlined and yet too hard to be really young, with a thin, almost unhappy mouth and very brilliant dark eyes, like cold white moonlight on cold black water. It was a face totally devoid of either expression or humour, pitiless without cruelty, too subtle for an android, too soulless for a man. She was reminded inexplicably of Hvern Tuoron, the central character in one of the Seven Plays, who murders his father because he is in love with his mother, only to find she marries his uncle after all. Accordingly he spends the rest of the play trying to murder the uncle, and inadvertently disposing of almost all the other characters instead. It is, of course, a black comedy, but Hvern himself remains utterly humourless, filled with hatred for the malignant gods who, he believes, are plotting his ruin, while in fact the Lords of the Universe merely wish to make him laugh. Looking at her companion, Tnoe thought he was one who would never laugh with the gods; if he laughed, it would always be alone. She wondered why he was going to Krake. As a rule, foreigners

[21]

only came to the Outmost System when a little scientific know-how was required to service veteran spacecraft, repair outdated computer networks, or work on the mineshafts in the employ of other powers many systems away. Tnoe decided this man was a scientist. She thought of Derec, poring over his medical books in an underheated laboratory somewhere in University Complex, and felt suddenly friendlier towards her companion, even though she had no way of knowing if her deductions were correct. Derec's hair was ginger and reared up in a sort of crest above his forehead, the bones of his face were knobbly and would grow knobblier with age, and he was studying to be a doctor; but to Tnoe all scientists were akin. She wanted to speak to the stranger, but although she was not at all shy she did not quite like to. He did not look the sort of stranger with whom one could fall into conversation easily.

Varagin Karel had summed up the girl in a single glance and dismissed her accordingly. He liked tall, slim, computeresque women with thin red lips and high cheekbones and geometric hairstyles. The girl waiting for the freightlift was short and (he suspected) stocky, with a square jaw and a resolute chin and the sort of forceful lower lip that denotes obstinacy. Her hair was too long and too curly, very dark for an Ifingen but not dark enough for Varagin, and her eyes were round and lashful and changed from blue to green according to her mood. Varagin liked slanting almond eyes which always stayed the same colour. Her luggage was contained in two carryalls, one old and one new, neither of which would tzip up properly, and her expensive boots were the wrong length with her expensive coat and the wrong colour with her expensive tunic, all of which (he felt) indicated a lack of mental coordination and an underdeveloped sense of taste. Varagin flicked a glance at the departure board and continued playing chess.

He was a scientist, as Tnoe had guessed, currently employed in a specialist capacity on the Kraken mineworks. This was his first trip. He was neither quite as old nor quite as bored as he looked, being in fact thirty-three standard years of age with a long education in emotional repression and general self-restraint. He had been born on a foreign planet at the wrong end of the galaxy and brought up in an experimental commune with three hundred other children who did not know what the word "parent" meant. The experiment failed. By the time they were twenty, fifty per cent of the experimentees had spent at least a short period in some sort of penal establishment. Of the other fifty per cent, many were equally amoral but too clever to get caught. Varagin was one of these latter. He went to college, gaining a good degree and a bad reputation. Then there was a girl—a girl from the commune who had undergone the metamorphosis from an uninteresting urchin into a tall beautiful creature with hair like black silk and a curling smile that lingered on her cheekbones long after her lips had grown solemn. By day, she worked in the laboratory with Varagin; by night, she danced in a cabaret and a grey-haired man, indifferent both to the size of the drinks bill and the presence of Varagin, sat alone at a table for six watching her with dispassionate eyes. The night before the wedding, his men met Varagin in an alleyway. They handled him with the sensitivity of true professionals, concentrating on all the soft places. Afterwards, Varagin lay in the gutter biting his tongue to keep himself from crying. When he could walk he bought a gun in a backstreet and went to a big house on the edge of the town and shot the grey-haired man between the eyes. In the middle, Livadya burst in and one of his companions panicked and fired. He could still remember the great red hole that opened in her stomach. After that, there was nothing to do but run. No one followed. The grey-haired man had many enemies. Two years later, in the mountains of Gwinid Cwoom on Stepsis, Varagin put on the robe of the Discipline of Nepeth and tried to learn how to endure the painful tedium of being alive. The Discipline of Nepeth was an illegal cult of atheist monks who believed in combining mastery of the spirit with mastery of the nervous system. From Brother Mind, Varagin learnt to regulate his pulse and adrenal flow, to wake and sleep when he wished, to order the subject matter of his dreams. From Brother Limb, he learnt to run thirty miles untiring and to kill an animal (or a man) without pain or noise, either with his bare hands or with the N'pethic scalpel. From Brother Thought, he learnt that death is final, and another man's life is all the immortality we can ever hope for. When he left, his body was at peace, if machines are peaceful, and he no longer dreamed of Livadya. His one ambition was legally or illegally to make a great deal of money, and to teach the grey-haired men of illicit power who was their master. In the meantime, he drifted from job to job and kept an eye on the main chance. When he and the girl were finally permitted aboard the cargoship, he did not offer to help her with her luggage. Tnoe, who had been brought up to the double standard, decided to dislike him all over again.

The flight was very quick, not because the ship was fast but because the captain had two Black Market calls to make before returning to Fingstar. Almost all cargoship pilots supplemented their income in that way. Varagin, with the savoir-faire of someone who has travelled half the galaxy, deduced what was going on and lay back with his eyes closed prepared to be blasé. Tnoe, accustomed to comfort and disagreeably affected by the resulting pressure fluctuations (the ship was not designed for speed), lay back with her eyes closed and felt sick. The tedium of spaceflight offered no distractions and after about an hour she decided she was really going to vomit. She reached for the switch to open the V-slot. But this was a cargoship; there were no such luxuries. Varagin opened an eye and indicated a disposable bag. He did not say anything. Tnoe did not say anything either, possibly because she could not. Afterwards, she lay back again wondering why she did not feel any better and tried in vain to go to sleep. The sort of thoughts that invariably come when the body is at a low physical ebb preoccupied her mind: her mother's death, her financial position, the hole in the lining of

[24]

her left boot. It did not seem to matter how important or unimportant these thoughts were : they all weighed upon her with an equal degree of leaden gloom. Her mother had died three weeks ago. No one expected her to die. She was still young, or at least, she still looked young : her skin had the well-kept texture of wax fruit and her hair was only faintly and elegantly silvered around the temples (she did not dye it since she was auditioning for the Wytch Voraste in the Third Play). "I have to go into hospital," she told Tnoe, the day before it happened, as though illness and hospital were the merest commonplace. "They say I need some sort of operation. I'm afraid it's quite serious. It's a dreadful bore : they don't seem to think I will be able to open at the Stardome next week. Don't let anyone come and see me, will you? *Particularly* Dani. You know what he's like. And for Inspiration's sake, no flowers. They always look just like a Reduction. But I shan't say any more, darling; I know you'll manage everything. You always do." The next morning, she went. Tnoe remembered thinking that she had never mentioned Reduction before. Not like that. In the late afternoon, someone came round from the hospital. They had mislaid her communication code, so they could not fetch her in time to see the body. It had already been sealed up when she got there. She did not cry at the time. Her head felt heavy and fuzzy inside, as though it was full of fluff, but she did not want to cry. The next day, at the Reduction Ceremony, she found herself looking at Dani's flowers, a huge, overstated bouquet of snowlilies and silverfringe and Evening Glory, and suddenly the tears came, angry, fiery tears tracing runnels through her make-up, tears of uselessness and misery and she knew not what. "She would have hated them so," she sobbed, clinging onto Derec. "They're so bloody *vulgar* .. ." Dani, who had been Tnar's Theatrical Orientator and the bane of her life, wandered round in a black silk dressing gown dabbing at his eyes with a white silk handkerchief. From time to time he declaimed, tragically. "She was the theatre's brightest ornament" (he said), "the First Star, the

[25]

Innemerle, in this our constellation of talents. We shall mourn our loss until the theatre is no more." Tnoe watched the little black box, scarcely bigger than her fist, sinking slowly into its appointed slot in the Chapel of Memory. Somewhere in the background they were playing the Constellation Symphony No. 5. It was all quite horrible.

Afterwards, there were the lawyers. A small round man with spectacles and a tall thin man with a drooping nose. Elts, Elts & Protion Assoc. She remembered with a strange sensation of blankness that moment when they had finally confessed to her that she didn't have any money. At the time, she hadn't understood. There had always been money, somewhere safe in the background, all her life. Plenty of money. "Your mother—hrmmm!—invested it." The small one spoke; the tall one cleared his throat. "Highly irregular. Yes, highly irregular. A most unusual woman." "But it can't be gone," Tnoe said. "Not all of it. Mummy was extravagant but she wasn't stupid. We've always been so *rich* . . ." I can't marry Derec, she was thinking, somewhere at the back of her mind. Not without the money. All through the Reduction, she had been sustained by the thought of marrying Derec. Not that he had actually asked her; she would have to do the asking. But now Tnar was dead, now the money had come to her, he could not tell her how poor they would be or how much her mother would dislike it. She would look after him and finance his researches and he would become the first great Ifingen doctor and would bring the rule of science to the Outmost System at last. Tnoe loved her mother and would grieve for her, but some time in the future, when grief was respectably over, she was going to be very, very happy. "I'm so sorry," said the small round man, with genuine regret, "but—well—there isn't any money. I'm afraid there's absolutely nothing left at all."

The next week Tnoe sold her pearl necklace (she did not feel she could sell Tnar's) and bought herself a one-way ticket to Krake. And that was that.

[26]

Beyond the window, the positions of the stars shifted ever so slightly as the cargoship fled through space. An hour to landing. Tnoe had forgotten her travelling companion altogether and found herself increasingly obsessed with the hole in the lining of her boot, which had worked uncomfortably over her big toe. She wondered briefly if she should have stayed after all, if she should have accepted the invitation from her aunt, who disliked her, or her grandmother, who was mad, if she should have moved in with Derec, as he suggested, instead of being self-consciously noble and insisting that she would not tie him down. She had even tried to tell him she did not love him, because that was what you were supposed to do under the circumstances, but he had brushed it aside. "Don't be so damned theatrical," he had said. "It doesn't suit you." She did not tell him when she was going. She did not want to say goodbye at the Departure Desk, to walk down the corridor, clutching her luggage, pausing, looking back, walking on and looking back. That sort of thing was always so unsatisfactory. If she had hoped he would find out, she did her best to repress it. What good would it have done, after all? She must concentrate on the future, such as it was: a new planet, a father she had never seen, a sister Tnar had hardly mentioned. Tnoe had never particularly wished for a sister. Effectively an only child, she had been self-sufficient, a little spoiled, needing nothing she could not have. But now all that was changed. She found herself thinking, optimistically, that it would be nice to have someone to learn to love.

At Castle Kray, Pzyche was expecting her. She knew she ought to take the Ita Spear (Goloro had polished it specially) and drive down to the spacestage, but she did not move. Perhaps she ought to send Goloro instead. From time to time he came and stood, expectantly, at a respectful distance, but she did not say anything. There was no point in asking the Doctor. When Pzyche brought him the incredible message which the computer had relayed to her (the actual communicator had died of discouragement long ago) he merely said it must be a mistake, he had never seen his other daughter and never wished to, Pzyche was not to bother him with the matter any more. "But —what if she comes?" Pzyche whispered. Nonsense, said the Doctor. She would not come. There was no regular flight. Pzyche looked at the end of the printout ("Arriving Krake evening 5.02 freightlift") and then back at her father. But he had returned to his studies (Territorial Violation, Subthesis 3301, Latent Connotations) and did not notice. Pzyche went away. From that moment she was quite sure Tnoe would come.

She sat by the tower window (there were no windows on the lower floors) looking out across the plain. A threadbare carpet of cloud covered the sky and the light was poor: the very grass looked grey. Every so often, her hand clenched on the window sill until the knuckles turned blue. When she noticed, she would make herself relax, very slowly, counting her breathing speed and loosening her fingers one by one, as if there was a Watcher somewhere who could see and criticize the perfection of her self-control. Occasionally, a faint shudder ran through her, as though a butterfly had escaped from her stomach and fluttered up her spine. Time passed. The drab light grew drabber and the acuteness of suspense gradually lessened. "She *must* come," thought Pzyche, torn between two fears. And then: "Perhaps I was wrong ..." A long time later, there was a movement on the plain, a grey shadow in the grey dusk. The sound of an engine carried faintly to her ears. "They are coming," the computer informed her, cryptically. Soon she could make out a landmovile. It was a heavy vehicle of a kind suitable for covering rough ground; Pzyche did not recognize it. The shield was down and she saw three white blobs in the front, moving about, in a nebulous way, like flowers nodding on their stalks. Faces. People. Pzyche could not believe it.

She did not move from the window. The landmovile came to a halt on the driveway below and she saw Goloro going out to meet it. The white blobs disappeared as the shield came up and then reappeared, outside the vehicle, with bodies attached. Two of them were men: miners, Pzyche supposed. The third must be her sister. Even in the dim light she could see how unlike her Tnoe was. Terror filled her. None of the pictures she had seen, nothing the computer had taught her, had prepared her for the differentness of people. This was another girl, her own sister, only a little less in age, and there did not seem to be any physical similarity at all. Somehow, Pzyche had expected a mirror-image of herself, a kindred spirit with whom conversation would be as effortless as thinking. How shall I talk to her? she thought in panic. She drew closer to the window, fascinated and fearful, pressing the palms of her hands against the pane as though to ward off the encroaching world. At that moment, one of the men happened to look up. Her hands, blotted against the glass, stood out like two little white starfish. She saw him point and seize his friend's arm, and she stepped back. But not before he had seen her. He had seen her *face*. (She felt the impact of his eyes.) No human being but Goloro and the Doctor had ever looked on her face before. Not since she had left Fingstar and the infancy she could not remember. She felt naked, exposed, insupportably vulnerable. In the safety of the room, well away from the window, she gave way to shivering.

Outside, the man who had looked up, a mining engineer called Forn, said to his companion: "*That* one was beautiful."

3

The accident occurred about three weeks later. Varagin was on Level 2 with the survey team. There was a deep booming noise underground and they felt a shudder run through the rock. Then silence. A thin trickle of rubble, dislodged somewhere far above, came pattering down the wall. Dust settled. "Listen!" said Varagin. And gradually they became aware of another sound, a growing murmur at first indistinguishable from the silence, and in the ground at their feet, faint but pursuing, a subtle vibration. For a long moment they stood listening. The sound swelled from a murmur to a rumour, from a rumour to a rumble, from a rumble to a roar. It was a sound at once disturbingly familiar and faintly anomalous. None of them could quite remember where they had heard it before. Then there was a clatter of footsteps in the intersection and a voice hailed them, echoes bouncing recklessly from wall to wall: "Water!"

They ran.

As he scrambled out of the liftshaft onto Level 3, Varagin knew he was afraid. His hands were busy with ropes, with shovels, with props. Someone called for pumps. But there weren't any pumps. This was Krake, the dry planet. No water, no pumps. No quick-dry insulating foam. No sandbags. Varagin found himself thinking in a series of staccato flashes, of soundings that had been too deep or too shallow, of rocks that were too solid, of vast hollows guessed or unguessed beyond impenetrable layers of stone. They should have known there was water. The instruments should have identified a reservoir half a mile away ... The floor was awash. Someone said: "Hold this!" and passed him a bucket.

"Don't be ridiculous," snapped Varagin.

He wanted more than anything to know what had gone wrong. His fear was there, but he could detach himself from it, keeping his mind clear for concentration and analysis although his pulse was irregular and his forehead clammy. Lower down, he found piles of shattered rock blocking the half-made passageway. Great metal screws, torn and heat-scarred, protruded here and there. The water came frothing up between the stones like saliva. At one point he caught sight of a hand flapping idly in a crack. He took hold of it and pulled but it came away too easily and he staggered and almost fell. By some spasm of muscles no longer there the limp fingers stiffened and closed about his own. Someone grasped his other elbow to steady him and made a would-be flippant remark which affected him with more nausea than the grip of the dismembered hand. Ahead, a voice cried out: "Back! Get back! We cannot—shut—the door! The lake . . . is coming in . . ." The echoes rang strangely far down in the earth. Then there was a slithering noise and voice and echo were lost in the roar of water and stone. A chain of lights extinguished abruptly, leaving them in a greenish semi-darkness. The man at Varagin's elbow, an engineer called Forn, said: "There's nothing we can do." Varagin watched with peculiar distaste the shudder of a muscle in his cheek as he fought to set his mouth firmly. He remembered, irrelevantly, that he had seen the man before and had not liked him then either. And suddenly, the smell of his fear seemed to go to Varagin's head. "Wait," he said fiercely. Out of the blackness ahead the water climbed towards them, streaked with luminescent clots of foam. He gripped Forn's arm, feeling the other man flinch and knowing a cruel satisfaction in his own superior control. He, too, was very much afraid. "Did you hear the echoes?" he said. "There's space down there. *Space*."

We cannot shut the door . . .

The *door*?

He hardly noticed when the water came over his boots. "It'll

[31]

find its own level," he said. "Let's go."

Behind them, long tongues of spume licked up the walls and swallowed the place where they had stood.

The day after she came to Castle Kray, Tnoe went to find her father. "So you are Tnar's daughter," he said, disowning her. Then he went back to work.

"He would not listen," Pzyche explained carefully, remembering to think aloud. She was not used to thinking aloud. Her father had never required a response to his rare monologues and when she gave Goloro an order or asked a question of the computer she would think it out first inside her head. To speak a thought as it came was a new experience. She never spoke on impulse.

"What do you do all day?" Tnoe asked her, trying valiantly not to be daunted by the silent corridors, the unfurnished rooms, the blank horizon beyond the windows. Pzyche took her to the library. (It was always easier to show her things than to have to explain them.) Shelves climbed from floor to ceiling. Cabinets were stacked one on top of another. On a table in the centre, catalogues years out-of-date lay where Pzyche had left them, halfway to reclassification. Some were draped with cobwebs. Tnoe looked round in horror.

"The library," Pzyche explained, belatedly. Tnoe's expression bewildered her. She was not used to reading expressions; she had seen so few. Perceiving the need for further demonstration, she selected a brainprint at random and plugged it into the recorder. On the keyboard, she tapped out a standard experience. Presently, coloured lights appeared on the screen, showing the expected reaction.

"You cannot mean," said Tnoe, "that something like this can tell you how *people* behave?"

"Of course," said Pzyche, glad of a question she could answer. "A brainprint is an automatic copy of a human psychotype. It reacts as a human psychotype would react. My father told me, they used to use rats. But brainprints are better. Here," her gesture embraced the countless shelves, the cobwebs, the shadows, "we have the largest collection in the whole world." Even so she might have said: here we have all the roses that ever blossomed, or all the jewels that were ever mined. For someone who had never seen expressions, Tnoe's face was a good face on which to learn. Suddenly, Pzyche began to pace about the room, wrenching open the cabinets, pulling out the drawers. "Look," she said. "*Look*. These are *people*. Real people. These. And these." Her words came raggedly, unplanned. Brainprints clattered to the floor, giving off little blue sparks. Dust stirred. "They have personalities—characteristics—reactions. Happiness is yellow. Anger is purple and green. All classified. They are people—people like us. Hunger is red —two red lights. Fear is red. Three red lights in an upside-down triangle. Do you want to see Fear?" Her voice went very loud and then very quiet, as though she could not control it, and Tnoe caught her by the shoulders to restrain her, moved with a sort of loathly compassion which she would have given anything not to feel. For a moment, she thought that was why Pzyche flinched away.

"It's just reaction," she said. "You're not used to people. It must be a shock. You need some kaffine." Derec had once told her kaffine was good for shock.

"You're touching me," Pzyche whispered. "You mustn't touch me. This is my territory. It's a violation of my territory."

Dimly, Tnoe remembered her father's theories, twenty years behind the times. "I am your sister," she said, groping desperately for the right words. "It doesn't matter if it's a sister. You must let in the people you love."

Pzyche responded, predictably: "I have read about love."

When Tnoe arrived at Castle Kray, her expectations had not been high. Nonetheless, she was an optimist by nature, and she had hoped; she was the sort of person who always hoped, unless

[33]

from some cause or other it seemed absolutely necessary to despair. (After her arrival, she sometimes thought the expectations of a pessimist would have been optimistic for Castle Kray.) She had expected her father would welcome her, and he had refused to notice her existence. She had expected the adventure of a strange planet, the thrill of something new and unfamiliar, and she had found silent corridors, unfurnished rooms, blank horizons. And she had hoped to love her sister.

She never forgot her first sight of Pzyche. A tall girl (too tall), awkwardly slender and as pale as a bug in the dark, with the cold green eyes of a Kraken dawn and a gleam of dead gold in her hair. She never smiled, hardly spoke. After a while, it occurred to Tnoe she resembled her mother. If you could imagine that flickering charm and parade of quick-change expressions caught in a still life like an overexposed photograph. She welcomed Tnoe with an antiquated greeting which she had found in the Third Play. By a strange chance, Tnoe had heard her mother utter those same lines at a dress rehearsal in the Stardome only a month before. There were no colours in Pzyche's voice: it was like a cold, soft note without pitch or feeling; but to Tnoe, it was familiar. And behind the blank eyes she thought she saw a furtive soul, too long desolate to look out. Having Pzyche, Tnoe felt, made up for everything: for her father, for Castle Kray, for the bleak plateaux and still winds of Krake. She loved her in spite of, or because of, her cold beauty, the improbable range of her knowledge (what was there to learn, on Krake, but education?), the horrifying blank of her experience, the questionable existence of her heart. Her sister needed her, or so she thought, as no other human being had ever needed her, and all her life Tnoe had adored to be needed. As a child, she had nursed injured birds, collected stray cats. As an adult, she had shielded her mother from audiences, from admirers, from Theatrical Orientators. Even Derec, forceful, self-sufficient, utterly sure of himself, even he had needed her financial and moral support. But the money was gone and she had re-

[34]

solved at the Reduction to despair of Derec. She did not like to think about despair. Only in the night watches, waking untimely, the dark would come down over her mind. Sometimes, she would stand by her window watching the green dawn paling the stars (Iscys, and Fosces, and Axum) and wonder how in all the wide and populous universe she came to be so alone. Those were the moments when she remembered Pzyche most lovingly, and loved her most fiercely.

Pzyche did not love her sister. She had only read about love. She would sit beside Tnoe, studying her passionately: the eyes that changed from blue to green, the colours in her skin, the constant mobility of feature and expression. She had never seen a face before other than the grey faces of her father and Goloro and her own white reflection, and she was totally absorbed by the wonder and the strangeness of it. At first, too, she was a little afraid. Fear passed quickly but the wonder still touched her every day when Tnoe said good morning. (Pzyche practised her own good morning in her room before she left, watching herself in the mirror. It was not a thing she was used to, saying good morning.) She had, of course, seen faces in pictures on the computer, young faces like Tnoe's, shapely and many-coloured, but no two-dimensional picture could conjure the texture, the solidity, the sparkle of real life. If anyone had asked her, Pzyche would have said without hesitation that Tnoe's face was the most beautiful thing she had ever seen.

The two miners who had given Tnoe a lift to Castle Kray came back once or twice, avoiding the Doctor, to visit the girls. "We don't see many women," Forn's companion, Udulf, explained a little shyly. He was an ugly youth with merry eyes and a nose that crinkled up when he moved his lips (Pzyche was fascinated by his nose). After the accident, when the passage had been secured and the roof shored up, they came to boast of the disaster. "Was anyone killed?" Tnoe asked, horrified. Udulf,

[35]

who had had little previous contact with violent death, endeavoured rather uncomfortably to shrug it off, launching into an
animated account of the clear-up operation. Pzyche sat watching his nose, saying nothing. Forn sat watching Pzyche. Too
many women had told him he was pretty and he was alternately
annoyed and intrigued because she did not seem to see it. ("The
other one?" said Pzyche, after they had gone. "I didn't look at
him much. His face was too still. There was just this muscle by
his mouth that wriggled sometimes: it looked very peculiar. As
though he had a worm in his cheek.")

"After the lake went down," Udulf was saying, "we got into
the cavern. They seem to think there were people there once.
The site manager says we may have to call in an expert. That's
the trouble with this system: it's too old. Millions and millions
of years ago it had advanced technology and a rising civilization,
and now there's nothing but dust settling on empty plains and
old holes way underground filling up with water. Even the
people don't seem to be able to think *forward* any more ...
Hiboryn, now, Hiboryn is *new*. That's where I come from. You
should see Hiboryn."

"I'd like to see the cavern," said Tnoe. "It sounds exciting."

"There isn't much to see," said Udulf. "Just stalactites. Huge
ones, hollow inside. They say the people lived in the stalactites.
Like rats in a wall ..."

"We'll pick you up in the Scrambler," said Forn, never taking
his eyes from Pzyche. "Tomorrow."

Tnoe had forgotten that she did not really like going underground. It was cold in the mines and she was glad when Udulf
offered to lend her his leathertype. Pzyche did not seem to
notice the cold. Her sleeves were folded back from the elbow
and Tnoe could see the scant, silvery hairs on her arm standing
on end, but she was evidently so accustomed to discomfort that
it did not penetrate her conscious mind at all. Tnoe hugged herself tightly in the leathertype and refrained from complaint.

[36]

The corridor sloped down from the liftshaft and in the poor light their descent was slow. Gradually her sense of perspective, of the bigness and smallness of things, began to distort, until the passageway seemed to be shrinking in upon itself and the weight of rock above was coming down on top of her like a falling hill. Round a bend, they came suddenly upon water. There was a boat drawn up on the stone, an inflatable autoraft such as all projects carry even when they have no use for them, and Tnoe allowed herself to be handed in, trying not to look reluctant. She did not notice how close Pzyche was sitting until she felt the touch of a small, cold hand on her arm. Perhaps it was instinct; perhaps, even in the bad light, Pzyche had seen the whiteness of her face and her lips tightly clenched to keep them from shaking. Tnoe felt the hand close over her own and then withdraw, as though suddenly shy, and for a moment she was so surprised she forgot to be afraid.

The Door was open. The passageway widened out and the roof climbed steeply beyond the range of the nitron lamps. On the stone panels many times their own height, they could make out a design of some sort, half-obliterated by the fungus of time: it looked like a monstrous beast or reptile, with a red cavernous nostril protruding just above water level and an eye enamelled in blue taupe under a horny eyelid. In the background, there was a suggestion of pale flanks peeling with scales and a jagged ridge of bone, like spines, but more than half the Door was submerged and it was difficult to make it out. The miners had named the caves for the doorway. "Behold!" said Udulf, "the caverns of Dragoncrake!"

As he had said, there was nothing very much to see. Once past the Door, the boat drifted out into a vast subterranean pool, as still as a mirror. Far below them hung a coved ceiling glittering with outcrops of greyish crystal and sprouting here and there into huge warts and mushrooms of stone. Stalactites of enormous girth were suspended improbably in between; in the greatest of them, ragged holes like windows showed a glimpse of chambers and passageways hollowed in the living rock. But the chambers were empty, the passageways led nowhere. Light filtered in somehow through invisible fissures and touched the depths of the pool with a faint grey shade. Everything was so still it seemed nothing had moved there for a million years. Then a ripple left their bows, and all that world of stone trembled for a moment in an impossible wind. "I told you," said Udulf. "There's nothing here but old rock and old shadows. There aren't even any bones."

"What is the crystal?" asked Pzyche, unexpectedly. "It is not very common, I think."

But Udulf did not know.

Afterwards, the girls went back to the barrack where the miners lived for kaffine and austracized biscuits. They were offered spirits of pterviti but Tnoe declined, doubtful of the effect on her sister. Pzyche sat by the window, watching, in case any other people went past. There was a man in a black leather-type with eyes that glittered darkly like the crystal in the cave, but his face had the closed-in look of a face that gives nothing away, and Pzyche found it uninteresting. She was only learning to read faces, and had yet to get beyond the large print.

Varagin went past without seeing Pzyche.

4

The next morning, Varagin stood waiting for the freightlift to Camarest. At Castle Kray, Pzyche was rerunning an old educational programme on the computer: essential physics, lesson 3, "Crystals and Crystaltypes". Presently, she found what she wanted. "Mammonite," the computer stated. "Found exclusively in sunsystem T1 303, called the Anchor. Due to its extreme rarity, it was chosen as the reserve currency in the principal systems of the Planetary League. Its value is essential to the balance of economy in the civilized worlds." On the screen, a picture appeared showing a single grey-black crystal, shaped rather like an irregular stick of celery.

"Information inadequate," Pzyche pointed out.

But the computer had nothing more to say.

The next day, when the miners came over, Tnoe decided she did not like the way Forn looked at Pzyche. Still, she was glad they had come. When she passed her father in the corridor that morning, he had looked the other way. And she did not much care for Goloro. She thought he was "creepy". In one of the Seven Plays there was a character called Blot, a hunchback with a sideways leer who crawled around after the supervillain licking his boots and strangling people who did not call him sir. She knew it was unfair, but Goloro always reminded her of Blot. She did not like the way he looked at Pzyche either. Forn, however, was young and good-looking, and in the young and good-looking she was prepared to make allowance for the lusts of the flesh. Let him look, she decided, thinking she might have found him pretty if it had not been for Derec, half a system away. She would take care he had no opportunity to do anything else.

But when Udulf came alone, she did not object to the idea of a walk without Pzyche. She had chosen to despair of Derec, and Krake was very dull. "We won't go far," said Udulf, glancing towards the distant plateau with a measuring eye. ("Get her out of the way," Forn had told him. "I want to see the other one on her own. I should like to know if she can actually talk.") They went off in the early afternoon. "We shan't go far," Tnoe told her sister. "You don't mind, do you?"

When Forn arrived he found Pzyche in the computer room, alone. Even the computer was switched off. If she had minded, she had not known how to say so. She offered him kaffine or greentea but he declined, preferring to sit, staring at her, waiting to see if it would make her feel uncomfortable. Perhaps it did. But Pzyche had done without conversation all her life and even when she felt uneasy it did not occur to her to try to communicate it. She only wished he would not look at her hands. Every so often her fingers would flex and clench as though of their own accord, and she felt increasingly inhibited by this evidence of uncontrol. It was like the muscle in Forn's cheek that jumped constantly, as though behind his closed lips his tongue was roiling round inside his mouth like a serpent. After a long while, he said: "Don't you ever *say* anything?"

"No," said Pzyche, comprehensively. (She was wondering how he managed to enunciate his words, with his tongue writhing round in his mouth all the time.)

"It is usual," remarked Forn, "to try to make conversation with a guest."

"I have never learnt any conversation," Pzyche explained. Presently, she felt required to elaborate: "I can answer questions. Like the computer."

"Good," said Forn. "Very good. You can answer questions. So few women can answer questions. Are you a woman? First question. Are—you—a—woman?"

"I am," Pzyche sought, confused, for the correct term, "gender, female . . ."

"But are you a woman?" Forn snapped, eagerly. "Are you vulnerable? Are you beautiful? Have you ever looked in a mirror, and thought how beautiful you are? All women are vain. But I could almost believe you aren't. I could almost believe you've never looked in a mirror at all." Suddenly, he got up, and came very close to her. Much too close. His eyes were glittering with moving needlepoints of light. When he spoke, his mouth looked lipless and drawn, as though some alien passion had sucked in all the skin of his face. His voice seemed to be full of tongue. "I want to touch you," he said.

His closeness appalled her. No, she wanted to say, but somehow she could not speak. The thought of his tongue, revolving greedily in the hot red interior of his mouth, paralysed her. If only she could stop thinking about his tongue.

He took her wrist. It was cold. He was fascinated by her coldness, her withdrawal, her disgust. He had expected her to struggle, to pant like an animal. She did not seem to breathe at all. Her tunic fell in thin, sharp creases from the points of her breasts. (He fancied her nipples were erect.) "I want to feel you," he said. (Her arm was icy.) "Are you a woman? Answer me. Answer. You answer questions, don't you? Like the computer. Are you a computer? How old are you? Where were you born?"

He laid his hand on her belly. Under the thin material, he could feel all her flesh crawling away from him. His voice came thickly, through his tongue.

"I want to make love to you," he said.

Pzyche whispered, almost inaudibly: "I have read about love."

Tnoe ran. The pathway streamed beneath her feet like a conveyor belt, like something in a nightmare, bearing her further

[41]

and further back the harder she tried to run forwards. Once, she stumbled, and knuckles of greystone, thrusting through the ground, pummelled at her knees. She had shed her coat long ago. (Perhaps Udulf would pick it up.) Fool, vain fool: she should have guessed it was just a ploy. She at least knew something about men. Pzyche, *Pzyche* . . .

Far behind, Udulf called to her. Tnoe did not stop to hear. Grey walls loomed suddenly through the mist; blank windows; unopened doors. High up, a single light, like a little white star. (The Doctor? Useless.) The back door was locked. She rattled the bolt, threw her shoulder against the panels, tore round to the front. The front door was open. Somehow, that made her more afraid. Sounds came from the computer room. Thumping, grunting. Sounds of violence and pain. She ran down the corridor.

Forn was standing by the far wall. He had Goloro by the shoulders, and he was beating his head against the stone. It was bouncing to and fro like a ball on a spring and there was blood in the grey hair. Presently, Forn became aware of Tnoe, wrenching at his arm. Abruptly, he released Goloro. The old man slid down by the wall like a doll. Tnoe's eyes blazed blue and green like copper in the fire.

"I didn't like the way he looked at her," Forn said. "The dirty old man."

Pzyche was shrunken into the corner, white as a ghost. She did not say anything at all.

That night, waking in the grey darkness around two o'clock, Tnoe found she was not thinking of Derec. She had bandaged Goloro's head herself, vaguely repulsed by the nakedness of his scalp under his hair and the way the skin went into withered brown creases on the nape of his neck, like leather. Forn's hair fell to his shoulders, slick and straight and dark as her own. In his neck, you could see the sharp line of the bone, the tautness of sinew, the flexing of an Adam's apple. His skin was thick and

[42]

pale from long hours underground. He's a Lippith, Tnoe thought, inconsequently. If he worked outside he would be as brown as a coppernut. (One of Tnar's admirers had been a Lippith.) If only Pzyche had said something. But even later, even when they were alone, she would not talk about it. "I am your sister," Tnoe had reiterated, over and over again. "You can tell things to a sister. It doesn't matter. It's a special relationship. You should be able to confide in the people you love." She always talked to her sister as if Pzyche loved her. But something in Pzyche's face had closed up. Trust me, said Tnoe despairingly, into the darkness, thinking of Pzyche's cold green eyes and Forn's slinky dark hair, falling about his neck. She did not want to believe he was lying. All her life, she had done only what she wanted. It had never been necessary for her to believe anything she did not like. Until now.

In the morning, Tnoe overslept. Pzyche had been in the library an hour before she got up. On the recorder, a mug of greentea was growing cold. (Pzyche had forgotten to put on the heatstop.) She had made it because Tnoe always made greentea, first thing in the morning; it was what they did on Fingstar, where greentea was a proper way to start the day. But she did not really want it. The acquisition of habits, the ordinary, everyday habits of ordinary, everyday people, on planets where people came two to the square mile, was something Pzyche studied, though she did not know quite why. Perhaps it made her feel less isolated, knowing somewhere else it was morning, and someone else, like her, was making greentea. ("In other systems," said Tnoe, "Derec says, they chew gum, or smoke hennebuhl, or drink raw spirits. In the Third System, on Grôm, they even eat eggs, fried in grease with pigmeat and black fungus. But you can't just get up.") That morning, Pzyche needed to feel she had something in common with the rest of humanity. All her reactions, all her instincts, were so *wrong* . . . She ran through the shelves of brainprints, carelessly, finding what she wanted without seeming to look. Not that there was anyone to see. But then, there never had been anyone to see. The early light came through the window and spread across the floor, a pallid oblong, full of dust. Pzyche plugged the brainprint into the recorder. Psychotype 78C, group 1101, lower grade. Example 7550. If the example had had a face, it might have been young and good-looking, with slinky hair. Pzyche pressed the keyboard. Not a standard experience, not this time. It was one she had made up herself, long ago, when Goloro came and she could not bear to touch his wounds. She had never properly understood the reaction. But it was always the same. Three red lights in an inverse triangle. After a little while, they turned white. Then they disappeared . . .

Pzyche unplugged the useless brainprint and threw it in the waste disposal unit. When Tnoe came in, she was sipping her greentea, long grown cold.

"The library," Pzyche told Forn, a few hours later. Forn followed her in, willing to humour her. Downstairs, he knew, Tnoe was discussing him with Udulf. He wondered how far he trusted his friend. "What is this for?" he asked idly, leaning on the recorder. Pzyche endeavoured to explain.

"You plug in the brainprint," she said, "here. A brainprint is a human being. When you plug it in, it is in suspension, unconscious. It thinks and feels only what the machine allows it to think and feel. You dictate the experience on the keyboard, here, and the reaction comes up on the screen, in coloured lights." After a moment's thought, she went on: "You can dictate any sensation. Comfort, warmth, touch. The reactions are in the manual. Happiness is yellow. Pleasure is pink: four pink lights in a flower. With extreme pleasure, a red light comes on, in the centre . . ." She added, a little wistfully: "It would be interesting to try it with a real human being. I have never used a real human being."

Forn thought: "She's talking. She's actually talking." Anticipation made him warm all over. "All right," he said. "Let's try it."

Pzyche sat him in a chair and attached the sensitisors. Two behind the ears, one on the forehead, one at the base of the skull. The last thing he felt was the cold soft touch of her fingertips. Then she connected the plugs.

Gradually, Forn's head fell back. His face was blank, his eyelids drooped. Presently, his mouth came open, and she saw the tip of his tongue lolling between his lips like a serpent. On the keyboard, she pressed out the experience she had used that morning. She called it "limbo". Absence of seeing, absence of hearing, absence of touch . . . Her hand closed on the time-switch. Accelerate fifty. One hundred. On the screen, three red lights in an inverse triangle . . .

After a little while, they turned white.

Then they disappeared.

When Tnoe came in a few minutes later, Pzyche was still standing by the machine, her hand on the timeswitch. Accelerate five hundred . . . In the chair, Forn did not move. His mouth was open. In the gap, a little scum of saliva was drying on his tongue. His eyeballs showed white under the drooping lids.

Tnoe did not want to call Udulf. But she knew she must.

When they disconnected Forn, he tried to speak. His eyes rolled with effort and the sweat gathered on his temples, shining like slime. A muscle in his cheek, gone out of control, throbbed like a bullfrog. But he could not get the words round his tongue.

"What am I to say?" Udulf shouted. "What the hell am I to say? Look at him. He's gone out of his mind. She's driven him out of his mind . . . Don't go there, they said. The Doctor's a lunatic. No one's ever seen his daughter. He hasn't *got* a daughter. Poor fool, Forn, he couldn't do without women. He said she was as cold as a slug and harder than geometry, but he couldn't do without women. Poor bastard, look at him now. I've got to take him back. You see that, don't you? If he was

[45]

dead we could bury him. But he's alive. I'll have to take him back . . ."

"I'm sorry," Tnoe whispered. "But he asked for it. He must have done. He must have touched her." She had always been a gentle person, or so she thought. But even when she saw the spittle running from his dry mouth, she could not quite forgive him.

They got him into the Scrambler somehow and Udulf drove away. Tnoe stood for a while, staring after him. She could not see the colony, but from behind a ridge a thin line of smoke, darker than the mist, climbed steadily into the green evening sky. Presently, she turned, and went back into the house.

She was very much afraid.

5

Tnoe never knew if it was luck or instinct that made her decide to go for a walk that day. "I should like to see the site of the accident," she said, "where you found Goloro." (Long afterwards, she was to remember that she had felt remorseful about Goloro.) The weather, like most weather on Krake, was dull. Mists lay above the ground. Where you could see the sky, O, the Ifingen sun, slipped between clouds, blinking uncertainly. It was neither hot nor cold. "On Krake," Tnoe remarked, "when you go for a walk, you never feel any better for it. I don't believe there's any fresh air here at all."

"We could stay at home," Pzyche pointed out.

But the castle was affecting Tnoe with claustrophobia. "I want to get out," she said.

The wreck of the spacecraft looked exactly the same as on the day of the accident. The hyperglass had melted in the heat so that only the honeycomb structure remained, but the outer hull, though blackened from the explosion, was almost intact. Tnoe picked her way through the entrance shaft, gingerly, waiting for something to disintegrate. In the pilot capsule, the dead controls still prickled with a faint static. The navigator's swivel chair had survived somehow and when she sat down it creaked slowly round to the left, like the flexing of a joint too long unused. "Where did they go," she asked Pzyche, "the dead?" But Pzyche did not know.

Outside, they sat together on the short grass. Suddenly, Tnoe felt homesick: for grass that grew tall and ragged, for wide cold skies, for straight country roads lined with spider trees going nowhere in particular. There was a little park in the heart of Camarest with a single spider tree, all drooping grey branches, which was said to be a thousand years old. It was only twice the height of Tnoe. And beyond, there was a walk paved with white stones between banks of flowers: snowlilies, and silverfringe, and Evening Glory ... "Long ago," said Tnoe, "before they invented Reduction, they used to bury their dead under flowers." And in her mind's eye she saw Goloro, six years earlier, digging and digging in the grey soil ...

"It must be terrible," she whispered, "having to bury the dead."

They never heard anything. At Castle Kray, the miners had been and gone. The bolt was torn off the back door and the passage was wet and slippery; someone had smashed the hydrant with a pickaxe. The austracisor looked all right until Tnoe found the feed tube, on the far side of the room. "Light," said Tnoe. "We must have light." But even the handlamps were broken.

Goloro lay beside the computer, in a little black heap. (Tnoe almost fell over him in the dark.) "Answer," said Pzyche, pressing the controls. But the computer would not answer any more.

Tnoe said: "We must find the Doctor." She would not call him father. He had not been a father to either of them. Somewhere at the back of her mind she was thinking: this is all his fault.

They found him in his study, above the library. His feet swung slowly, left and then right, with a faint creaking noise like an old swivel chair. One of his shoes had fallen off. There was something so disgusting about old men's toes, Tnoe thought. None of it seemed real, not yet. She remembered that kaffine was good for shock, but of course there wasn't any water. "The library," whispered Pzyche. Tnoe followed her down the stairs.

They had not touched the library. A single light, the only

light in the whole castle, glowed wanly in the centre of the room. On the endless shelves, dust and shadows lay undisturbed. Pzyche went over to the recorder, pressed the keyboard. (There was a brainprint already connected.) Presently, coloured lights appeared on the screen. "It works," Tnoe said. "What can it do?"

"Nothing," said Pzyche.

A long time later, they started to clear up. At Tnoe's suggestion, they piled all the rubbish in a back room, and then locked it. (The waste disposal unit was broken.) The castle, always bare, looked like a house where even the rats had moved out. "What shall we do," asked Pzyche, "with the dead?"

"We'll have to bury them," Tnoe said.

They slept that night in the same bed, under Tnoe's anapuma coat. The heating system was damaged beyond repair and gradually the castle grew colder. Tnoe woke at moonset, with the light on her face. She got up to close the shutter, her feet shrinking from contact with the bare floor, and looked out across the plain. Fossil, the greater of the two Kraken moons, hung low over the horizon in an irregular blur of cloud, faintly pink like the blotching of blood vessels seen through thick pale skin. It was almost at the full. The lesser moon, Wormwood, was a mere cusp of silver on top of the tower to her left. Evaporation had almost stopped and only a few wisps of mist lay across the plain. She could see a long way in the moonlight.

They had buried the Doctor by the big rock, about half a mile distant. It cast a long black shadow across the newly turned earth. ("There ought to be flowers," Pzyche had said. "You told me, they buried the dead under flowers.") Goloro was behind the castle, out of sight. Tnoe did not want to look at Goloro. The Doctor, she felt, had merited such an end: a cold grave on a desolate planet, with a standing stone to watch over him like the tombstones of the ancients, whose thoughts and dreams had perished from the world over a millennium ago. But she did not want to think about Goloro. Somewhere, she had read that the worms ate the bodies of the dead, and the birds ate the worms, and the people ate the birds, and this was the cycle of life and it was good. Tnoe had never eaten a bird. (She wondered what you would do with the feathers.) She had never eaten raw food at all. The idea filled her with horror, like eating excrement. But the austracisor was broken and people must eat to live. And suddenly she found herself filled with a great love of life, of the cold floor under her feet and the night beyond the window and the diseased face of the Kraken moon, like one of Derec's cultures of bacteria. Life had always come easy to Tnoe. There had been food from the austracisor, drink from the hydrant, enough money, enough love. She was not going to give up the first time things became difficult. She would even eat birds, if it was necessary. (Perhaps she could spit out the feathers.) On Ifings once, she had seen raw fruit, growing on trees. Maybe she could find fruit. She imagined the thick, coarse peel, curling away from her fingers like leather, the pink, squelchy flesh, oozing juice, the feel of that flesh in her mouth, the juice running down her tongue . . . A shudder of uncontrollable nausea ran through her. For a moment, doubled up over the stone sill, she wondered if she could bear to survive after all.

Something swooped past the window, chittering, and it occurred to Tnoe that she had never seen any birds on Krake. She had never seen fruit trees, either. She wondered if you could eat bats. In the bed, Pzyche breathed evenly, sleeping like a child.

"Do you think they will come back?" she had asked.

"Why should they?" said Tnoe. "They have done all that is necessary."

It was curiously difficult to imagine still being alive, the day after tomorrow.

In the morning, they found water, in a shallow cave. "We must boil it," said Pzyche knowledgeably, "to destroy the bacteria."

"Derec likes bacteria," Tnoe remarked, without thinking.

"Who is Derec?" asked Pzyche.

"Oh, someone I used to know."

Pzyche said, her voice grown suddenly cold: "Did you love him?"

"Yes," said Tnoe. "Yes, I did."

"I shall never love anyone," Pzyche stated. "I don't think I should like it."

"The way things are going now," Tnoe snapped, unreasonably annoyed, "you probably won't get the chance. Is this fire-pot going to work? It's badly dented."

Carefully, Pzyche switched on the flame and adjusted it to "medium". "I put in a new flint," she said. "There were some in the cupboard over the austracisor, at the back."

After a while, the water came to the boil. There was no kaffine. "There's a herb called sisley," Pzyche volunteered, "which you can use to flavour boiling water. I saw some growing outside. In the Cold Season, it has green seedpods, with little grey seeds. They are poisonous. But in the Hot Season, it's edible."

"What season are we in?" asked Tnoe.

"The Cold Season," Pzyche said.

They were so thirsty, they drank the water before it had cooled. It tasted tepid, flat; like water which has been boiled and has not yet cooled. Tnoe tried not to remember that for hundreds of years it had been lying at the back of a cave cupped in naked rock, open to all the phantoms of the air.

"You can eat beetles," said Pzyche, "if you boil them first."

"How do you know?"

"The computer told me," Pzyche explained. "It's biology."

"Can you eat bats?" asked Tnoe.

But that Pzyche did not know. "At the mineworks," she said presently, "they must have plenty of food. Proper food, I mean,

[51]

which has been austracized. Perhaps we could manage to take some. The miners are at work most of the time, down the mines. When we were there, with Forn and Udulf, I only saw one other person. If we were very careful, perhaps nobody would notice."

"You mean," said Tnoe, "*steal?*"

"I suppose so."

Tnoe said: "I have never stolen anything . . ."

Pzyche was not particularly concerned with survival. Other humans were so alien, so entirely different from everything she had dreamed or imagined, she had come to feel there was no place for her in a world peopled with such beings, and the only thing she could do was to die, unobtrusively. Even Tnoe evidently had hidden depths which Pzyche would always find horrible. Watching her sister, covertly, she tried to reconcile what she knew of those secret urges with that vivid open face, so familiar now, and so precious. It was incomprehensible. "It must be me," Pzyche thought, logically. "I am the one who is all wrong. 'Natural', means what is natural to the majority. I am one, alone, the minority. I am unnatural. But I cannot change. Things which are quite natural, will always seem terrible and strange to me. It is better, much better, that I should die . . ." There was a precedent in these matters. Fleacrows, she had learnt, somewhere in the assorted rubbish of her education, if they found one white bird among a flock of black ones, would always kill it. If only she did not feel quite so resentful. The miners, like the fleacrows, could not help themselves. They were only acting according to their nature. But Pzyche had read about the gods, in the Seven Plays, and she knew that somewhere there was a Power which had created that one white crow. At times she felt a certain affinity with a character called Hvern Tuoron, who had claimed he would be happiest living in a coppernut. He had been afraid of dying, Pzyche remembered, in case he had bad dreams. But she had seen her father and Goloro, and she was quite sure the dead did not dream.

[52]

Tnoe had caught a beetle. It did not look very appetizing. "Not that kind," said Pzyche. "The bigger ones, with claws." It occurred to her suddenly that she did not want Tnoe to die. Whatever went on behind her face, no matter how natural, that face was still beautiful, still special, and Pzyche could not endure to think of it lying in the dirt, with all the colours draining away. If it was necessary for Tnoe's survival that she should be there, then she supposed she, too, would have to survive. At least for the moment.

"Tomorrow," said Tnoe, surveying a bigger one, with claws, "we'll go over to the mining colony. Just to have a look."

That night, Pzyche woke to see her sister standing by the window. The shutter was open and the dreary moonlight spilled across the floor. Pzyche got up. Fossil, now at the full, hung over the ridge: a flat, discoloured disc. "It looks like an old bone," said Tnoe, "which has been passed from hand to hand for hundreds of years." (In the Outmost System, the coins are still called bones, in memory of the currency of primitive days.) The plain was lost under a pale sea of mist from which the ridge rose in a long black peninsula. Nearer at hand, the tip of a single big rock stood out like a marker buoy. A thin column of smoke from the mineworks trailed across the face of the moon.

"Look at the mist," said Pzyche. "It must have grown warmer. We do not usually have such mists in the Cold Season."

"I am not warm," said Tnoe.

"If we were to lie back to back," Pzyche suggested, "you might be warm." She added, by way of explanation: "The computer says, that is what some animals do, when they go into hibernation."

Tnoe said: "That would be violation of territory."

"You are my sister," said Pzyche.

They closed the shutter and went back to bed. Even through

her shift, Pzyche's back felt cold. Tnoe could feel the shoulder blades jutting sharply through her skin. "I shan't sleep at all," she thought, on the edge of oblivion. She slept.

They were woken abruptly, shortly before dawn. Pzyche sat bolt upright, her eyes wide with listening. Tnoe said: "What the *hell*—?" The shutter was open, banging against the wall. All the glass seemed to have gone from the window. Beyond, the sky had turned red.

Pzyche got there first. Over the plain, the mist was scattered and whipped into ragged waves, trailing gouts of spume which glittered on the wind like cinders. Half the ridge seemed to have blown away. And above what had once been the mining colony, unfurling slowly into the sky like a huge inverted umbrella, was a dense cloud of smoke, ghastly white above from the light of the second moon and lit from beneath with an evil scarlet glare. Everything was absolutely silent. The ground still throbbed from the sonic boom. "Heaven and hell," whispered Tnoe. "What have they *done*?"

For a long time the two girls stood by the window. Gradually, the umbrella opened out over the whole sky, eating up the stars. Presently, thought Tnoe, we will die of radiation sickness. She knew very little about bombs. In any case, it did not seem to matter.

"It is all gone," Pzyche said at last. "The other austracisor. Everything. I think perhaps we will starve."

"But the *people*," said Tnoe. "Hundreds of people . . ."

"They are dead," said Pzyche, struggling vainly to assimilate the enormity of so much death. But the scale was too great. She added: "We will not have to bury them, I think. They are buried deep . . ."

They waited two days before going to investigate. "If it was a bomb," said Pzyche, "it wasn't a very big one. I think in two days it will be safe."

[54]

"It looked big enough to me," said Tnoe. "Whatever it was."

But Pzyche knew about bombs. "Bombs," she explained, "come under philosophy."

They were beginning to be very hungry now. Tnoe had caught a lot of beetles, but she could not bring herself to do anything with them. Pzyche had told her with an air of authority that they had to be dropped alive into boiling water, and Tnoe had never been able to kill anything. However, she found a bottle of glucose tablets in a cupboard which the miners had missed somehow, and she hoped those would give them enough energy to last a little while. They both drank a great deal. Sometimes, Tnoe wondered if the impurities in the water were affecting her mind. There were moments when even the green Kraken dawn looked beautiful to her. "Soon," she said, "there must be a freightlift. Or perhaps they know about the bomb, and someone will come to investigate."

Freightlifts had never formed a part of Pzyche's routine. Her father and Goloro had always dealt with supplies. "I suppose so," she said, without enthusiasm. She found the certainty of a rescue vaguely disagreeable.

They climbed the broken ridge and looked down at the colony. There was nothing left. Where the barracks had stood yawned a shallow crater, filled up with rubbish. Here and there thin spires of smoke, dirty yellow in colour, climbed skywards. Ragged vapours veiled the entrance to the mineshaft. Overhead, the evil pall of fume was beginning to disperse, and a single shaft of sunlight slanted down, glimmering with dust. "I wonder," said Tnoe, "if the caves are still there? The caverns of Dragoncrake . . ."

"They were over that way," said Pzyche, pointing, "and far underground. They must be almost undamaged."

They had come as far as they could. Beyond, the ridge ended in a sheer drop, where the blast had torn half the hill away. A single tongue of rock remained, jutting precariously over the gap. Pzyche walked along it. Tnoe, who did not like heights any more than she liked going underground, followed carefully. "Is there anything to see?" she called, about halfway along.

Pzyche stood on the edge, her hair lifted off her face in an unenthusiastic wind. "Only rubbish," she said, "and desolation."

They walked back along the ridge. "Are you sure it was a bomb?" asked Tnoe.

"There's a crater," said Pzyche. "Bombs always make craters. An explosion underground would have looked quite different. I have seen pictures."

"Then," said Tnoe, "if it *was* a bomb, somebody must have dropped it."

For a few minutes they were both silent, wondering why the question had not occurred to them before.

"Perhaps it was the gods," suggested Pzyche. Her ideas on religion came exclusively from literature, and she was consequently uncertain as to how far the immortals were liable to interfere in real life. "Perhaps the gods were angry." She did not say why.

"Gods don't drop bombs," said Tnoe. They both looked back, a little nervously, half expecting to see some huge greywhiskered djinn come writhing out of the smoke. The wind whipped at the pall of cloud and in the widening gap there was a sudden gleam of silver.

"Look," Tnoe whispered. "*Look.*"

It was a spaceship.

PART II

6

At Sunset City on the planet Teuxis, at the other end of the
Hiboric Chain, express spaceflight 335 was coming in to land.
It was about a week earlier. In the blue and green corridors of
Spaceport Sunset, girls in white suits with beaded hair went
about their business, their epaulettes flashing like indicators as
they pressed appropriate buttons. Automatic doors opened and
closed at will. In the neutral areas, passengers sat in waiting
bays on First Class cushions, drinking essence of pathé. Other
passengers stood in Second Class queues, shuffling their feet.
On the departure board, flights appeared in yellow and were
cancelled in red. This was the Inmost System. This was science
and technology. As he came out of the disembarkation corridor,
Varagin Karel heard the familiar seductive female voice over
the tannoy: "We apologize to passengers for the delay to space-
flight 335 from Fingstar and Hiboryn. This was due to an air
bubble in the fuel pumps. We apologize to passengers, and
regret the inconvenience caused ..." Through the customs
office, Varagin followed a corridor marked with yellow arrows
down to the liftshaft. In the enormous lift, liftfreaks, or lifties,
as they were called, sat around in the leathertype chairs playing
push-button chess and drinking interminable cups of kaffine.
They did nothing else all day. Most of the passengers ignored
them. At the top of the shaft, Varagin stepped out into a vast
round hall roofed with glass. The floor was divided into seg-
ments, like an orange, and in each segment were pictured the
landscapes of different planets in the Hiboric Chain: mountains on Ossor, steppes on Golad, yellow forests on Ozray, green

forests of Teva, raw red hills on Qara and skyblocks on Qateng. Beyond the glass dome it was sunset, and the whole sky was like molten bronze. (Most outsystem flights were scheduled to arrive at sunset, by special dispensation of the tourist board.) Round the walls, there were the usual notices: "Public Communications", "Bar", "Autocars", "Enquiries and Information". Varagin headed for the exit.

He emerged onto a terrace about halfway up the Sunrock. Above, there were the palaces of the Establishment, cylindrical towers glittering with windows, many-faceted domes, vast cubes of obsidian and glass. Below, the villas of the Established dignitaries, set among rockeries of crystal and groves of electronic trees. (No living things grow on the Sunrock.) And then the Rock ended abruptly in a sheer drop to the plain, and the rest of Sunset City was spread out beneath. The sunlight flashed golden from every window and the thousand antennae of the city glinted like needles: aerials, spiragira, delicate webs of sensitisors monitoring traffic, pedestrians, crime levels, consumption of alcohol and astralburgers. On the terrace, newcomers paused to gasp and wonder. Once, it had been called Desert City, a cluster of tumbledown shacks clinging perilously to bare rock and bare earth. There was nothing to look at but the sunset, which lasted two hours every day. Now, it was the most beautiful city in the whole of the Hiboric Chain. But Varagin had seen it before. He left the terrace and made his way down Centre Street.

At the Thousand Steps, one of the lifts was out of order. The other was at the bottom. Varagin went down on foot. He did not, like most people, try to keep count. (On a previous occasion he had given way to scientific curiosity, and he knew quite well there were only seven hundred and ninety-three.) Once, a man had gone mad, losing track around five hundred and eighty, and had thrown himself off in despair. Now, there were electric railings, so that anyone trying to jump would be electrocuted first.

[60]

In the Lower City, it was the law that all windows had to be built facing the sunset. The light was failing now and over the darkward horizon the sky was turning from violet to blue. In the endless windows, there was a last glint of dying gold. Varagin turned aside into a narrow road skirting the base of the Sunrock. Presently, he came upon a tunnel, going back into the cliff. In the unlit entrance there was a gate which opened only in response to an assortment of personal codes. Varagin selected one at random which he had learned from a man with whom he had once shared a taxi in Spacecity Lunamundi on the far side of the galaxy, and tapped it out on the keypanel. The gate opened at once and Varagin passed through into the Undercity.

The tunnel was narrow and ill-lit, winding erratically deep into the rock. At intervals, unseen animals scurried away into holes, leaving behind a faint acrid smell and a trail of pawprints which gleamed briefly in the darkness and then faded. On either side there were openings through which Varagin glimpsed alleyways of what looked like interminable back doors. Presently, he came to a spiral stair with no lights at all. He emerged at the top into an underground street lined with clubs and restaurants and hung with green and scarlet lamps. This was Midnight Street. Through arched windows inlaid with waterlight he could see cushioned floors and murals which seemed to have been inspired by the oldest legends in the world. Music of all kinds floated through curtained doorways: from audiograms, zitars, three-pronged Lippith pipes, fantastic tintinabula constructed of wine-glasses filled with varying levels of liquid and struck with silver forks. The smell of the strange animals, like overspiced hnim curry, lingered elusively. Varagin turned into Sorg Street. This was devoted almost exclusively to bordellos. In the windows of the cheapest, girls sat with their breasts exposed and price tags round their necks. The more expensive showed a single foot peeping through chiffon curtains, with gilded toenails and an anklechain. The most expensive had no windows at all. At the far end, Varagin slipped

[61]

through a covered doorway, murmuring a password. (He knew it was the wrong password but such was his assurance that the man on the door decided his own information must be out-of-date.) Varagin went down a long passage, through a room where a very fat man was making love to a very thin prostitute, and into a courtyard. The ground was studded with electronic stars in equilateral triangles. There was no other light. Opposite, Varagin could make out a huge door with a stone mask in the centre. As he approached, its eyes lit up, and a single deep note, like a gong, sounded somewhere beyond. Presently, the door opened.

"Varagin Karel," he said. "Tell Krater. He isn't expecting me."

"Let us talk," said the man called Krater, leaning back in his chair. Like all major villains, he liked to discuss the meaning of life, particularly after dinner. It went well with the digestifs.

The chair in question was a curious construction lined with scarlet cushions, which adapted itself to his shape no matter what position he assumed. On his bad days, he found it extremely irritating.

The dinner had been excellent if a little bizarre. Vegetables from the austracisor, dyed to recapture their natural hues: green peas, red carrots, yellow leeks (the result of a disagreement between the artist and the cook), white onions and black olives. Cutlets, ornamented with butterflies and impregnated with scarlet spice. Yellow sauce with green flecks. Green sauce with yellow flecks. Several different kinds of wine.

The digestifs were equally varied. Spirits of pterviti, zaragon, Sunset Special. Varagin had a Sunset Special. "I would mix it myself," said Krater, "if I wasn't employing someone to do it for me." Varagin watched carefully as the drink changed colour according to the different additives: from colourless to green to yellow to orange to pink. It was said there was no drug or poison which could be added to a Sunset Special without affecting the standard colour changes.

Krater drank zaragon, well watered. "Let us talk," he said.

Reaching out a long leg, he pushed the table aside with his foot. He did not stand up. It was said, no one but his personal bodyguard had ever seen him standing up. He was supposed to be a big man, too big, over seven spans in his bare feet. His waist had thickened a little over the passage of time but otherwise he was as fleshless as a robot, with bones like steel girders. From a distance, he might have been in his early thirties. Varagin thought he was fifty at least. Regular cosmetic surgery had affected his face, giving it a curiously bland look, as though there were muscles around the jaw line which had been tightened up a little too much and pads of flesh on the cheekbones that did not belong to him. Only the skin around his eyes looked loose and old, crumpled like paper into innumerable wrinkles. Sometimes, people did not notice his eyes. They were small and deepset, and they glinted in the dim light like pebbles. His mouth was thick-lipped and much too large; that was why, long ago, they had called him Krater. He had taken up the name because it suited his sense of humour, but nobody laughed any more. His teeth were rotten, his tongue black from too much hennebuhl. It was said he had once murdered his dentist. He wore skins which did not fit in all the wrong places and a shirt open to the waist; the web of muscle across his chest rippled as he tightened his fingers on the stem of his glass. One sleeve was rolled up, and the skin of his forearm showed mottled, pale and dark, and bristling with little white hairs. On his fingers, he wore several rings with very big stones, set in spikes. Round his neck, there was a sundisc on a silver chain, left over from the days when he believed in God.

Outside the Undercity, no one had ever heard of Krater. In the Establishment, if they knew his name, it was not mentioned. But the people of the Undercity, pimps, ball dancers, waiters, zitar-players, petty thieves, supercrooks, people just passing through who had lost a purse at Zinthe's or woken in an open drain by somebody's back door, they liked to tell stories, over the very last bottle, in whispers that would not go beyond the dark. They said he owned all the Undercity and most of the Establishment. They said he was rich enough to buy a planet and such was his influence that if he dropped a pin, shares in the steel industry would fall three points. They said he had arthritis, cancer of the liver, athlete's foot. They said he liked boys. Some of the stories were true, some were less true. Some were totally apocryphal. When they got back to Krater he would smile a little, with an effort, pulling at the stiff mask of his face. Stories bred terror, and terror bred power. He was a powerful man.

"One day," he remarked to Varagin, "you will drink zaragon, and I shall know you trust me."

"And then?" queried Varagin, very softly.

"I shall have you killed," said Krater, and laughed, without moving his face, deep down in his throat. "It gets to be a habit," he went on, "having people killed. All you have to do is give an order. It's the simplest thing in the world, giving orders. That's the secret of success: never do anything yourself. Never rob a safe or commit a murder or mix a Sunset Special. Just give an order. I have killed very few people myself. I daresay you may have heard I strangled my first wife?"

"No," said Varagin. "Your second."

"One forgets," said Krater. "She asked for it, whoever she was. I couldn't manage that kind of exercise now. The joints grow stiff. One doctor told me, in half a year I shall be completely crippled. I have a wasting disease, he said, something to do with hardening of the sinews and imitating the action of a dangerous animal. King's Evil or Queen's Fancy or Prime Minister's Relapse. One of those sort of names."

"If you say so," murmured Varagin, politely.

Krater laughed again. "You know, Karel," he said, "I like you. I really like you."

[64]

"If you say so," said Varagin, through his teeth.

A servant came in carrying an inlaid box of hennebuhl and two long-stemmed pipes. Varagin declined. "Haven't any vices, have you?" snapped Krater, lighting up. "There's too much of this damned self-control about these days. Bad for the heart. One of my doctors told me, it puts a strain on the ventricles. You'll drop dead before you're forty. If you're not careful."

"I'll take my chance," said Varagin, allowing himself to smile.

"The sod I'm sending with you," Krater went on, "he hasn't any self-control. Healthy bastard. Or he would be if it wasn't for the women and the drink. You know the type."

"I thought I was to be in charge of the Kraken project?" said Varagin, in an edged voice.

"I always send two," said Krater. "Keep an eye on each other. You'll love Vinya Borogoyn. It's a delicate business, you know, delegating power. It doesn't matter who does things but it matters like hell who gives the orders. I like my project managers in the field to have a very special relationship. If they get on too well, they'll form their own syndicate. You have to pick very carefully."

"This Borogoyn," said Varagin, evidently resigned, "what's he like?"

"He's an educated man," said Krater, "if logs are educated. Likes a fair fight, three to one. Thinks before he acts, at cards. Honest as the day on the dark side of the moon. A silver-tongued conversationalist, after a couple of drinks. A profound thinker, after a couple more. Choosy: fornicates anything with a hole in the right place. Refined: eats with a knife and fork, especially on Sunday. I could go on forever. Anyway, you know the type. Have fun."

Krater was a very powerful man; he did not need lighting effects. Varagin's face was in shadow.

"They say," he went on, "he used to love his mother, until he discovered he wasn't born from an austracisor." He refilled his pipe. "A practical sod, Karel: you ought to appreciate that."

"I appreciate it," said Varagin. "If I wasn't practical, I wouldn't be here."

"I like a man who knows his limitations," murmured Krater, through his pipe. "You had the luck; I have the organization. You are one, alone; I am universal: the government, the underworld, the crime, the law. Don't you forget that, Karel. Not even in your sleep."

"I am a student of Nepeth," said Varagin. "My dreams are my own."

"I always understood the Discipline of Nepeth did not care to advertise," Krater remarked.

"It's hardly an advertisement," said Varagin, "telling you something you already know."

"As you say," said Krater, shortly. He relapsed into a silence which the other felt no particular inclination to break. He knew everything, naturally; a man in his position had to know everything. But he did not like having to admit it. He was not curious, merely efficient. He thought people should mind their own business and get on with their own lives. He probably knew about Livadya. But he would have considered it unethical to say so.

Presently, he resumed briskly: "Anyway, what were we talking about? Vinya Borogoyn. A stupid man. That's why I thought of him. Thinks like a rhinoceros: with his horn. He's got the right experience: ran the Gold Rush for me on Voltis, a couple of years back. I lost a fortune; a pity. But it wasn't Vin's fault. That's one thing you learn, Karel: never pass the buck. It's too damned easy when you're right at the top. If something goes wrong, it's your fault, or God's, or whoever. I'm a good atheist now, thank Heaven. But not the middleman, or the manager, or the man who mended the drains. Vin's all right. His men hate him. Have another drink."

The bottles were out of reach. Krater pressed a button in the arm of his chair and a servant appeared, too promptly, as though he had been poised for action in a cupboard just outside. Varagin said, belatedly: "No thank you."

Krater ignored him. "Zaragon," he ordered. "Lots of water. More . . . Have you got the material I asked for?" The man nodded. "Good. Put it by my bed; I suppose I'd better look it over. It'll make sweet bedtime reading. I need bedtime reading, now Mortan's cleared off. And order a survey team to look over the site. I don't want any witnesses. We had too much trouble on Voltis, paying people off. I want the mines cleared out completely; Scharm knows the routine."

"Anything else?" said the man. He did not call his master sir. None of Krater's people ever called him sir. He could not stand it.

"Yes; why not? Take my guest next door. He would like a little entertainment. I think, Sateleptra . . ."

Varagin sat on a lizardskin sofa surrounded by sensile cushions. He was bored. The room was furnished like something in an expensive bordello. The walls were inlaid with a leaf design in green taupe and covered with hangings in transparent silk, showing luscious-looking orchids with very fat bees masturbating on over-developed stamens. Above one door the West Wind, carved in alabaster with pursed-up lips, exhaled a pale lilac vapour, smelling of roses. Above the other door the East Wind, in ebony with a constipated grimace, exhaled a rose-coloured vapour, smelling of lilac. Music began to creep up out of the floor. At the far end of the room different-coloured curtains drew back, one at a time, like the slow unfurling of a rainbow. There was a rustle of soft bare feet, a tinkle of ankle-bells . . .

Presently, the most beautiful girl in the world came in and proceeded to take all her clothes off.

Varagin told himself that he had seen it all before. The drugged vapour, the pulsating cushions, the music. Krater was discreet: she did not look like Livadya. Her skin was dark velvet, her breasts as firm and upstanding as though cast in

[67]

bronze. Muscles rippled, tantalizingly, in her abdomen. When she had finished, she gave him a long smouldering look out of her long smouldering eyes. Then she went out.

A section of the wall slid back to reveal Krater, lounging at ease in his scarlet chair. "Nice, isn't she?" he said. "She likes you, too; I could tell. I forget where I found her. She's very dark, even for a Lippith. I'll send her to you tonight."

"Thank you," said Varagin, icily, "I prefer to sleep alone." He did not like being manipulated, even for his own pleasure. And he wanted Krater to know that there was nothing he could not do without.

"As you wish," Krater shrugged. "You know, Karel, you want to be careful. Go on giving things up at this rate, and even abstention will become self-indulgent. Borogoyn, now, he wouldn't have said no. He'd have swallowed her in two bites. Yes, I think I'll give her to Borogoyn. She'll hate that. She likes to think she's got class. Whores are the worst snobs in the world. I'll give her to Borogoyn and he can take her to Krake. That should keep the three of you happy."

"If you don't mind," said Varagin, uninterested, "I'll go to bed. I'm tired."

"Of course," said Krater. "Time lag; I forgot." He pressed a button. "Sweet dreams."

In the bedroom, Varagin undressed slowly and lay down naked on the bed. The cushions were a little too soft, the heating a little too warm, but he was determined not to think of Sateleptra. His moods were rarely sensual. When he had the money, he visualized himself sleeping in a cool white cell, with a window in the roof and very little furniture. There were no women in the picture, no fountains running with alcohol, no feasts of forbidden meat. There were, perhaps, somewhere in the background, the resources of modern technology, the many fingers of power ... There were distances beyond light and time, familiar and unfamiliar stars, old memories erased like stains. But all that was beyond the hermit's cell. Varagin had grown wary of anticipation. He let himself think only of a bleak luxury, and an expensive solitude. If he had considered it at all, the exotic vulgarity of Krater's apartments would have filled him only with a kind of amused contempt. Krater was right: he had the organization, the resources; the allegiance was unfortunately necessary. But evidently it was going to be difficult. Varagin found all allegiance difficult; he preferred to be alone, to take orders from no one. Krater, he thought, did not like to work with a man he could not control. But Varagin was determined to remain just outside his plans, watching any attempt at manipulation with a detached eye. He had come a long way from the other side of the galaxy, in more ways than one.

He did not speculate about Krater's probable methods. "Everyone has a conscience," he had learned, in the monastery of Nepeth. "The most important thing is to tell yourself no lies." Varagin did not think he was given to self-deception. It was wrong to kill, and he had killed; it was wrong to corrupt the corruptible, to exploit the exploited, to steal from thieves. The world was wrong. Varagin told himself he might have lived by certain standards, if the rest of mankind had not shown itself so regrettably deficient. To survive in the rat-race, you must learn to run like a rat. Trained in the Discipline of Nepeth, he slept well. He always slept well. But sometimes, he was afraid to lose control of his dreams.

7

Thousands of lightyears away, towards the heart of the galaxy, lay the seat of the Planetary League in sunsystem Sc 0771, called the Ring. There were only three planets orbiting the sun, Schiv: Ovolt, the closest, wreathed in hot red gases; Quent, the farthest, a cold wilderness; and Orgo, a reclaimed planet with an artificial atmosphere, where the countless member systems that constituted the League did their best to sit round the conference table making boring speeches, rather than bombing each other with their little black bombs, or shooting each other with their blue and green lasers, or giving each other exciting diseases out of test-tubes. Adjoining the vast complex of conference buildings and a network of hotels so glamorous that even those who paid the bills did not know what they actually came to, lay the Galactic Culture Centre, a fairly recent and very ambitious project covering high-level teaching and research facilities. In the World University, the most intelligent students in the galaxy, or those with the most influential parents, filled the glittering lecture halls to listen to the audio-magnified words of the wise and the venerable, or sat in the hanging gardens under the shadow of ivory towers, smoking hennebuhl and talking about Truth. In the Department of Archaeology and Anthropology, some of them had even heard of the Outmost System, and a planet called Krake.

Professor Galbrenzil stood at a long bench in Laboratory 5, talking to himself. Nobody was listening. He had been in the department for many years now, and it was a rule of courtesy not to listen when he was talking to himself. In any case, it would have been very difficult for the uninitiated to understand what he said. The words came out in a sort of low-key scramble which, it was claimed, only his fine, sensitive brain could re-assemble into a form that made sense. Every so often, while he talked, he would lean absent-mindedly on the keyboard of the second-hand laboratory computer, known affectionately as the Toaster, so that all the lights flashed on and off. Then he would break off to stare at the machine in faint astonishment, before resuming his conversation with himself. He was a little, brown, wizened creature, more like a gnome than a man, with a round blobby nose and round brown eyes, like little bright buttons, and a quantity of thick upstanding hair which was still occasion-ally black. All his life, it was said, he had looked just the same, merely getting a little browner and more wizened with time. Even among the wise and venerable he was regarded as antique, but his students were fond of him, and some of them even called him sir, just to make him happy.

Beside him on the bench part of a time-and-space chart was spread out, showing a section of the twenty-fifth circle on a very small scale with all the minor planets omitted, and poring over it was a postgraduate of indeterminate sex with long fair hair and cold violet glasses. The air was full of fumes of toluene, and as the ventilator fans were not working everybody was mildly stoned, except the professor, who was used to it. At the far end of the bench two young students were rebuilding the skeleton of an ancient cterethin. One of them, a girl, had taken most of her clothes off. The Professor did not notice. Even if he had, he would probably have attributed it to the strange customs doubtless obtaining on her planet of origin, and smiled with pleased tolerance at the fascinating vagaries of the wide world. The postgraduate did not notice either, possibly because of the cold violet glasses. "The quickest," he said (on his application, he was listed as male), "would be for me to go to Garth, in the Octopus, and pick up a direct flight to Hiboryn. After that—"

("Me," muttered the Professor. "Me, he says. Twenty-five, or perhaps thirty-six, so he thinks he can say 'me' like that.

[71]

What about ME? I know: I am just a useless old man. Old.
Old. Like an old horse in a pretty green field, which is not good
for pulling carts any more. Garth: the Age of Horsepower. I
have the back-ache in my back and the knee-ache in my knees
and the lumps in my stomach which they pretend are not there.
Stupid doctors. Do they think I don't know? My uncle, he had
lumps in the stomach. It is to be expected. Soon, they will put
me in a hospital, and I will sit in a nice white bed till I die.
Perhaps it will take years. That stupid historian, he wrote a
book first. *History!* Now, I could write a book. A great, great
book. All the things I have discovered. When I was thirty-six,
and found the Hidden City, in the jungles of Ioa. Or perhaps it
was the Lost City, in the snows of Gol. Or the Forgotten City,
in the rose-red mountains of Omarth. I forget. But it will be a
great, great book. I will get a secretary to write it for me. A nice
young girl, with pretty teeth. You can always tell the pretty
ones by their teeth. That Topioc skull must have been a *very*
pretty girl . . . All the same, it will be dull. I would rather go to
the edge of the galaxy, and discover the Oldest City, in the
underworld of Krake. Galbrenzil, they said, how do you know
it is so old? How do I know it is so old? I have the rock samples.
Not many, but enough. *I* do not get my dating all wrong. *I* do
not come up with two different interglacials from the same
piece of burnt flint. Stupid men. Besides, I can feel it in my
stomach. I may have the back-ache, and the knee-ache, and the
imaginary lumps, but my stomach is still the stomach of an
archaeologist. My stomach is never wrong. That nice young
man with the glasses, I forget his name, he will go out there and
prove it for me. He is fit, and strong, and quite clever. But perhaps he will not draw the proper plans? Perhaps he will mix
up the samples. He is a nice boy, but is he truly *systematic*?
Bah, Thiodor Galbrenzil, you are not fair. You are old, and
jealous, and you want to go yourself. So you are not fair. It is
too late, you stupid old man. Too late for Forgotten Cities, and
Hidden Cities, and Cities of No Return . . .")

[72]

"This man Brant," commented the postgraduate, looking down at a sheaf of notes and adjusting the focus on his cold violet glasses, "he says he's trying to start an Archaeology Department on Fingstar. He studied in the Distaff, somewhere obscure. Apparently, there are problems. The natives aren't very science-orientated, I gather. And he says something about danger—"

"So the site is unsafe," said the Professor, this time for the general ear. "You take a helmet. You take protective clothing. Sometimes, you remember to put it on. You take beams, and props, and suspension leads. Obviously, this Brant, he knows nothing. He has no experience. Danger! Bah!"

"He hasn't seen the site," said the postgraduate. "Apparently, it's been taken over by some profiteer. No, privateer. I assume there's treasure of some kind. It all sounds rather improbable."

("Treasure!" sighed the Professor. "Danger! And is he excited? Do his eyes light up behind those ridiculous glasses? They do not. It is 'rather improbable'. Life is rather improbable. The creation of the world was rather improbable. He is blasé. All these young people, they are blasé. They have their health and strength, and they slouch around like damp dragonflies, turning up their noses at adventure. Was I a damp dragonfly, when I found the Tombs of the Ancient Kings at Araquat? Was I daunted by danger, or curses, or the flux? Of course not. I was prepared to die for the cause of knowledge. I was even prepared to catch the flux. This poor young man, he will die, and he is not even excited. He will be stung by poisonous snakes, wicked privateers will shoot him, and rocks will fall on his head. Perhaps there will be a curse, and his old mother will find his pet mongrel howling in front of the family sundial, which has stopped, while a thousand lightyears away he has fallen down a pothole. 'It is rather improbable,' he will shout, from the depths below. His last words. Pathetic, truly pathetic. Such a brilliant young man, too. What a waste. One day, he

[73]

might have been a great archaeologist. Not so great as me, but quite great. He is a young man with his life before him, and he must die, while I, who am old and unnecessary, must go on . . .")

Down the far end of the bench, the girl student removed another item of clothing. "Sir," she said to the Professor, "do you think this is part of a condile?"

"No, no," the Professor responded, absent-mindedly. "Mammary glands. When is this flight to Hiboryn? I have changed my mind. I go myself."

"Sir—"

"Do not argue! I am old, and doddering, and there is danger. Danger is for the old and doddering. You are young, and have your life before you. Besides, you are not systematic. Book me on the first direct flight."

"You have to go to Garth. Sir—"

"I do not want to go to Garth. I have been to Garth many times. Arrange a special flight. I go now to kiss my wife. She will have the life insurance. She will be sad, but happy. You will go and have tea with her sometimes and tell her that I was the greatest archaeologist in the world."

"Sir, it is rather improbable—"

"I know," said Professor Galbrenzil.

On the day Professor Galbrenzil flew out from Orgo (more or less: it is always difficult to synchronize galactic time) Derec Rolt was sitting in his college room on Fingstar contemplating the evolution of the spleen. He was frowning horribly. His eyebrows, which were paler than his hair and rather bristly, would obviously become grey and beetling with practice. His eyes were deepset and usually narrowed to slits of intense concentration. He was a serious young man, and he frowned often, particularly when tangling with the deficiencies of advanced medical education in the Outmost System. The Ifingens believed in the dominion of the mind (and indeed almost any

[74]

other intangible and unproven theory), and doctors concerned with the mundane details of ordinary biology were regarded in much the same light as dustmen or sewer operators: a necessary evil. Fortunately for the Health Service, there were several foreign specialists practising in Camarest, but no native Ifingen was expected to take medical science seriously. What made Derec Rolt want to become a doctor he never knew. Perhaps it was a result of his adolescent rebellion against his parents. Most Ifingen adolescents rebelled against their parents: the psychiatrists expected it. Derec, however, rebelled against the psychiatrists. He sat, an uncooperative and taciturn fourteen-year-old, through various lengthy and rather one-sided sessions with analysts who called him "unique", "challenging", and finally "unresponsive". In the end, bored, he walked out. When he said he wanted to be a doctor his mother, an artist, shut herself up for three weeks painting a picture of disembodied hands washing themselves, presumably in blood, and his father, a financier, spent a whole day playing therapeutic Patience while the Ifingen Stock Market, always shaky, disintegrated about his ears. Not surprisingly, Derec left home. After two years basic medical studies he managed to obtain a grant to do an external advanced course with the University of Hiboryn, still using the limited facilities of University Complex in Camarest. He worked hard and had very few friends. The authorities regarded him with suspicion because he was never seen smoking hennebuhl, vandalizing the facility room, or otherwise expressing his personality. The students regarded him with suspicion because he refused to join any social clubs and had once admitted that he never wrote poetry. His only outside activity was cross-country running. The countryside on Fingstar was nothing much to look at, being largely flat and featureless, but it meant he avoided team games, which he hated, and was left alone to think. And on Sundays, he visited the caretaker at the old monotheist chapel. Monotheism was out of fashion and sometimes no one came near the place for weeks. The caretaker was not conversational but he made good greentea, so strong it was almost black, and Derec always said, by way of self-justification, that as a practising atheist he liked the feel of a place where they had given up on God. He did not add that the week Tnoe went, he had stood for a long time by the dusty altar, trying hard not to pray.

He had never meant to fall in love with Tnoe. They met in a bar, over breakfast; she was with a gaggle of theatrical friends and an expensive fur jacket was coiled about her shoulders like an affectionate cat. She looked, he thought, rich, spoiled, and artificial. They fell into an argument and when breakfast was over she offered to pay. "You're a student," she said simply. "I've got lots of money." "Rubbish," he snapped. "I'll pay for myself." He had no intention of owing anything to anyone, particularly gratitude. She took out her purse, without answering, and he found himself noticing the obstinacy of her mouth and the misguided sincerity in her eyes. Suddenly, he felt ungracious. On the way home, reluctantly, he decided to fall in love. Even now, when he remembered bitterly that she had gone for all the wrong reasons, and without even saying good-bye, he found himself thinking of her, in unguarded moments, with futile longing.

He looked down at the spleen in front of him, a photographic diagram in glorious technicolour, and decided it was as meaningless as an austracized bean. Outside, rain was running down the window in little trickles, dividing and rejoining like transparent blood vessels. Suddenly, he wanted to get wet. He went out without a jacket and headed for the Meeting Hall. He was expecting a consignment of books from the Inmost System and although he knew it would not arrive on schedule (they never did), he could take a look at the general notice board, just in case. Needless to say, it had not. However, another notice, lettered in red, caught his eye. "Krake. Reports of a unique archaeological discovery . . ." He read on. At the bottom, he saw the name of Caleth Brant, Lecturer in Archaeology. No one was studying it, but this did not deter the Ifingen authorities from paying a lecturer. Derec contemplated the notice, darkly, for a minute or two. Then he went to enquire where Caleth Brant lived.

The spleen might never have evolved.

In Caleth Brant's flat on the edge of University Complex, Professor Galbrenzil said, shocked: "You mean there really *is* danger?"

"I'm afraid so," said Caleth Brant apologetically, passing him another drink.

The flat, by Ifingen standards, was exceptionally bare. The walls were tinted in green; so were the lights. There was only one picture, a still life of maggots in a cucumber, selected presumably because it matched the colour scheme. The furniture consisted mostly of rather uncomfortable cubes, either covered in green padding or welded into cabinets. Above the autobar hung a stone hand-axe, about thirty thousand years old, which constituted the principal feature of the university collection. "I want to do a display," Caleth had said, on arrival. "You'll have to find something first," the Vice-Chancellor had told him, happily. Caleth found the hand-axe in the bottom drawer of a filing cabinet.

"You don't have to come," he went on, unobtrusively refilling Derec's glass.

"No, no," said the Professor. "I am prepared to die for archaeology, of course. It's just that I did not expect it would be quite yet. In a year or two, maybe . . ."

"Nobody does," said Caleth. "That's the secret of being alive. Knowing that whatever happens you'll never, never die. Death is like the ghost of an old legend that feeds on credulity. Once you believe in him, he's got you, and you're dead already."

"Death," said Derec Rolt, shortly, "occurs when the brain ceases to function. I believe in death. He is my oldest enemy."

"No, doctor," Caleth smiled, "you see, but you do not

[77]

believe. Otherwise you would just give up the fight." He called Derec "doctor" to please him, although it would not be true until Derec had passed his finals the following year. Derec felt that his arguments suffered from inverted logic, but he did not say so. He was not yet sure that he disliked Caleth Brant. Normally, he disliked all intellectuals: they were, he suspected, empty-headed, pretentious, and interested in art. But this man was different. His manner was a curious blend of courtesy and mockery, straightforwardness and reserve, as though behind the gentle deference he was so perfectly self-assured he could afford to give way, smiling quietly, knowing he was in the right. To look at, he was short and extraordinarily ugly, with a pale, unhealthy face and dark lines under his eyes. His hair was coarse and very thick, too dark for a native of the Hiboric Chain, and cut raggedly as though he had done it himself with an old-fashioned razor. His mouth was almost bloodless, a shadowy line, twisted on one side by an old scar, so he looked as if he was always just about to smile. Somewhere in the past, his nose had been broken. He surveyed his colleagues without illusion, and approved. A clever, slightly pompous young man with red hair and an aging professor who talked to himself. Caleth smiled. He liked people, all kinds of people; he was not a man who took pleasure in *things*. And he had not really expected a response at all. He had been too long in the Outmost System for that.

He had come there three years earlier because it was as far as possible from the planet where he was born. He stayed because there was space. He could look out beyond Ingellan, low in the evening sky, and see space going on forever. Once, he tried to paint it, the great white star hanging on the edge of nothingness, the rays of light streaming out into the void until lightspeed itself grew tired of the journey into infinity. (Even with decelerated time, we have yet to cross the gap where time and light are not.) But he was not much of an artist, and he kept the picture in a drawer, to look at by himself. On the planet from which he came, there was no space. The people teemed together

[78]

in endless tenement blocks, committing suicide like lemmings, mugging and being mugged, dying of lack of light, lack of air, lack of life. The planet had a disastrous history of social problems and an even more disastrous history of social therapy. Caleth was the tenth child of careless parents who were into smoking concentrated hennebuhl, meditation, and getting close to the earth. Which of these factors produced the ten children is not clear. Caleth's mother beat him, when she was not stoned. (His father was always stoned.) When he was seven a social investigator took him away and put him in an experimental commune with three hundred other children who had never known their parents at all. In the commune, no one was ever beaten. A child who misbehaved was sent to the principal and given a sugar biscuit and a lecture on personal relationships (if anyone noticed). The adult assistants were changed every three months to prevent them turning into mother figures. It was forbidden to write reports. The children grew up in a kind of sociological Utopia, without hunger or cold or punishment, without mother complexes or father complexes, without ever being told that "life isn't fair". Childish teasing became mental sadism. Childish tantrums became homicidal. There was nothing against which to rebel. By the time the children were in their teens the powers that be had decided to revive the family, but for those three hundred it was too late. Only Caleth had had seven years of parental mistreatment, and he never felt he was quite like the others. He was their leader, the one they looked up to, imitated, envied. Aged ten, he had beaten the commune bully, who was much bigger than him, at chess. The secret of winning, he knew, was to pick your own battleground. At thirteen, when sex was in vogue, he slept with most of the girls. (There was one he had tried to love, but she had not known what he meant.) At sixteen, he packed a carryall, and went away. Nowhere in particular: just away. In the end, all the commune children went away. Wherever they found themselves, they moved on. They were always restless, always alone,

[79]

looking for something or trying to leave it behind. Caleth did not want to forget his childhood; he was not a person who ever wanted to forget anything. But he wanted to look back on it from a very long way off. Perhaps that was why he took up archaeology, to look back, over a great distance, at a past grown grey and peaceful with time, quietly accumulating the dust of the years. Arriving on Fingstar, he invented a degree for himself and persuaded the Ifingen authorities to install him as a lecturer. Archaeology was considered rather scientific, but he was a very persuasive man. The other lecturers invited him to dinner, though he did not come. It was rumoured the vice-chancellor liked him. When the report came in from Krake, he saw it as a challenge. "Challenges," he said, "are like windmills. You cannot pass them by without taking a pot-shot with a short-range missile." (He had read the Seven Plays.) The next day, he sent a communication to the Planetary League, and re-stocked the autobar.

In Caleth's flat, under the green-tinted lighting, Professor Galbrenzil was growing mellow. "This wicked privateer," he said, comfortably, "who is he? What do we know about him? And what is this wonderful treasure which he is trying to steal?"

"As far as we know," said Caleth, "there isn't any treasure. That's what makes it so interesting. According to my information, the mining colony was completely wiped out. A bomb, I understand, at a time when everyone was off duty. I gather the unions insist on what they call a total relaxation phase, in the middle of the night. Anyway, about two hundred and fifty people were killed. That seems a trifle extreme, when there isn't any treasure. And on Fingstar, nothing has been done. In the Outmost System, of course, one would not really expect anything to be done, at least for a year or so. Nonetheless, that, too, is interesting. My informant—"

"Might we know," interrupted Derec, "who that informant is?" (He wouldn't believe Tnoe dead. Not till it was proved.)

Caleth smiled. "I have many friends," he said. "Some of

[80]

them are not, perhaps, what you would consider respectable. My informant, now, he seems to think that someone has been pulling strings. There are puppets in high places, here or anywhere. Of course, we shall never see the puppeteer. But we can see the colour of his money. Corruption costs money. Death costs money. There is altogether too much money about. And money means money. Forgive the repetition. But there is a smell about this affair, a smell of recklessness, of greed, of wildcat gold. It reminds me of the discovery of platinum, on a planet called Ax. Unfortunately, I don't know enough about geology to know what might be found on Krake. Can you help, Professor?"

But the Professor, intrigued, had lapsed into a private harangue, and Caleth was too considerate to break his concentration.

"What happened," asked Derec, thoughtfully, "on the planet called Ax?"

"The people came," Caleth said, "and went away again, leaving their plastic bags behind. They blow around the ruins of the old town like indisposable ghosts. As for the platinum, the poor men stole it for the rich men, the rich men sold it to the jewellers, and the jewellers made it into rings and brooches for the rich men's wives and sold it back to them at twice the price. All that wheeling and dealing for a little cold metal. Are you sure, doctor, that you want to involve yourself in these things?"

"If you are going to get killed," said Derec, "you'll need a doctor."

Caleth looked amused. "Very well," he said. "The day after tomorrow, there is a freightlift on schedule, to Tzorn. It will, I gather, be stopping elsewhere on the way. My informant knows the cargo handler. There will also be a little spare room in the hold."

Unexpectedly, the Professor emerged from his soliloquy. "Good," he said. "Always I travel with my equipment. Otherwise, the stupid porters, they bang things that are fragile, and put upside-down things that should be the right way up. It is

[81]

very important that we come back in the hold as well."

"I hope," said Caleth, "that can be arranged."

In a shabby solicitor's office somewhere in Camarest a tall thin man sat behind a desk, clearing his throat. "Very difficult," said his associate, who was short and fat. "Really very difficult. Tnar Meliander was a most extraordinary woman. And to find out now, with the situation as it is . . . Of course, one is glad to know that the money was not *wasted*." (He did not sound particularly glad.) "But to invest in such a way, without taking the proper advice—! It's all in order, I'm afraid. Miss Meliander, Miss *Tnoe* Meliander, now owns sixty per cent of the Kraken concession. The rest, of course, is owned outside our system. She could be a very rich woman, a *very* rich woman, if there is anything there. Archaeology. Wildcat gold. It really is most difficult."

"Hrmmm!" said the tall thin man.

On the other side of the desk a younger man, taller and, if possible, even thinner, sat looking extremely uncomfortable.

"Of course," continued Mr Elts (and Mr Protion), "she may well be—hrmm!—dead. That would be shocking. Yes, very shocking. I gather there are several people out there who are, or seem to be—hrmmm!—dead. It is all highly irregular. Then there is the sister, if she survived infancy. Miss Pzyche Corazin. Doctor Corazin was a very strange man, a very strange man indeed. He may even be alive himself. Many of the individuals concerned may be either alive or—hrmmm!—dead. The legal possibilities are endless. It is *essential*—that is, you do appreciate—"

"Yes," said the young man unhappily. "Yes. Of course. Yes."

"Young Mr Protion," said his uncle, and his father's brother-in-law, "you are a credit to the firm. A credit. In the legal profession, we have a duty. Hrmmm! Perhaps you would like to draw up your will."

[82]

8

At Castle Kray, the austracisor had been mended and a new hydrant installed. The heating was working again. In the dim corridors, lights could be switched on and off. "It feels rather strange," said Pzyche, "to be still alive." She did not go into the library any more. One day, Tnoe had found it locked. Pzyche said it was to keep the newcomers from damaging anything.

"It's a good thing," said Tnoe, squinting at her face in the mirror, "that Mummy was a famous actress. This man Borogoyn hadn't heard of her, but some of the others had. I don't think they're all foreigners. I only hope they don't realize how little I take after her." (Yes, the left eye was definitely darker than the right. She picked up the kohl pencil.) "Fortunately, they're probably too stupid. Just a band of underpaid thugs who need lots of alcohol and entertainment to keep them happy. Not like the miners . . ." Now she had smudged her kohl. It wasn't Udulf especially; just the thought of death. "If only we weren't so helpless," she went on. "If only someone would come. Having to bargain with Borogoyn makes me feel so frightfully cheap. But what else could I do?" Pzyche did not answer. "Anyway," said Tnoe, "at least I know most of the Seven Plays by heart." She could remember, even when she was quite small, reading the cues for her mother. Do it with feeling, Tnar had said. Don't just give a prompt. I want you to *be* the person you're reading. Which person? Tnoe had asked. All of them, said her mother. "I never wanted to be an actress," Tnoe remarked.

"He's got a woman with him," Pzyche said unexpectedly. "I saw her yesterday, when we went over there. I *think* she is beautiful."

"I hope so," said Tnoe. She did not like the way Borogoyn looked at Pzyche. Sometimes, she found herself thinking with longing of absolute desolation, and the contemplation of beetles for dinner. She did not feel particularly hungry now. Or particularly safe.

"He is going to get me some flowers," said Pzyche, "to put on father's grave. I have never seen flowers."

"You didn't tell him anything?" said Tnoe sharply.

"Of course not," Pzyche said.

In the passenger compartment of a cargoship bound (indirectly) for Tzorn, Varagin Karel was playing push-button chess. The calculator was losing. On the seat behind him, there was a huge box of flowers: yellow ambrosine, goldenwand, winter roses. He had learnt, on enquiry, that Borogoyn had ordered them. He wondered if they were for Sateleptra. He had met Vinya Borogoyn already, and he found it difficult to imagine him ordering flowers, particularly for someone like her. Such evidence of delicacy and consideration seemed somehow a little out of keeping with his recollection of a big, swarthy, coarsely good-looking man, whose resident sneer and brackish complexion suggested overindulgence and an alcoholic temper. He found the thought of Sateleptra, enjoying or being enjoyed by Vinya Borogoyn, peculiarly distasteful. For no particular reason he remembered Livadya, an undersized twelve-year-old with legs that seemed to consist mostly of knees, dragging eagerly at his arm.

"But Varik, all the others have done it. I *must*. I can't be the only one who hasn't. Please, Varik." (No one else had ever called him Varik.)

"Liv, can't you see I'm busy? Ask Rif, or Tristin."

"But I want it to be you! You're my best friend. Rif's a bully

[84]

and Tristin's just stupid; he would be sure to get it wrong. You're so clever, Varik. *Please!*"

"You won't like it," Varagin warned her, with all the superiority of fourteen. "It'll hurt dreadfully and you'll probably bleed. Most girls do. And I haven't got much time. There's something on tonight."

"Thank you, Varik. Thank you *very* much!"

"Well, don't say I didn't warn you."

Afterwards, he remembered, she had cried and cried. "I told you so," he said.

The calculator made its usual predictable move and Varagin, almost absent-mindedly, abstracted two pawns and a rook. He had gone to college at sixteen and stayed for postgraduate research; for five years he had not seen Livadya at all. Not that he had missed her. Then she had come up to do a year's training as a lab assistant, and one summer morning she had walked into his laboratory to say hello. He had not even looked up. (He could still remember every detail of the diagram he had been studying at the time.) The other male students were staring, wide-eyed. One of them dropped a pencil. "Hello Varik," she said. He raised his head.

He saw a tall girl, reed-thin, with a long pale face and high cheekbones. Her black hair hung down her back in a single fine braid. There was a tremor about her mouth as though she did not quite dare to smile. The strange thing was, not that he realized she was beautiful, but that he saw a beauty which had always been there, a hidden potential, like the white perfect form of a classical virgin dimly envisaged in the primitive idol of some ancient goddess. Presently, she ventured to finish the smile. "Hello Varik," she said again.

"Hello Liv."

Years later, lightyears away, he saw a small furry animal on a bleak plateau, curling up to a rock in search of warmth and shelter. But the rock did not move. It just stood there, silent and cold. The wind came across the plateau, howling. Snow fell.

[85]

Presently, the animal died. Varagin, trained in the Discipline of Nepeth, did not pick it up and tuck it inside his coat. It had come to the rock for shelter, and the rock had failed. He watched the small black body stiffening in the cold, and the snow stung his eyes.

To his annoyance, he discovered the calculator had laid a trap for him. "You're improving," he murmured, forced to concentrate on the game. Inside him, there was a still small voice, crying out in pain, but he had learnt not to listen.

Down in the hold, the stowaways were playing cards by the light of a handlamp. The cards were green, with the four suits in red and gold: leaves, stones, rubies, tears. There were four red angels and four black devils. Professor Galbrenzil held the Key, but his mind, as usual, was elsewhere. Young Mr Protion, rather to his own surprise, was winning. "Who is our travelling companion?" asked Derec, jerking his head in the direction of the passenger compartment.

"Someone in charge," said Caleth. "At a guess, he's been a long way away, sounding the market for whatever it is they've found out there. My informant couldn't tell me his name." He did not add: I know him. He would have recognized the children of the commune anywhere, even at that distance. A pale, secretive boy with a tight mouth, a few years younger than Caleth. He had not changed all that much. Paler now, with more secrets. Not a pleasant face. There had been an incident with a flick-knife, Caleth remembered. In the commune, such things were frequent, but this one had been particularly nasty. And there had been something to do with a stink bomb which had blown a boy's hand away. Childish teasing, that was all. But after that, they had not teased him any more. Karel, that was his name. Karel something. There had been a little girl with black hair who used to follow him around. Looking back, Caleth thought she might have turned out pretty; those dark, bony ones often did. He could not remember her name at all.

[86]

"Your play," said Derec, looking at him thoughtfully.

Caleth answered the unspoken question in his usual oblique way. "Distant stars cast long shadows," he said. "It may not be important. I will tell you, when you need to worry."

He discarded the Ace of Tears.

On landing, the cargo handler let them out of the hold. It was dark, and there were several men milling round the improvised spacestage. No one asked them any questions. The Professor checked off the equipment on his fingers. Young Mr Protion sat down on a packing case and was severely reprimanded. "I told you," said Derec, "I don't know how to get there. It may be five miles or fifty. We need transport."

"Wait," said Caleth.

Varagin Karel had disembarked and was standing only a little way off. In the glare of the nitron lamps Caleth could see more clearly how the planes of his face had fined and hardened with time. He was speaking to someone, giving an order. Two men disappeared into the belly of the ship and for a few moments he was left alone. Caleth went across to him, stopping deliberately just outside the circle of light. Presently, Varagin wandered over, nonchalantly, like someone who has nothing better to do. "Caleth Brant," he said softly.

"Karel," said Caleth. Now, he remembered. "Varagin Karel."

"It has been a long time," remarked Varagin with careful irony. "Did you come, or were you sent?"

"Let us say, I have arrived," said Caleth. "As you see."

Varagin stared past him, narrowly, towards the packing cases stacked in the shadow of the hold. Caleth seemed to see him summing up the other three like a machine, assessing their ages, their fighting weight, their probable function. Presently, Varagin said: "You must have had an uncomfortable flight."

"Fair," said Caleth. "I stowed away in the wall space, once. That was much worse."

[87]

"Are you going to tell me," asked Varagin, "what you are doing here?"

The two men had emerged again, but they did not approach. "There's a fortune here," Caleth said, guardedly. "You know that."

Varagin remembered an independent eleven-year-old with a crooked nose, who would not take fifteen tela for his favourite finger-whistle. "In any case, you probably stole it," he had told the would-be musician, as if stealing were wrong. The next day, he had given the whistle to one of the girls, when somebody blacked her eye. He had always been an unnatural child, Varagin reflected bitterly. Afterwards, the girl had sold the whistle back to the first boy and bought herself enough sweets to be sick for a week.

"I have come to seek my fortune," said Caleth.

"If you say so," murmured Varagin.

Caleth gave it up. He had not really expected to learn anything, anyway. "I am interested in archaeology," he explained. "I gather the caves here are worth looking at. There is a representative of the Planetary League among my companions, one Professor Galbrenzil, from the Galactic Culture Centre. You may have heard of it. We've come in search of the Dragon of Dragoncrake."

"That is much more likely," said Varagin, ignoring the sarcasm. "You always wanted to try your hand at slaying dragons, didn't you? A pity they're extinct. In the meantime, I suggest you avoid the caves. The air down there is unhealthy. And try not to run into my colleague. He is an uneducated man and may not have heard of the Planetary League. I don't think you would like him."

"I never liked you much either," said Caleth.

"How very distressing."

"All right," sighed Caleth. "I didn't expect a welcome. Perhaps you would be kind enough to direct me to Castle Kray." This time, he spoke without sarcasm. He had never found it

[88]

difficult to be polite. Often, it seemed to surprise people, as though he had put them at a disadvantage. But Varagin was merely curt.

"Ask her," he said. "She lives there."

On the far side of the spacestage, Tnoe had pulled up in the Ita Spear. Her performance was over and she had come on Borogoyn's instructions to collect the flowers. She had done the Song of the Wytch Queen from the Third Play. The audience had not appreciated the song but they had appreciated Tnoe, and she was still flushed with humiliation and useless rage. If only Pzyche would throw the flowers in Vinya's self-satisfied face. But of course, he would not be there, and Pzyche had never seen flowers. She would open the box, aglow with rare pleasure, touching them only with the tip of her finger so as not to violate their territory . . . Suddenly, Tnoe felt so helpless she could almost have cried. Pzyche was right, she knew: they had to live with Borogoyn, or not at all. They might as well make the best of it. And at least he would not see her, pale with rapture, touching his flowers with her cold fingertip. Better anything, than for him to see *that*.

They put the flowers in the landmovile. Yellow ambrosine, goldenwand, winter roses. They were extraordinarily beautiful. "Sweet Inspiration," thought Tnoe, "where do we go from here?"

They were putting the packing cases in the back now: insulated containers with red labels and black straps. Three or four of them. Presently, a little brown man like a hirsute gnome climbed in and perched anxiously on the top. "Packing cases?" Tnoe registered, startled. She opened the door.

Derec Rolt shut it again, firmly. "No questions," he said. "Just drive."

Some time later, Varagin and Borogoyn were sitting in the main tent, in a section curtained off from the bar. The tent-flaps were of grey weathercloth, covered with faded drapes in a colour that had once been garish. The chairs were not particularly comfortable. Everything looked as if it had been used and misused several times. The sickly rays of a low lamp lit Vinya's face from beneath, showing the sagging muscles around the mouth, the eye-pouches, the incipient jowl. Between the thick eyelids Varagin could see nothing but blackness, with maybe an occasional elusive gleam that flickered when he moved his head. He was drinking ptermix from a tin mug. It was old, and had gone very sour. Varagin did not drink. He sat a little beyond the light and surveyed Borogoyn without expression.

"Explain," he said.

"The Doctor's dead," Vinya said shortly. "Died of shock when we dropped the bomb. Heart. He must have been off his head anyway, shutting himself up in that hole. It's as cheerful as a morgue and much the same amenities. No heating, no hydrant, and the austracisor was broken. When we got there, the two girls were boiling all their water and eating blackbeetles. They'd have died anyway, if we hadn't turned up. You can't kill people like that: it's just not human." Varagin contemplated Borogoyn's profile, with its low forehead and paleolithic jaw. It was not, somehow, the profile of a convinced humanitarian. "The mother was a famous actress," Vinya continued. "She'll have friends. Too many friends. You've got to be careful. On Fingstar, a good actress is as precious as royalty."

"Krater has friends, too," remarked Varagin.

But Borogoyn was not listening. "Alive, they're no problem," he said. "Tnoe's useful. The men like her. Keeps them happy. The other one's different."

"I have seen Tnoe," said Varagin. "The other one?"

Borogoyn was getting drunk. "Beautiful girl," he said. "Cold as ice. It's something you can't put your finger on. She's been here all her life: never seen any men, not till we came. I don't count the mad Doctor. She walks round all the time like something that isn't really there. You would think, even her hair feels cold. She wanted some flowers, you know, to put on the

[90]

old man's grave. Seems they had to bury him themselves, and someone had told her the dead need flowers. Funny thing was, she had never *seen* flowers. Didn't even seem to know what they were."

Varagin said nothing. He had heard this story, he knew, somewhere before. There had been a miner he had not much liked who had got a little drunk one night and talked about a desolate castle and a girl who had never known men. There had been someone else in that story, Varagin recalled, a servant or something. Deaf and dumb, or deaf, or dumb. Possibly just uncommunicative. And there had been nothing at all about black-beetles. He felt vaguely dissatisfied. Of course, perhaps this story, like so many others, had merely grown in the telling. Perhaps the servant, too, had died conveniently of shock or perished with the miners: Scharm's routine. Varagin was not inspired by Scharm's routine. It was very difficult, when so many had died, to sort out one death from the rest. Looking at Borogoyn, he found himself thinking of the credulity of the simple criminal mind. There was something about it in one of the Books of Nepeth: "The folly of deceivers who believe they have a monopoly of deceit . . ." Varagin knew better. He had yet to find a consistent morality anywhere in the world.

"What harm can they do?" said Borogoyn with a shrug. "Two girls on their own."

"I don't know," murmured Varagin. "Yet." He ought to mention the stowaways, and Caleth Brant. But he did not. Perhaps he thought it was unimportant.

Borogoyn drained his mug. "What harm can they do?" he repeated, contemptuously. "We need women. They're in short supply."

"What of H'ara Sateleptra?" asked Varagin, very gently. "I thought she was supposed to offer—entertainment."

"She does," snapped Borogoyn. "To me." Under his low forehead, his eyes were blacker than the ptermix and equally sour.

At Castle Kray, they were having supper. "You brought *food*!" said Tnoe ecstatically. "Decent vegetables. Sourbeans. Do you know, we've had nothing to feed into that useless machine but grass? I've tried coding it for something other than string beans but it never works. And the meat substitute tastes perfectly disgusting. Pzyche wanted to use toadstools, but I didn't trust them. This is lovely."

"Your father must have been very disorganized," said Derec, disapprovingly. "Surely he could have arranged for proper supplies."

"Oh, well . . ." Tnoe shrugged. It was a long story, and not one she wished to relate. Not just now. The other three were strangers to her, and even Derec, though she knew he loved her, could not be expected to love Pzyche quite yet. Later, of course. she would tell him everything . . .

Caleth had even brought some wine. "We are starting on a great adventure," he said. "Nobody can be expected to start a great adventure without a bottle of wine. I have often thought, if it wasn't for alcohol, no one would ever have adventures at all. We would all stay at home in mundane sobriety, growing old. Those who have adventures very rarely grow old. It is one of the risks."

He gave a glass to each of the girls. Tnoe sipped; Pzyche, who was thirsty, drained hers at one go. She found conversation with one other person difficult enough; with more than one, it became unmanageable. She had never learnt the civilized art of interruption. It was much easier to eat her supper, although she was not very hungry, and to keep on drinking. After the second glass, there was a tingling sensation inside her head, but it was not disagreeable. People, she reflected, looking round the ring of faces, were really quite pleasant, when you got used to them.

"That man at the spacestage," Tnoe was saying, "he was here before. I thought he would have been killed with the others, when they dropped the bomb, but he must have got away. Do you suppose—"

"I got the impression," Derec said to Caleth, "that he was an acquaintance of yours?"

Caleth nodded. "In a way." (We grew up together, he thought, and smiled a little; it sounded so strange.) "I hoped to learn something from him. But he never was very communicative. Don't worry. I told you, I will let you know when you need to fear. Varagin Karel is a very dangerous man. Quite possibly he is on the wrong side. But there is still honour among thieves. They will know we are here soon enough, but not from him. Tnoe, you have been to the caverns: tell us again, what did you see? There must be some clue."

But Tnoe could not help. "Everything dripped," she said. "It was like an old, old laundry, where all the stalactites have been hanging up to dry for thousands of years. But they still dripped. Some of them were huge, full of holes, like gigantic hollow trees. I told you. There was nothing that looked like precious metal anywhere. Just rock crystal, and traces of ore, greenish or red. But that's copper and iron, isn't it? Even I know that."

"Probably," said Caleth. "Anyway, it is inconceivable that the miners would have overlooked gold or platinum or anything of that nature. No: whatever they have found, it must be so rare that even a person with a certain knowledge of geology would not recognize it."

"Somebody must have done," Derec remarked drily.

Caleth said: "I have my own ideas about that." (He did not elaborate.) "Let us consider. We are in the Outmost System, on the farthest edge of the galaxy. According to Szaal, who is currently in fashion, this part of the twenty-fifth circle constitutes what is supposed to be the oldest sector. Unfortunately, planetary dating is still accurate only to the nearest thousand years or so, but some scientists believe the Hiboric Chain may even contain the oldest stellar systems of all. Certainly it had the first oxygen-based atmospheres and the first manifestations of life. What went wrong is another story: perhaps evolution, like civilization, wore itself out with time. We are living in an

[93]

ancient pocket in the universe. There are very few young, hot planets, very few boiling seas and breaking continents. The rocks are old and cold. The stars are shrinking. The seconds are too far apart. Time itself has grown slow and tired."

"This is all very poetic," said Derec, "but is it getting us anywhere?"

"All physics is poetry," said Caleth. "The whole universe is a poem, if we could only make it scan. Look at it logically. If we are on the oldest planet in the galaxy, then there can be no precedents. Nothing else has ever been this old before. We have no way of telling what to expect. Anything might happen. In the caverns of Dragoncrake, there may be substances which should not be there, or which have never been anywhere else. We are on the edge of the galaxy, and even the universal probabilities are less probable. With geological know-how, we can work out what *should* be there, but not what *might* be there. Liquid crystal. Diamond gas. Of course, as you say, somebody recognized it, whatever it is. A herbalist would recognize spidergrass, if it was growing on the bottom of the sea. But spidergrass does not usually grow on the sea-bed. All that tells us is that there is a herbalist about, and we know that anyway." ("This is not archaeology," said Professor Galbrenzil, who had stopped thinking in order to listen. But his eyes were very bright.) "Pzyche," said Caleth, "tell me: what did *you* see?"

But Pzyche had reached her third glass of wine, and she was falling asleep.

"Do you mean," said young Mr Protion, bewildered, "that there truly *is* a fortune here? My uncle didn't really believe it. He thought it would just be a few old bones and amulets, or a single vein of gold which would run out in a couple of weeks. Does that mean Tnoe is rich after all?"

"She would be," said Derec grimly, "if it wasn't for those crooks."

"I wonder why Mummy did it?" remarked Tnoe. "Do you suppose she *wanted* me to come here?" It was strange, but the

[94]

thought of having lots of money did not seem particularly important any more. Not even to her relationship with Derec. At the back of her mind, Tnoe was conscious that she had grown, although she was not yet sure in what direction.

"I think," said Caleth, "it's time Pzyche went to bed."

Lying alone in her cold bedroom, Pzyche began to wake up. She hoped Tnoe would come soon. Even after the heating was mended they had continued to share a bed, just for comfort. But perhaps Tnoe would not want to, now Derec was here. At the thought of Derec, Pzyche was conscious of a pain, a thin, angry pain that did not seem to belong anywhere in her anatomy. She tried to analyse it, but could only come to the conclusion that she must be very selfish. Living alone, Pzyche had never learnt to think of others. It was difficult, trying to understand selfishness. She reasoned with the pain, but it would not go away.

Much later, Tnoe came to bed. "Are you awake?" she whispered. "Are you happy? Do you know, I feel ridiculously brave."

Pzyche turned over and buried her face in the bolster. It was easier, somehow, to be asleep.

In the camp of the enemy, Varagin Karel was dreaming. Students of Nepeth can control their dreams. When her image comes into your mind, he had learnt, replace it with something else, something that makes you feel at peace. As a child in the commune he had once seen a picture of poppies in a cornfield, on a distant planet where the cornfields stretched from horizon to horizon and there was nothing in the sky but clouds. He still dreamed of that cornfield now and then. But the feeling of peace, of wildness, of infinite space had gone long ago. It had become a place of secrets, full of countless listening ears. The poppies were the colour of blood. He walked the boundaries of the field from sky to sky, looking for something that he could

[95]

not find. It was there somewhere, he knew, but he could not find it. He was always alone. Sometimes, the surface of the corn moved strangely, as though there was something there, hidden, crawling among the roots. But no one ever came. The cornfield went on forever.

This time, there was somebody else. He could not make out any details of form or feature: it was too far away. Just a small white figure coming towards him through the corn, gathering poppies to lay on a grave . . .

9

In Sunset City on Teuxis, it was, as usual, sunset. An invisible animal ran across a courtyard in the Undercity, leaving luminous footprints among the stars. Behind the masked door, a young male prostitute called Mortan had come to collect his second-best socks. "Aren't you afraid I may have you killed?" said Krater from his chair.

"Don't be so melodramatic," snapped Mortan.

Krater laughed, sourly. He was not at all melodramatic. Some while after Mortan had gone, he pressed a button. "Is my financial agent here yet?"

The financial agent, it transpired, had been there for some time.

"Well, show him up," said Krater. "What are you waiting for? If there's one thing I can't stand, it's people with tact. Bring me some kaffine, and a smoke."

The financial agent came in behind the kaffine, carrying a large red file. His name was not important, which was just as well, since Krater had forgotten it. He invariably forgot things which he did not consider worth remembering. The file was locked. Krater pressed out a number on the index card and opened it. Inside, there were several computer printouts, headed "Treasury of Fingstar: Confidential" in one of the more elementary computer codes.

"The information *is* confidential, sir," said the agent, who was relatively new to Krater's employ.

"Good," said Krater. "I hope you haven't read it. And don't

call me sir." He shut the file with a snap. "Well, what have you done about it?"

The man looked surreptitiously relieved. "We have acquired forty per cent of the concession already," he said, adding: "Zebadar didn't want to sell."

"I heard," said Krater. "An obstinate man, Zebadar. Narrow-minded. I must remember to order a wreath. So far so good. The great thing about crime is to make it legal. What about the other sixty per cent?"

The agent looked slightly less relieved. "It belongs to an Ifingen," he said. "An actress. It seems she invested all her money in it shortly before she died."

"Dead already?" commented Krater. "Very efficient."

"She died naturally," said the agent, apologetically. "Every-thing was left to her younger daughter. I have tried to get hold of her, but there isn't a private line and I didn't think it was a good idea to go through the Inter-Planetary Exchange. She seems to be rather inaccessible—"

"Where is she?" said Krater, with increasing resignation.

"Krake," said the agent baldly. "If she's still alive, she's on Krake."

Startled out of his resignation, Krater tried to sit up, but the chair foiled him. "What the *hell* is she doing there?"

"Her father," murmured the agent, endeavouring in vain to make himself invisible. "A mad doctor, I understand. Psycho-specialism. Lived all alone in a haunted castle surrounded by human cassettes."

"Rubbish!" said Krater. He thumped a button. "Get me my secretary. I want an urgent message to go to Vinya Borogoyn. No: Varagin Karel. He should be back by now. Vin lacks subtlety. Among other things. Send someone out via Fing-star, top secret and all that garbage. I don't care if it takes four days; do it in two. This is important. I want the rest of that con-cession. If I don't get that, it's stealing. And, you with the warts—"

"Yes, sir?" said the agent, lapsing.

"I'm surrounded by yes-men. You're fired."

The following day at the Castle was spent unpacking the packing cases and sending scout-parties to survey the terrain. There was a rather lax rota of sentry-duty at the top of the mineshaft which lost enthusiasm towards evening, but Borogoyn, not unnaturally, did not see the necessity for the caverns to be strictly guarded. Young Mr Protion fell down a hole on the bomb-site, but fortunately there was no one around. Caleth lay on a narrow ledge for three hours hoping to overhear something of interest and got a bad attack of cramp in the legs. Professor Galbrenzil discovered, with a certain morbid glee, that some extremely sensitive electronic equipment had been irreparably damaged in transit and he would have to improvise with a plumb-line and a tapemeasure. Tnoe spent most of the day in the kitchen, preparing the one thing she knew how to cook: casserole of mincemeat substitute with green spice and five different vegetables. Derec, partly (though he would not admit it) to impress Tnoe, and partly (though he would not admit that, either) to impress Caleth, pinched a protective helmet and fell into conversation with some of the men at the head of the shaft. He learned nothing, and nearly gave himself away when one of them made a personal remark about Tnoe. As for Pzyche, she sat watching her flowers, waiting for them to open and close like the films she had seen as a child, and no one paid any attention to her at all.

"You ought to tighten up the guard at the mine," Varagin remarked to Borogoyn, after he had taken a brief look round.

"No need," said Borogoyn. "Who'd try to get in? What's eating you, Karel? You don't look the nervous type."

Varagin shrugged. "This is a big planet," he said. "There's plenty of room to hide. I suppose you know those props in the lower corridor aren't particularly safe?"

"We haven't got time to be particular," said Borogoyn. "Krater wants the job done fast. That's what the men are paid for. They know the risks. Anyway, safety costs money. Krater buys cheap labour with no insurance and that's what he gets. He doesn't care if one or two get killed in a rockfall and nor do I. Nor do the ones who survive to get paid. I didn't know you were supposed to be a bloody public benefactor."

"I heard your men hated you," remarked Varagin. "I'm beginning to see why." He switched on the communicator to the mine. "Secure those props in the lower corridor. If the ceiling comes down somebody will get killed and we'll be two days digging through. No, not later. Do it *now*." He turned back to Borogoyn. "You're a fool, you know," he said lightly, and went out.

They had pitched camp in the lee of the ridge, presumably to shelter from the wind. There was very little wind on Krake, but Borogoyn's mind, such as it was, lacked elasticity. It was early evening, and in one or two of the tents a dull glow of light shone through the grey weathercloth. Above the horizon a wall of cloud rose into the sky, blotting out the sunset. It was still too warm for the season, a damp, sticky warmth that slowed the brain without reaching the bones. Mists crept out of the ground, shrouding the desolation of the bomb-site. The half-finished walls looked like something from an ancient world. Varagin passed the deserted spacestage and took the road round the ridge. He had enquired the way that morning. Borogoyn's men had cleared the road when they first came, and it was just wide enough for a Scrambler and dangerously uneven. At intervals, Varagin saw the antennae of some hidden insect groping out of a narrow crevasse. Enormous moths, the colour of dust, brushed past his face. It was dark when he reached the grave.

He switched off the handlamp. The newly turned earth made a pale scar against the withered ground. There were no flowers. In the distance, he heard the cough of an engine. Eyelights shone through the mist, turning the drifting curtains into pallid shafts of smoke. Varagin waited in the shadow of the rock.

The landmovile pulled up a little way off. He was quite sure

[100]

it was the Ita Spear. He heard a door open and close, the sound of a voice. (Tnoe?) Presently, something white began to materialize out of the mist, walking towards him. A girl. A girl in a white tunic. Her long hair looked almost colourless in the darkness, like a pale shadow. Her arms were full of flowers. She walked straight to the grave with unseeing eyes, like a blind man in a familiar room.

Through the mist, Varagin heard Tnoe calling: "Come away, Pzyche. I don't like it. It isn't necessary. Let's go home."

Pzyche placed the flowers on the grave. Her bare arms gleamed in the darkness, as white as her tunic. Varagin was standing very close to her. He could see the shadow in the corner of her eye, the single strand of hair that fell forward over her face. "You told me, they buried their dead under flowers," she said. Her voice was very clear and almost devoid of intonation. "He was my father. I wanted to do it properly. Besides, I had never seen flowers."

"Yes, I know, but did we have to bring them here? The Doctor won't care, wherever he's gone." (Thinking of Derec. Tnoe remembered she was an atheist.) "You didn't love him. I didn't love him. There isn't any *point*."

"No, I didn't love him," said Pzyche. She did not sound regretful or even interested. "Do you know, I watched those flowers all day? I thought, if I was very careful and quiet, I might see one of them move. In the films I saw on the computer, the flowers moved all the time. That was speeded up, of course. But I did think, if I was patient—"

"Pzyche, do come away!" pleaded Tnoe, unhappily. "Please come now." Varagin heard her climb out of the landmovile and the sound of her footsteps approaching through the mist.

"They didn't move," said Pzyche. "They might as well have been made of wax." She looked down at Borogoyn's offering in disillusionment.

A little way off Tnoe stopped, a small dark figure against the eyelights. Varagin heard the note of desperation in her voice.

[101]

"Come away, Pzyche. I don't like this place. He should have had a Reduction. It's not right. Please, Pzyche." But she did not come any nearer. Varagin thought: she's afraid. She's afraid of the grave.

Pzyche waited, as if lost in thought. But Varagin could see her face. He remembered how he had lingered on Level 3, needlessly, defying his fear, while the water climbed towards him. There was no thought in Pzyche's face.

"You mustn't get morbid," whispered Tnoe. "It wasn't your fault . . ."

Varagin stepped out from behind the rock and watched them walk away. He saw Tnoe half turn, peering into the darkness, and give a slight shudder. "For a moment," he heard her say, "I thought there was someone there . . ."

After they had gone, Varagin bent over the grave. In the light of the handlamp the flowers acquired a faint tinge of colour. When he moved them, two or three petals fluttered to the ground. He dug carefully, using a flat piece of stone. He knew it would not take long. They had been tired and half-starved; they would never have had the strength to dig deep.

Doctor Corazin lay under about two feet of earth, wrapped in an old weatherblanket. Cautiously, Varagin pulled the cloth away from his face. The body was already far gone in the process of decay, but he could still see the belt drawn tight around its neck, where the girls had not been able to prise it loose . . .

At supper, Sateleptra put in an appearance. Away from Krater's apartments, without the aphrodisiac vapours and the background music, she looked definitely less beautiful and more like an ordinary human being. The suntan of Teuxis had already begun to fade, and her dark skin was growing sallow. In the unsympathetic lamplight, her velvet arms had a faint sheen, like the furred wings of the moths which had brushed Varagin's face in the dark. Her eyes still smouldered at him over the rim of her glass, but they were no longer the eyes of a beautiful

[102]

animal in season; they were the eyes of a woman, a personality, with qualities and fallacies, neither of which were particularly interesting. She wore a tunic of sensile chiffon, the colour of the inside parts of a sunset orchid. Her toenails were gilded; her long hair was threaded with pink Lippith pearls. She looked expensive and glamorous and totally out-of-place.

The food was unexciting, consisting mostly of nondescript vegetable matter. Sateleptra concentrated on the meat substitute rather as if she wished it was real. Borogoyn drank too much ptermix and conversed exclusively in grunts. Varagin's eyes, meeting Sateleptra's, neither accepted nor refused. He did not really want any trouble, if only to disappoint Krater. When the meal was over he left them to each other's company and went to bed.

That night, she came to him. "I suppose," said Varagin, "you doctored his drink."

"It wasn't necessary," said Sateleptra. "He drinks too much anyway. When he drinks too much, he is no use. He will snore half the night now. Maybe I refilled his glass once or twice, when he was too slow. I wanted *you*."

She wriggled up close to him like a seal. Nothing else had quite the texture of human flesh, he thought: that quality of firmness and yielding, of coolness and warmth. He could feel the muscles moving under her skin. Presently, he said: "Borogoyn would not like this at all. I hope you realize that. He is not a man who likes to share."

But Sateleptra was not thinking of Borogoyn. Her hands felt greedy and too skilful, like the hands of a professional thief. "You are very good," she murmured, a little while later. "Very good. So few men know how to *concentrate*. I knew the moment I saw you. There is a man, I thought, who is capable of serious concentration . . ."

Varagin concentrated.

Afterwards, when the physical satisfaction had drained away, he felt curiously empty. She had come easily, with all the sensi-

[103]

tive touches. Her body arched and sank and shuddered. Her nails buried themselves in his shoulders up to the hilt. When it was over, she fell asleep almost at once. Lying beside her, Varagin found himself wondering, unwillingly, what sort of a person she was. Unsubtle, arrogant, overdressed. The type of woman, he thought, who judges all things by the amount on the price-tag. A shoplifter. He did not feel cheap: she had come to him, and that was that. He did not feel particularly sorry for her. Later in the night, he woke her and made love to her again, just for the exercise. In their gentler moments, she told him things about herself, things she evidently considered appropriate. Her childhood on Lippe (upper-middle-class), the financial misfortunes of her father, her passionate hatred of having to do without. Not that she had ever been hungry, he realized, merely unable to overeat. "Compromise is so dull," said Sateleptra. "Compromise, economy, second-best, second-rate. All those words. They sound so *tatty*. I wants lots of everything. The most expensive, the most beautiful, and *lots*."

"So what are you doing on Krake?" murmured Varagin.

Sateleptra made a face. "Krater is stronger than me," she said. "I have to do what he wants. For the moment. But we will outwit him, won't we? You will have lots of money. Tell me, what will you give me, when you have lots of money? Tell me."

"The strap," said Varagin, shortly.

Sateleptra laughed.

"You must go now," he told her, a little while later. "It would not do for Borogoyn to find you here."

"Perhaps *he* will beat me," said Sateleptra, idly. "That might be interesting. All the same, I would prefer it to be you. I should think you would hurt like you make love. Deliberately. With concentration . . ."

In the end, she stayed another hour.

When she had gone, Varagin did not go to sleep. He was quite sure Krater knew all about Sateleptra. The childish lusts, the petty values, the snatching at life. To Krater, women were infinitely dispensable. Varagin had gone to him because he was rumoured never to have cheated at cards, but they said in the Undercity his sense of humour was mortal. Varagin did not really appreciate the idea of making him laugh.

10

Varagin was up early the next morning. "You looked tired," said Borogoyn, meeting him at the minehead. Varagin looked him straight in the eye and said nothing. Later, he had plans of his own. Sateleptra, he noticed with satisfaction, stayed out of sight and hopefully out of mind.

At Castle Kray, all the men had gone out. "It is for tonight," said Tnoe, addressing the washing up. "We have no time to waste." That was what Caleth had said, the previous evening. No time to waste. In the dark, at a council of war, huddled round a firepot and a jug of kaffine, it had sounded exciting and even rather frightening. But in the cold light of day, over the washing up, it was not difficult to be brave. Tnoe stacked the plates in the circulator, which was attached to the hydrant. Bits of mincemeat substitute, twelve hours old, glued themselves to her fingers. By the time she had finished she felt positively blasé. When she heard the door open, she did not even look up. "Pzyche?" she said. "Can you pass me a cloth? This thing always leaks at the beginning."

She reached out a hand and presently it was full of cloth.

"Good morning," said Varagin Karel.

Tnoe said: "Oh," but no particular sound came out. She stood up, awkwardly, fast and then slow. "I'll call Derec Caleth . . ."

Varagin looked bored. "Do you imagine I'm a fool?" he said. "I have been waiting for some time. They are all out. The circulator is leaking; I suggest you use that cloth."

"Yes," said Tnoe, obediently. She was frightened, she told

herself, but not very. Without turning her back on him, she crouched down by the machine. The water soaked through the cloth, turning it black. She tried to think of something else she could do.

"I want to talk to you," said Varagin, "about your sister."

"You have never seen my sister," said Tnoe, startled. It was not quite what she had expected. But she was still not very frightened, not yet.

Varagin let that pass. "You worry about your sister, don't you?" he said. "You are obviously protecting her from something, or trying to. Perhaps from Vinya Borogoyn. She bears the unmistakable hallmark of someone with little or no sexual experience, and that is something he probably finds as rare as white rhinohorn and equally exciting. You ought to be losing sleep over that."

"Of course I am," said Tnoe. "I—"

"Of course," said Varagin. "I was merely wondering, who it was you were really trying to protect."

There was something niggling at her memory. A story she had heard as a child, an old, old story, about how, if you did not have a Reduction, the spirit would stand over the corpse, watching, until all the flesh had fallen in and the bones came through. She had had terrible nightmares, when she was five or six, about the bones, shining in the darkness, and the blank implacable features of the watching spirit. It was only superstition, of course.

"You've been spying on us," she whispered. She was very frightened now.

"I have made certain investigations," Varagin admitted. "I know certain things. I know, for example, that the Doctor did not die of a heart attack. I know there was a servant, who also appears to be dead. You did not see fit to mention him to Borogoyn, naturally. His grave is round the back. I conjecture he, too, did not die of a heart attack, although I have yet to see for myself."

[107]

"See for yourself?" echoed Tnoe, horrified. "You don't mean—?"

"Doctor Corazin was hanged," said Varagin, watching her disgust with faint amusement. "I hope you won't try to tell me it was suicide. Your sister—"

"Oh no," said Tnoe, hopelessly, denying she knew not what. "Please listen. It's not her fault. Pzyche isn't like other people. You can't judge her by the same standards. She can't help it if her conditioning is all wrong. She was badly brought up. The Doctor—my father—had some very strange ideas . . ."

"He must have done," said Varagin. "They cost him his life. I'm afraid I don't belong to the environment-and-glands school of thought. I have seen your sister. She is perfectly sane. She may be as pure as a nun and as innocent as a flower, but she is, as they say, responsible for her actions. She will have to live with that responsibility. She—"

"How dare you sneer at my sister!" Suddenly, gloriously, Tnoe was angry. "How *dare* you! Yes, she *is* pure and innocent, and that's still something beautiful and special even if it's so far out of date that nobody remembers what it means any more. Who the hell do you think you are, setting yourself up as a judicial committee? What about you, anyway? What about *you*? It was your fault, wasn't it? The bomb, and all those miners. You were here before. It must have been you. All those deaths. And you *dare* to blame my sister . . ." She was crying now, unconsciously, carried out of herself, crying with terror and rage. Varagin took her by the shoulders. His face was deadly, but he spoke very low.

"The action was not mine, but I accept my responsibility. Your sister killed her own father. How do you imagine you can justify that?"

Tnoe stared, blank with shock. "No," she whispered. "No . . ."

"Hadn't you better tell me about it?" said Varagin.

[108]

"N—no," stammered Tnoe. "I mean, you don't understand. She didn't *really* . . ."

They were so absorbed, they had not heard the door. "Did you want me?" said Pzyche.

Tnoe would not have thought she had heard anything, if she had not been so white. She was quite calm. For a minute, Tnoe wondered if she was frightened at all. Perhaps she did not realize . . . Her very eyelids were steady. Only Varagin saw the fingers of her left hand flex and clench, before she remembered to keep them still.

"Come here," he said. "Pzyche, isn't it? Come here. You can answer for yourself."

Abruptly, Tnoe found her voice. "Don't touch her!" she said. "You mustn't *touch* her!"

Her anxiety, thought Varagin, was out of all proportion. He was holding Pzyche by the wrist, and he felt a kind of shiver run up her arm from the touch of his hand. But she stood quite still. Her eyes watched him warily, wide and dark, like the eyes of a wild creature in a strange place, missing nothing. When she spoke, her voice was more than ordinarily devoid of expression.

"I have seen you before," she said. (It was almost an accusation.)

Varagin raised an eyebrow, an art he had perfected at college in imitation of a lecturer whose blighting sarcasm he had much admired. It was instinct now.

"We went to the barracks," said Pzyche, "with Forn and Udulf. I saw you there." She added, rather obviously: "You didn't see me."

"Forn I remember," said Varagin. "Not a particularly inspiring human being. Attractive to women, or so he thought. What did you think, Pzyche? I heard he found you—interesting."

Pzyche said, stupidly: "I don't know."

"After the bomb," Varagin went on, "it becomes a little difficult to sort out who died how. It was really very convenient for you, that bomb. You ought to thank me for it. It enables you to

[109]

explain any inconvenient absence without difficulty. But not, I think, the doctor. *I* have seen *you*, Pzyche, at your father's grave. 'It wasn't your fault,' I heard your sister say. What did she mean by that? Tell me. No, not you." (Tnoe fell silent.) "Your sister is an adult, at least in years. Let her speak for herself."

"I didn't kill him," Pzyche said, at last. "She meant, it was my fault. But I didn't kill him."

"As it happens," said Varagin, "I never thought you did."

"But you said—" In her indignation, Tnoe was rapidly losing her fear of him. In any case fear, like other strong emotions, is very difficult to maintain at fever-pitch.

"Never mind what I said," snapped Varagin. "I doubt if Pzyche would have had the necessary strength. There is also the little matter of the broken austracisor. Borogoyn told me, when he arrived here, you were boiling all your water and eating blackbeetles. I had heard that Castle Kray was isolated, but not that it was barbaric. I want to know what's been happening here. Let us go back to Doctor Corazin. If Pzyche didn't kill him, I should like to know who did."

Tnoe said: "Why should we tell you anything?"

Varagin smiled, not very pleasantly. "I don't wish to hurt you," he said. "Unlike Borogoyn, it does not amuse me. But I do not intend to leave here without *all* my questions answered. Naturally, you may rely on my discretion."

"Thank you," said Tnoe.

"Don't mention it. Incidentally, you haven't, have you? The Doctor's grave is quite a long way from the Castle, but you went without male protection. I don't believe even your red-headed friend knows what's been happening. None of them do, do they? After all, they don't know Pzyche. Perhaps they might not *understand*."

Tnoe sucked at her lips, helplessly.

Varagin turned back to Pzyche. "You tell me," he said. "Come on. You can't hide behind your little sister all your life.

I want to know who killed the Doctor. And I want to know why." He took her wrist, very gently, in his two hands. Tnoe saw Pzyche's eyes widen and then narrow. Her pale face became, if possible, a little paler. Presently, a drop of blood appeared on her lower lip. "Tell me," said Varagin, softly.

"Leave her alone!" cried Tnoe, tearing at his arm. (Varagin shook her off like an insect.) "You mustn't touch her! It wasn't her fault. It was the miners. Please leave her alone . . ."

Varagin released Pzyche's wrist. She stood there, looking down at her hand as though it did not belong to her. She had never felt pain before, not like that. When it stopped, the relief was so great that for a moment she thought she was going to be sick. Her pulse throbbed, disagreeably, in her throat. There was a stinging sensation behind her eyes like a kind of weakness. She tried to blink it away, to control herself: self-control was important, when your feelings were all wrong. She did not want to talk about the miners. She did not want to talk at all. Inside her, there was a hard cold fist, squeezing. But the pain had stopped . . .

"You're crying," whispered Tnoe, shocked. "You mustn't cry. Are you all right?" She had never seen Pzyche cry. But she did not touch her.

Varagin found himself remembering Livadya, on two occasions, finding relief crying into his shoulder. Once, as a child; once, as an adult. In the commune, you learnt to cry alone. "Really, Liv, I'm not a social investigator," he had complained, at twelve. As an adult, he had accepted it, in silence. It seemed the natural thing to do, to put his arm round Pzyche. He felt her stiffen immediately.

"Don't *touch* her," cried Tnoe. "It's territorial violation. The Doctor—"

"That outdated rubbish," said Varagin. "A germ of truth, and three volumes of superstition. I've read it. Corazin. I should have known. Zonderlinc discredited that stuff twelve years ago." He drew Pzyche's hair back from her face, making

[111]

her look at him. "You can forget all that. Grow up. You can't live outside the real world forever, I'm afraid. The real world is here and you must face up to it or perish. Take your choice." He went on, without change of tone: "I'm sorry if I hurt you. I regret the necessity. If you relax and cry about it you will feel much better. Then we can talk."

Pzyche looked at him, then at Tnoe. Her eyes were unsteady and overbright. Everything seemed to be sliding away from her, colliding, collapsing: self-control, emotion, sensation. It no longer seemed important that Varagin was standing far too close. Suddenly, his advice sounded quite practical. For a brief moment she laid her head against his shoulder and gave way. It was a feeling at once beautiful and horrible, an alluring, insidious weakness. The more she cried, the more she wanted to cry. She hated it.

"That will do for a start," said Varagin. "Why didn't you tell her about Zonderlinc?"

"You can't undermine the conditioning of a lifetime just by telling someone about Zonderlinc!" said Tnoe furiously. "The first five years are the most important. Vard says so. Anyway, I haven't read Zonderlinc."

"I might have guessed," said Varagin.

Presently, Pzyche lifted her head. "I have finished now," she informed them, surveying Varagin without enthusiasm. "Thank you very much. We can talk, if you wish."

"You don't have to—" began Tnoe, but Varagin shut her up.

"Good," he said. "Perhaps we can get through the rest of these explanations without any more violent emotion. Firstly, I want to know *why* Doctor Corazin was killed. I assume it had something to do with the uninspiring Forn. Did he do it? Or is that too easy? Tell me about Forn, Pzyche."

"It was violation of territory," she explained, very pale. "He —he liked me. He said—he wanted to touch me. He didn't mention Zonderlinc."

"I expect," said Varagin, "he hadn't read Zonderlinc either. Go on."

"He talked about love," said Pzyche. "Love is pleasure. Love is nature. Everybody has to be natural. Even Tnoe said she . . . Only, you see, I don't feel natural. I couldn't *make* myself feel natural. I don't know why. I used to think, it would be better if I died. Only it seems so *unfair*—"

"So he kissed you," said Varagin, "and you didn't like it. That sounds fairly natural to me. Initial encounters with sex frequently produce shock or repulsion in both girls and boys. It is, as your sister will tell you, in Vard. The only difference is that this usually occurs at twelve or thirteen rather than—" he considered her "—twenty-three. As you are older, the reaction would probably be intensified. Like tonsilitis. It means nothing." He added, derisively: "I am sorry to have to tell you that you are perfectly normal."

"Am I?" said Pzyche, doubtfully. "Are you sure?"

"Quite sure," responded Varagin.

"Oh," said Pzyche.

Varagin murmured: "I am afraid it must be very disappointing for you."

Perhaps it was something in his tone of voice which awoke in Pzyche an impulse of violent irrationality. It was a sentiment she had felt so rarely she could barely identify it. "How can you be sure?" she said. "You think you know everything, don't you? Just because it's in some books by these people I have never heard of. If I don't know about them I don't see how they can know about me. Why should I behave like someone in a book, particularly if I have never read it? I am an individual. I have freedom of choice. I behave like myself. You can't possibly know if I am normal or not."

"Pzyche," said Tnoe, "are you sure you're all right?"

"Of course I'm all right," Pzyche said. "It's just that I am a person, not a paragraph in a book. I have senses and feelings. Perhaps I have an immortal soul, if people have souls. But he

[113]

talks as if I am an object, an experiment, a brainprint. Pzyche Corazin, type 92Z, group 0033, higher grade. Example 5730 . . ." Suddenly, the impulse had gone. Pzyche stood very still. She remembered reading about nervous habits, like biting your nails, or sucking your hair, and wondered if she ought to acquire one, just for moments like these.

"Shall we get back to the point?" said Varagin. "I still want to know what happened to Doctor Corazin—and to Forn."

"I will show you," said Pzyche. Thought slid across her face, as blatant as a shadow. "No, Tnoe. You must not come. I must do this by myself."

Sometimes, thought Varagin, she spoke like someone remembering an old script. He followed her warily.

In the library, she sat him in the chair. "The recorder," she said.

"I have used a recorder," said Varagin.

Pzyche attached the sensitisors very briskly, so he would not have time to think. She did not want time to think herself. Then she switched on the machine. In the chair, she saw Varagin's face grow empty. She pressed out the code. Absence of seeing, absence of hearing, absence of touch . . . She waited. It would not take long. The time lag never varied by more than a few seconds, although she had used a hundred different psychotypes. She fixed her eyes on the screen. Nothing happened.

Her hand hovered over the timeswitch. She did not want to look at Varagin, not any more. On the screen, still nothing. Perhaps the machine was not working properly. Next to the timeswitch, there was a button marked with a red arrow. Emergency Cancel. Her hand wavered, undecided. On the screen, three red lights in an inverse triangle. They flickered for a while and then grew steady. Her hand was on the timeswitch. Unwillingly, she looked at Varagin.

She pressed the button.

Emergency Cancel.

The machine died. As she tried to detach the sensitisors, she found her hands were shaking. As soon as he was disconnected she saw the sweat spring out on Varagin's forehead. But his eyes, when they opened, were deadly sane.

"So that's what you did to him," he said.

Pzyche did not answer.

"If I did not have N'pethic training," said Varagin, breathing rather carefully, "I would be a gibbering idiot by now. I presume that's what happened to Forn. And the other miners—?"

"They came back," said Pzyche. "They destroyed everything."

"What about you?" asked Varagin. "I suppose you hid somewhere?"

"We were out," said Pzyche. "We had gone for a walk. I wouldn't hide."

Varagin was beginning to feel like himself again. "So why did you spare me?" he said. "Why didn't you go through with it?"

"I don't know," said Pzyche. She could see he was very angry.

Suddenly, he stood up and caught her by the shoulders. "Sit down." She opened her mouth to protest, then shut it again. He was too strong for her. All she could do was control herself. She sat straight and still while he connected the machine.

"Are you thinking, I don't know what to do?" he said. "I told you, I have used a recorder. And your little experiment isn't original, you know. There's even a name for it. Condition X. They were going to use it for interrogation purposes, but the effects are too rapid. Don't worry, I won't get it wrong. You need to know—"

There was a faint prickling sensation as he attached the sensitisors. Then oblivion.

She woke up. She knew she must be awake because she could feel her mind. She stretched her eyes until her eyelids vanished inside her head. She saw nothing. No darkness, no light. She had no eyes any more. She tried to call, but she had no voice.

No lips, no sound. No silence. She could not tell where her consciousness ended or began. She reached out, and her reach went on forever. She thought she had never understood the meaning of infinity before. She had learnt, the universe is curved, finite. Somewhere at the end of space there are walls of night, stuck with stars. She tried to remember Krake, normality, existence. But Krake seemed to be receding in her mind into a wilderness of space. Now, it was no bigger than a fist. Now, a coppernut. A microdot. Then it was gone. The universe was folding in on itself, a disintegrating forcefield. Smaller. Smaller. Soon, it would disappear.

"I must not go mad," she thought, desperately. But there was no madness, no thought. Nothingness was all round her, inside her, going on forever ... She screamed. Voiceless, endless, without sound or silence. She screamed with her mind. And even as the scream began it seemed to be dying away, receding into the void like a dream, until consciousness itself would be gone ...

She tumbled forward into waking. Daylight swam up to meet her, stinging at her eyes. The whole library was full of daylight. The gloomy shelves, the brainprints, the dust. Everything glittered and sparkled. Her mind reached out, thankfully, into her fingertips. She clung to Varagin without thought or fear, wanting warmth, contact, touch as she had never wanted anything in her whole life ...

When they went out, Pzyche locked the door. "Give me the key," said Varagin.

"I wouldn't—"

"Of course you wouldn't. I have a suspicious nature. Give me the key."

Downstairs, Tnoe said: "You were a long time."

"We had a lot to discuss," said Varagin, briefly. "I'm taking Pzyche for a walk. She needs air. Not that the brand on this particular planet is very invigorating. You can sit here worrying about it, if you really want to. We'll be back shortly." In the doorway, he paused. "By the way, I suggest you empty the circulator first."

He left Tnoe in a mood of uncertain exasperation. Reluctantly, she decided to take his advice. The machine leaked again and she knelt on the floor beside the seepage, staring forgetfully into space, trying not to feel anxious.

"How do you get on with the others?" asked Varagin, as they walked.

Pzyche shrugged. She looked all right, but she still felt pale. She hoped all of her brain was back in place. "They are quite kind," she said at last. "They never ask me to do anything."

Varagin did not comment. "It's probably unethical to question you," he went on, "but why are they really here? Mere archaeology?"

Pzyche nodded. "They never mention the crystal," she said. "Sometimes, I don't think they even know it's there."

"How did you know," said Varagin, softly, "about the crystal?"

"I looked it up on the computer," she explained, "after we went to the cavern. I knew it wasn't rock crystal."

"Evidently," said Varagin, "your ignorance is not to be relied on. I wonder how I ever came to believe in it?"

Pzyche said: "Sometimes, it's easier if people think you're ignorant. Like Borogoyn. That's why he sent me the flowers."

"So you dissemble?"

"N—no," she said. "If someone chooses to get a false impression, I do not always correct it. Besides, I *am* very ignorant. There are so many things I have never seen."

"Never mind," said Varagin. "This is the Outmost System. Here, everyone sits at home on their native planets, growing tentatively decrepit. There is nothing very much to see."

"Yes, but—"

"But?"

"I didn't mean this system," Pzyche said. "I meant, *outside.*

The Four Systems, the Ark, the Distaff, the Wheel. I want to see real mountains, with snow on top. I want to see cities, and trees. I want to see the sunrise when it is pink. I want to learn to be like other people. To drink spirits, and smoke hennebuhl, and talk too much." She looked doubtfully at Varagin, trying to read his expression, and failed. "Sometimes," she admitted, "I daydream."

"Kiss the prince," said Varagin, flippantly. "You might even turn into a toad." He was still looking inscrutable.

"I don't want to fall in love," said Pzyche. "Tnoe is in love. I think it affects the brain."

They walked for some time in silence.

"Have you ever been in love?"

"I expect so," said Varagin. He had no intention of telling her about Livadya. He had never discussed that with anyone, outside the white friendly walls of the N'pethic monastery. Before, it had hurt too much. After, he had learnt self-control . . .

"I don't understand," said Pzyche. "If she was in love with you, why did she marry the other man? It isn't logical."

"She was afraid," said Varagin. "For herself. For me. It isn't worth regretting. There were so many things I should have done."

"But why?" said Pzyche. "She was a free individual. It was her decision. She must have been very stupid. Did you fall in love with her, because she was stupid?"

"You," said Varagin, icily, "know nothing about anything." They parted in monosyllables.

Back at the castle, Tnoe was waiting for her sister. "We had an argument," Pzyche said, when she came in. "I have never argued with anyone before. It was very stimulating." She added, by way of explanation: "Computers don't argue." There was more colour in her face than usual, and her eyes were very bright.

Tnoe stared at her in astonishment.

[118]

Walking quickly, Varagin reached the camp in the late after-noon. On the edge of the bomb-site was a place which had been turned into a rubbish dump, already piled high with whatever organic and inorganic matter the elementary disposal instal-lation had decided to reject. A questionable smell hung over it, and wingless Kraken insects crawled gleefully in and out. As Varagin approached, he saw there was something on the top which had not been there that morning. A body. A naked, flam-boyant, voluptuous body. Her head was thrown back and her long hair hung down, unbraided. It looked as if someone had undone a tzip from her belly to her throat. Her thighs were open, and in between Varagin could see the place where he had been the previous night.

He was just able to get behind a wall, before he began to vomit.

PART III

11

"We will need weapons," said Caleth, placing the gun on the table. It was a gun unlike any they had ever seen before, small and yet curiously heavy-looking, with a short, ugly barrel and a grip of greenish wood, very highly polished. Derec picked it up, cautiously. In his hand, the wood felt as warm and responsive as flesh. There was no safety lock. The trigger seemed to quiver under his finger. "This is a denominator," said Caleth. "It was invented by a socialist who wanted to reduce everyone to a state of absolute equality. He was a believer in the Revolution. Whether there is famine, or disease, or mice under the stairs: the Revolution. What he did for constructive social-ism is not remembered, but his invention caused large numbers of people to be equalized for good. Hence the name." He added: "It is a collector's item now, but it will do us very well. In its day, it was illegal."

"I suppose," said Derec, "that's meant to be a recommen-dation."

Caleth smiled. "It fires good old-fashioned bullets," he went on. "Like these." Derec picked one up. It looked rather like a worn-down tube of lipstick, but about the nozzle there was a faint, evil phosphorescence. Caleth showed him how to load.

"I'm afraid I shall be a very bad shot," said Derec.

"Good," said Caleth. "I wish I could say the same. Pro-fessor?"

"I am an intellectual," said the professor. "Intellectuals do not carry guns."

("This is not good," he said to himself. "When I discovered

the Hidden City, on Ioa, we did not have guns, although the jungle was full of tigers. And on Omarth, there was a curse, and we all caught the flux, but we did not have guns. Perhaps I am a little afraid. I do not think I want to kill, or be killed, not even for archaeology. I want to die in hospital, in comfort. I should have sent that nice young man with the glasses. I am old and doddering, and danger is not for the old and doddering. Danger is for these young people, who enjoy it. Bah! Thiodor Galbrenzil, you are a coward. Yes, I am a coward. It is very true. All my life, I have been a coward. It did not matter until now. Never mind. This Caleth Brant, he is a nice young man, and sometimes he uses his head. But undoubtedly he exaggerates. He wants to have adventures, he wants the world to be full of danger, and guns, and privateers, so he exaggerates. Archaeology is not enough for him. It is very natural. Probably, no one will kill anyone at all . . .")

Young Mr Protion was examining the gun, at once nervous and excited. "You know," he remarked, unexpectedly, "it's quite different in books, isn't it? I mean, in books and plays and things, they just pick up a gun and start shooting. But in real life, you can't do that. It's—it's like picking up a candle in a church . . ."

"I'm an atheist," Derec said shortly.

"Oh," said young Mr Protion. "Oh, yes. Of course. But you do see what I mean, don't you? There's a kind of aura, awful and sacred . . . If you're religious, that is. Only with a gun, it's an aura of *evil*. I feel almost as if it might run away from me and start killing people all by itself."

"What's your name?" asked Caleth.

"My *name*?"

"Your firstname."

"It's Tirril," said young Mr Protion. "But—"

"Well," said Caleth, "yes, Tirril, I do see what you mean."

Tnoe was getting ready for her performance. At such times, her mood was normally once of reluctance and resignation. As a child, Tnar had encouraged her to play at dressing up, perhaps looking for some hereditary trace of her own talent, but Tnoe was awkward and self-conscious and obviously had none of the instincts of an exhibitionist. Tonight, however, she felt different. She had lost weight since her arrival on Krake and she wriggled with difficulty into a tunic made for her mother which she had never thought to wear. It clung to her in all the right places like a second skin two sizes smaller than the first. She put stardust in her eyes to make them glitter, as she had seen Tnar do. A lot of it stuck to her eyelashes and when she had finished blinking she thought her eyes looked monstrous and luminescent, like a caricature of an oversexed owl. Her toenails were gilded and her fingernails, which were fortunately well grown, were painted red underneath (Pzyche had done it for her). She looked in the mirror and, because she was quite alone, she stuck out one hip and tried to pose. "H'ara Tnoe," she said, using the ancient Lippith title for a chief concubine. She did not feel at all like a chief concubine. Inside, she was wearing chameleon green and a revolutionary beret, like pictures of old-fashioned commandos. Under the thick make-up her lower lip stuck out, resolutely. (She thought if she stuck it out it would be less likely to tremble.) She looked, she decided, like a low-class hetaira, but she did not feel cheap any more. Even her usual stagefright was swallowed up in other, different fears. Presently, Pzyche came in. "You look very strange," she said.

"I feel very strange," said Tnoe. With some difficulty, she returned to one of her most private anxieties. "Do you think Varagin will *do* anything?"

"I don't know," said Pzyche. She considered Varagin's character with a certain detachment, like a child studying a computer puzzle. "When he isn't angry with me any more," she concluded, "he might come back."

"Yes, but—" It was no use. She could not find the right words. Pzyche, she thought, was somewhere else; she always

[125]

had been. Before the others came, when they were alone to-gether and trying to survive, it had not mattered. But at the sight of Derec's face (such a lovely, plain, *civilized* face) the world had fallen into perspective, as it always did, and all the huge distorted shadows had gone back into their corners, leav-ing her life full of electric light. Now, when she looked at her sister, all the vast wastelands of Krake seemed to lie between them. Not that she loved her any the less; Tnoe's capacity for love had always been overambitious. But when she reached out, there was nothing there any more. Pzyche's personality seemed to fade in electric light like a ghost.

"I haven't said anything to the others," Tnoe ended, help-lessly.

"Of course not," said Pzyche, with an air of understanding which her sister found vaguely disquieting. Presently, she en-quired: "What are you going to sing?"

"Dirty songs," said Tnoe, gloomily. "The kind you sing at handball games, or in League Week when you're rather drunk. The sort of songs Borogoyn's men will really appreciate."

Pzyche said: "I hope you'll be all right." There was a faint shadow in her face. "I am the eldest," she added, unexpectedly. "I suppose it should have been me."

"You don't know any dirty songs," Tnoe pointed out.

"I know," said Pzyche. "But it should have been me."

Downstairs, Tnoe poured herself a drink. "A good idea," said Caleth, passing the bottle round. Professor Galbrenzil made everyone look for the plumb-line until he discovered it was in his pocket. Tirril Protion placed the denominator gingerly inside his jacket and forgot to take any ammunition. The Ita Spear wouldn't start.

"Rendezvous at the bomb-site," Caleth said to Tnoe. "Wait for us."

"You know," Derec remarked, noticing her appearance for the first time, "you look rather different."

[126]

Pzyche stood on the doorstep, watching them drive away. Only Tnoe remembered to say goodbye.

They were in luck. The guard at the top of the shaft had already wandered off, presumably to watch Tnoe's performance. The lift creaked horribly, but no one came. Everything was pitch-black. On Level 3, Caleth pressed the button to return the lift to the top.

"What if they come after us?" said Derec, whispering, for fear of the echoes that might be lying in wait in the darkness.

"What if the guard comes back," said Caleth, in a normal voice, "and finds the lift has gone?"

Everything he said, Derec reflected irritably, was quite un-answerable. In the light of a handlamp they picked out the right passageway. The roof had been shored up and there was a chain of nitron lamps which would probably have worked if they had known where to switch them on. Discarded tools were propped up against the walls. ("These men are not professionals," said Caleth.) They went forward cautiously, using only one light. The beam danced strangely in Caleth's hand, catching itself on an outjutting rock and throwing a huge, wheeling shadow against the wall, then slipping past to comb out the crevices in the floor or chase an itinerant bat from some hollow up above. There was no sound but the chattering of Tirril's teeth and the occasional cryptic monologue from the professor, in code. Presently, Caleth said: "It is much warmer than I had expected." Realizing they had no further excuse, Tirril's teeth fell silent. It was, in fact, quite warm. There was a sort of tense stuffiness in the air which was like nothing Tnoe had described at all. The Professor appeared to find the subject of some muttered significance and for the first time Caleth found himself wondering what he was talking about.

In the cavern, the water level had fallen. The beam of the handlamp flickered over the great Door, catching a brief glimpse of the blue reptilian stare and the glister of scales.

[127]

Lower down, huge claws could be clearly seen, white as ivory. But at the bottom the design faded and the Door was blackened as though with fire. The Professor pulled out an inspection lens. "Not now," said Caleth. They waded forward into the water. Suddenly, there was a splash and a startled cry. A couple of yards from the Door, Derec, who had taken the lead (if only to put Caleth in his place), seemed to have lost his footing and was floundering in the water as though out of his depth.

"Step!" he cried, spitting out a quantity of underground lake. "Mind—the—step!"

Caleth's handlamp picked him out, arms flailing in an attempt at crawl. "Can you swim?" he enquired, and in the dark no one could see whether he was smiling.

Derec got to his feet beside him, shaking the wet hair out of his eyes. "There's a sort of step down," he said. "It's deep there. Ten spans. Maybe more."

Cautiously, they made their way along the shallow side of the pool towards the edge. Using the professor's plumb-line, they discovered Derec had gone in at the deepest point; by the time they came out of the water, the step was only a couple of spans high. Behind them, the cavern wall arched into darkness. The air moved faintly as though somewhere far above there was an opening onto the planetface. By the light of Caleth's handlamp, they saw they had come to a dead end. On the far side of the pool, the beam fell on huge stalactites which seemed to waver and tremble in the flickering light. Shadows leaped in the ragged windows. High above, there was a brief glitter of crystal and the flash of dull ores. But there was no boat, and they had still to cross the pool. The rocks closed in around them. In the light of the handlamp they saw gargoyle-faces drooling down the walls, some of which might have been deliberate. "You know," said Derec, "this could almost be a kind of defence. Like a moat."

"Very good," said the Professor unexpectedly. "You are not as stupid as you look. But not, I think, a *moat* . . ."

[128]

"We can't get across," said Tirril. "Don't you think we should go home?"

("Why a *dragon*?" mused the Professor. "It is, perhaps, a kind of god. Or a demon, to frighten away evil spirits. No, I think I prefer a god. It is very rare to find a dragon-god. That Topioc monster, the one Lokke found, that is no dragon. I tell him so many times. It is a worm with the head of a grasshopper. But this, this is a genuine dragon. The guardian god on the gateway to the city. Even to this Derec who knows nothing, it was perfectly obvious. But not a moat. Dragons breathe fire. They must have kept the pit full of fire. The doorway was blackened; when we go back, I will do a test. Or perhaps there was a real dragon, kept on a chain and fed with the blood of maidens. Perhaps, when the water has fallen, there will be a huge skeleton, greater than a legserpent or a fossilized cterethin . . .")

"I think," said Caleth, "we will have to risk more light."

He lit a slow-burner and tossed it towards the Door. It fell on the very edge of the water, hissing and spitting as the fuse got wet. Then there was a soft explosion and suddenly the cavern was floodlit. They saw the roots of the stalactites writhing up out of the sunken lake like vast prehistoric trees. Beyond, there was a whole city of monstrous pillars, intertwined with convoluted spires and whorls of living rock which might once have been roads and bridges, flyovers and underpasses. At intervals, strange stone shapes sat like watchers, images of paleolithic beings too ancient for humanity. It was as if the city lay under an enchantment, turned into stone by a malignant witch. But if they could only find the right spell a flood of colour would wash through it, brown and golden and cream, grass would lap at the verges, voices would spring up in the silence. As they stood there, they seemed to see the whole city unfolding before them like a picture. Drapes fluttered from every window. White bats with ears like rose-petals swooped to and fro, singing like birds. And round the corner came the band, playing a strange riot of

[129]

minims and quavers on a stranger array of instruments. Twisted horns wreathed with gold. Big drums like enormous truffles. Small drums like cloves of garlic. Vibrating bubbles wailing with human voices. Everyone was shouting and cheering. The roof opened, and sunlight poured in, real sunlight from the days when the sun was young. Boats crowded at the quayside to listen. The water was deep blue; the reflections were red and yellow, gold and green. Everyone was happy, because the enchantment was broken, and the city had come to life . . .

Afterwards, they never talked about it. But for a few moments the spell was there, half a thought, half a heartbeat away. Already, they almost knew the words. Then the vision faded. There was an instant of loss, of anguish beyond bearing, and then the pain was swallowed up in the onset of endless years. All over the galaxy, a million different Times ticked away. The stars grew older before their eyes. The world darkened.

Suddenly, they realized the slow-burner was weakening. In a moment, the ancient night which they had dared to break would return forever. Automatically, Caleth registered the way round the pool, a narrow ledge under a bulging wall of rock which they had missed in the light of the handlamp. But his attention was elsewhere. "That passage off to the left," said Derec, "beyond the pool. I think it slopes upwards. I wonder if there could be another way out of here?"

"It's possible," said Caleth, abstractedly. He was considering an outcrop of greyish crystal, not far away. In the glare of the slow-burner he could see that each separate crystalstructure was shaped rather like an irregular stick of celery. Suddenly, he seemed to return to the present. "We are in great danger," he said. "There is a treasure here such as I never imagined. We must go quickly. This way. Before the light goes out."

They picked their way over the rocks towards the ledge. Already, the shadows were rushing up to meet them. Halfway along the ledge the slow-burner extinguished, and they were left in the dark.

Afterwards, Tnoe always said those last few moments before her performance that night were the worst moments of her life. Many of the other things which happened, both before and after, *seemed* much more frightening, but only then was she so completely alone. Everything depended on her. Her knees turned to water, her tongue was dry, her heart battered horribly against her eardrums. She knew her vocal chords would not work. It was going to be a hopeless failure. And it would all be her fault. "Go on," said Borogoyn. He drew aside the curtain and thrust her through into the main tent.

There was an outburst of cheering, whistles, catcalls. (That was the tunic.) Before, Tnoe had always hated it. But this time she felt almost reassured. They liked her. They wanted her. They would stay to listen. She opened her mouth, and her voice came out. She winked, experimentally, stardust entangling her long lashes. And suddenly, she knew it was going to be easy. These men were no longer a group of low-class, low-intelligence criminals. They were her audience. They loved her, worshipped her, desired her. They would do whatever she wished. Inside Tnoe, something that had long lain dormant, something of her mother, seemed to wake up and take over. In that moment, she was not a singer or a conspirator, but an actress.

Tnoe sang. She sang old songs, naughty songs, songs to which everyone knew the chorus. She sang crude songs, lewd songs. She sang songs she had learnt from a handball-player consisting entirely of four-letter words. The men drank and cheered and stamped their feet. Tnoe's repertoire ran out and she started all over again. She sang till her throat ached.

At the back, Varagin watched, unsmiling. Early in the proceedings he slipped out. When he got to the minehead, he saw the guard had gone. He went back to the main tent and gave certain orders. Then he collected a couple of men and returned to the shaft.

Caleth and the others had just crossed the ledge when a light sprang up behind the Door. "Stay quiet!" said Caleth, listening. Inside the cavern, a chain of nitron lamps came on, one right over their heads.

"We could hide in the city," said Derec. The lights did not reach far beyond the pool. And the city, he felt, was somehow friendly to them, although he did not say so. He had no desire to sound fanciful.

"No," said Caleth. "If we stay here, we'll be trapped. We must get out. We have a rendezvous to keep." In the mouth of the lefthand passage, there was a breath of cooler air. "We'll try the passage," said Caleth. "Professor!"

The Professor was still standing on the ledge. In his hand a small, maladjusted instrument filled with a red liquid was endeavouring to measure air pressure. "Professor!" repeated Caleth.

("I have felt this before," the Professor decided. "This stuffiness, this lack of air, lack of breath. But where? Where? Thiodor Galbrenzil, you are a stupid old man with a bad memory. It is important. It is *unsafe*. This feeling of tension, of . . . Now, I have it! It was Gnossos, Gnossos of the golden pillars, with the great temple, and the mosaic, and the statue of the Bull God in beaten bronze. A thousand years ago, they said, the Bull God was angry and shook his horns, and the roofs fell down. There was great anger there still. I walked the roofless corridors, and I could not breathe. He did not mind the archaeologists, no. But there were thieves who came to steal the gold off the pillars. Bah! it was all stories, tall stories. But when I was gone the Bull God shook his horns, and that nice young man from Ogen whose name I cannot remember, he was buried in the temple . . .")

The Professor looked down at the still surface of the lake. He

[132]

imagined great cracks opening in the floor and swallowing up the water. Flames leaped in the gap. The walls shook. "Professor!" cried Caleth, beginning to climb up to him. In the doorway, the figure of a guard appeared, silhouetted against the light. Derec was too stunned to reach for his denominator. Tirril's mouth was open. There was a shout, and the silhouette spat green fire. The shot was guided by fate or ill-fortune. Almost in slow motion, the Professor's body leapt into the air and then bounced off the ledge like a doll, hitting the water in a sheet of spray.

"The man who did that will pay for it." Varagin's voice, coldly furious. "Take them alive."

Only Caleth had drawn his weapon, and he did not use it. "We must go," he said, gently. "Let us hope this passage of yours will lead us out."

Derec and Tirril followed him without a word.

The Ita Spear wouldn't start. Varagin had dispatched two men to locate it and move it into the camp, but the temperamental behaviour of a vintage landmovile was beyond their skill. Eventually, one of them stayed to keep guard while the other went off in search of further instructions. Caleth took the guard easily, from behind.

"Tie him up," he said to Derec. "There's rope in the back. We must get out of here."

The engine came to life at his touch.

"No," said Derec, stubbornly. "We wait for Tnoe."

"B—but—" stammered Tirril.

"We wait," said Derec.

But Tnoe did not come.

12

Tnoe was not particularly surprised when they told her to wait. "Remember," Caleth had said, "if anything goes wrong, we can't help you. They'll probably hold you as a hostage. Later, we'll do a deal, or get you out somehow. You're on home ground; you might even be able to escape. They won't hurt you. But we have to take the risk." He added: "I don't really expect anything to go wrong." Perhaps he was placing too much faith in the loyalties of a loveless childhood. He had not known then, how much was at stake.

She did not discuss the danger with Derec. Possibly he did not see it. "Don't worry," he said, "I'll be all right. Best of luck." And now the show was over, and her luck was out. But it did not seem to matter. She felt exhausted and uncaring. They put her in the partition by herself and sat her at the low table. Presently, someone brought her a drink. She gulped down about half of it and then leaned her head on her arms. She thought at least an hour went past but she was not sure. Much later, she heard voices just outside, cursing the Ita Spear as she had frequently done herself. "They got away!" someone shouted from across the camp. "They got away in the bloody landmovile!"

"Oh good," Tnoe whispered. "Good. Good . . ." She knew she was relieved, but she felt so tired even relief seemed little more than the relaxing of a few taut nerves. The others were all right. Now, there was nothing for which to stay awake. She felt limp, uncoordinated. She tried to pick up her drink, but it fell over. No one came in. Presently, she thought she was asleep.

"You *fool*!" Varagin. Tnoe tried to wake up. "Did you really think you would get away with it? You stupid little fool."

"It doesn't matter about me," Tnoe managed to say. "Caleth said, they might take me. The others got away."

"Caleth," said Varagin, "is nearly as unprincipled as I am. Or hadn't you noticed? The difference is, for the first seven years of his life he was brought up to be a hypocrite. It's all in Vard. I'm afraid I have some bad news for you."

"The others got away," Tnoe repeated, uncertainly.

Varagin smiled unkindly. "Three of them," he said. "We shot the academic."

"Professor Galbrenzil?" Tnoe could feel the blood draining out of her cheeks. She was wide awake now. "No," she said. "No. It isn't true. You're trying to hurt me, to frighten me. Please say it isn't true . . ."

"You can identify the body, if you like," said Varagin.

"No," Tnoe whispered, in answer to she knew not what. She wanted to say that Professor Galbrenzil had been a sweet old man, and it wasn't fair to kill sweet old men. It was cruel, and tragic, and unnecessary. But she knew Varagin would only mock her.

"Don't worry," he said. "It wasn't your redhead."

Tnoe shook her head, blindly, fighting the tears. He was right, of course. She was relieved all over again because it wasn't Derec. She hated him for being right. She hated him for not caring, for being aloof and in control. For a moment, he made her feel she had condemned a sweet old man, selfishly, just to save her lover . . .

Varagin considered Tnoe dispassionately and decided she had abandoned herself to unreason. He called the guard. "Get me some disposables. With all that make-up, her face is going to be a sight."

"Disposables?" The guard looked blank.

"Use your head," snapped Varagin. "There should be some among Sateleptra's things, if they haven't been thrown out."

[135]

Tnoe wondered if Sateleptra was Borogoyn's mistress, the one Pzyche had thought beautiful. Evidently she wasn't there any more. She might have been a possible ally, but it did not really matter. Not now. Tnoe struggled to stop crying. The mascara had run into her eyes, making them heavy and sore. Her lips tasted of tears. Her nose felt like a hot red blob. "Here," said Varagin. She mopped at her face with the disposables. They were soft and pink and smelt of rose-petals. The unknown Sateleptra must have had expensive taste. Tnoe sniffed gratefully.

"Get her a mirror," said Varagin, sadistically.

"Oh no," said Tnoe. "For Inspiration's sake . . ."

She felt a little better now. "What are you going to do with me?" she asked.

"Send you to sleep," said Varagin. He went out, and came back with a mug full of some kind of soup. It was pale green, with darker green flecks, and it smelt of austracized cabbage. Tnoe knew that if she had been even moderately spirited she would have thrown it in his face. She was quite sure it was drugged. "Drink it now," said Varagin, "before it gets cold. If you scald your mouth enough you won't be able to appreciate the flavour." Tnoe resigned herself to the fact that she was not at all spirited. She did not even care if the soup was drugged. All she wanted to do was sleep, and sleep, and sleep . . .

Varagin lay on his camp-bed, dreaming. Lately, his dreams seemed to have gone off on their own, independent of N'pethic control. He was in the cornfield, but the corn had been broken and flattened as though by a monstrous wind. Someone had picked all the flowers. Enormous combine-harvesters with spiked wheels came rolling across the field, and the earth churned in their wake. Suddenly, Varagin was aware of himself, crouching among the corn-stems. In his dream he was afraid, but he could not control that fear any more: it possessed him, mind and body.

[136]

The combine-harvesters had gone and the field was empty. Presently, the architects came, with tapemeasures. Huge grabs with rows of glittering teeth crunched up the stubble. Concrete-mixers growled. At one end of the field they were building a skyblock. This is quite ridiculous, thought Varagin, in his dream. He was not frightened now. He knew he could wake up.

Afterwards, lying in the darkness, he tried to picture Livadya. In the past, when her face came into his mind, he had always sought to obliterate it with other thoughts and other images, until the necessary mental readjustment had become a reflex action. Now, when he wanted to see her, she was not there any more. Her face had become blurred and distant with time, over-laid with other, different faces which he thought he had for-gotten. ("One day," they had told him, in the white-walled monastery far above the clouds, "one day, you will be cured. You do not believe, but it is so. With time, all things are curable. Hence the survival of humanity, and their undying regret. When you can no longer remember the tone of her voice or the shape of her smile, then you will understand. Nothing is forever. The anguish of man is eternally superficial, and so they have outlived the other intelligent races, and they rule the stars. But they will never be immortal.") Varagin reached for Livadya's face, but the memory eluded him. Instead, there was the girl who used to feed the rabbits, in the Vivisection Centre on Lok. The swan-dancer of Cetis, whose offer he had (politely) de-clined. The geologist on Wetwinter, when he was studying the Ten Volcanoes, waiting for the great eruption. When it came, she was at the Project Station. The last thing he remembered was imagining her die . . .

Suddenly, Varagin's mind was full of volcanoes. Mountains grew up overnight, like mushrooms. Craters opened, vomiting ash. Clouds of gas, thicker than porridge, obliterated the atmos-phere. Lava crawled. He stood on a lone hill making notes, but he knew that, presently, he too would be swallowed up . . .

[137]

To his annoyance, Varagin realized he had fallen asleep again. He struggled into waking. Livadya was forgotten and he had never even considered the problem of Tnoe. But he was very disturbed.

When Tnoe awoke she was lying on a camp-bed at the back of the partition, wrapped in a blanket. What was left of her make-up had dried in tight patches on her cheeks. Her eyelashes were stuck together and her tongue felt as if it was covered in fur. She was desperate to urinate.

She got up and went to the curtain. Beyond, she could see the shadow of a guard, sitting in a chair. She put a hand through the curtain and tapped him on the shoulder. The guard, who was half asleep, nearly fell off the chair.

"I want to have a wash," said Tnoe, "and so on."

They took her, under escort, to a small tent with very primitive facilities. Tnoe held her nose and relieved herself. Afterwards, she asked for a bowl of water.

Instead, she got Varagin. "No," he said, thinking of Borogoyn, who was beginning to get restless without Sateleptra. "You look better as you are. You can have some kaffine, and something to eat."

The kaffine was bitter and the austracized biscuits very dry. Tnoe felt she ought to say something witty and sarcastic about the falling standards in hotel service these days, but she thought better of it. In any case, she was very hungry. Even the taste of the dry biscuits made her mouth water. Varagin stood watching her but she could not be bothered to feel uncomfortable any more. "What happens now?" she asked, towards the end of her second mug of kaffine. "Do the others know I'm all right?"

"I sent a message earlier this morning," said Varagin, "on the local communicator." He had not consulted with Borogoyn. Since the death of Sateleptra, their conversation had been restricted to the barest essentials. Her name was not mentioned. The incident lay between them like an unopened drain.

[138]

Tnoe had remembered something which had been troubling her. "Pzyche told me," she said, "you had an argument. I don't suppose you would tell me what it was about?"

"No," said Varagin. "I wouldn't. Your sister," he added, rather to her surprise, "is not only ignorant, but arrogant. A disastrous combination for a potentially intelligent human being. You ought to take more care of her. One of these days she is going to get herself into a lot of trouble."

"She's in enough trouble now," said Tnoe. "Thanks to you."

"No," said Varagin, again. "Let's get it right. Now, you're the one who's in trouble."

Tnoe said crossly: "No seems to be your favourite word."

Varagin smiled slightly. "Yes," he said, and went out.

He wished it was not necessary to go out on a further survey that day, but they could not afford to lose any more time. On Teuxis, he had listened to Krater's long-term planning, and told himself the geological anomalies he had encountered were of no particular significance. They would start on a small scale, with a limited number of unqualified personnel, and the project could be expanded according to necessity. By the time the Ifingen authorities had decided to take any action, no one would remember it was illegal anyway. But that was on Teuxis. On Krake, the anomalies increased: inexplicable vibrations in rock a hundred miles thick, feverish fluctuations of temperature, grumblings far underground which only the most sensitive instruments could hear. It was as if the whole planet had stomach ache. Varagin had a long experience in unwanted facts. He had returned with the most sophisticated equipment, and he did not like what he found. But there was no point in facing disaster until he was absolutely sure it was there . . .

Outside the main tent, he saw Borogoyn. Varagin decided he must speak to him before he left. Tnoe might be useful if she was kept undamaged; her presence in the camp would act as a restraint on Derec if not on Caleth. He was under no illusions about Caleth. There had been expensive educational facilities in the commune, for the few who were interested. (He remembered Livadya, all hair and bubblegum, trying to understand what he found so beautiful about molecular structure, and weeping with boredom and frustration.) Caleth Brant would know the value of mammonite, down to the last milligrain of potential corruption. And he would not count the cost, either to himself or Tnoe. It would be a question of priorities. Caleth, Varagin reflected savagely, had a disproportionate sense of responsibility, a twisted desire to serve in a world where fools and criminals ruled. He was a victim of his own integrity: his ideals were out of date, his standards out of bounds. Ideals were all very well in an idealistic world. But the world had grown old and wise in corruption and Varagin was uninspired by last stands. For no reason that he could explain, he felt a sick anger against all of them: Caleth and his overdeveloped conscience, Pzyche, unnaturally innocent, Tnoe with her reckless affections. He at least lived in a real world, cold and hard as fact. Life and death mattered little to him, but he would survive. He thought of Sateleptra, sprawled among the vegetable decay and empty tin cans, Sateleptra who had been beautiful and greedy and very much alive. To his surprise, he found he was angry with her, too, angry with everyone who died unnecessarily. He did not like unnecessary death. It was a long time since he had killed anyone himself, and that had been a matter of acute necessity. Sateleptra had died on impulse; Borogoyn's impulse. If he felt any more such impulses, Varagin decided, they would have to be curbed.

In the partition, Tnoe had finished her last biscuit. She sat with her elbows on the table, staring into space. No one had ever told her how boring it was, being captured. She was not surprised prisoners spent so much time trying to escape. There was nothing else to do. She contemplated the weathercloth tent-flaps, but the seams were sealed in and there were no gaps anywhere. An examination of the wall-pockets produced nothing but a couple of empty bottles. "When someone comes in," thought Tnoe, who preferred thrillers to serious fiction, "I suppose I could hit him over the head with a bottle." Beyond the curtain, she could see the back of the guard, looking very square and solid. In the main tent, there always seemed to be someone moving about. But it would be a start.

These things are easier in books. After a short struggle in which Tnoe acquired several uncomfortable bruises, she found herself sitting in the chair again with her hands tied behind her back. Presently, Borogoyn came in, looking disconcertingly sober. Afterwards, she was to remember the glitter in his eyes. "Right," he said. "We'll have to keep you quiet for a bit."

His fist encountered her temple, and the world went blank.

At Castle Kray, the argument had been going on all night. "You must listen," said Caleth, for the fourth or fifth time. "The issue is not just one of money or even of crime. Mammonite reserves form the basis for the economies of all the galactic superpowers. The wealth of a planet can be measured in a single crystal. Our hidden puppeteer is not dealing in platinum or wildcat gold; he is dealing in governments and spacefleets, in empires and men. The souls of presidents will be his small change. The balance of power will be his plaything. We must stop that, at any cost. In ourselves, we are unimportant, except that we are here. I am sorry about Tnoe. She has grown very dear to me. In moments of danger, your companions become soulmates, and I have grown fond of you all. You will not believe me, but if I survive, I shall regret the professor's death every night of my life."

"You're right," said Derec. "I *don't* believe you."

Caleth shrugged. "So be it. These are details, and we must look at the whole. Mammonite is mined in the Anchor: the seven planets are uninhabitable, and the League owns the mines. If any attempt is made to sell this stuff to the Big Six, they will naturally want to know where it came from. But a lesser power, an up-and-coming nation with too weak a hold on its sister planets and too few supercraft in its spacefleet, such a

[141]

power will be only too ready to purchase half the future at the cost of the other half. You can imagine the consequences. The security of the galaxy could well be at stake."

"Your friend Karel," said Derec, with furious sarcasm, "where does he come in?"

"I am not sure," Caleth admitted. "I can only guess. It is many years since I knew him, and I never knew him well. Some people are born bitter. What the years have done to him, who can say? I trusted him, because of an old, old loyalty, but when the wealth of the worlds is at issue, even old loyalties come up for sale. However, I do not think he will harm Tnoe, not unless it is absolutely necessary. He is seldom violent, rarely for pleasure, and never without provocation."

"That must be a great comfort to all of us!" Derec retorted. "The professor is dead, Tnoe has been captured, but we need not worry because Varagin Karel will not use violence without provocation! I wonder why it is I have no confidence in your judgement any more? Don't you realize this is all your fault? If you hadn't spoken to Karel at the spacestage, he wouldn't have been expecting trouble, and we might have got back last night in one piece. If you—"

"There is no point in all this speculation," Caleth said, as gently as he could. "In any difficult situation, the range of potential ifs is virtually infinite. It will not help us or Tnoe to run through them all."

"Difficult situation!" said Derec. "Is that *all* you can say? Are you really so absorbed in high ideals and galactic politics that you just don't care about *people* any more? It sounds very impressive, I agree, talking about the wealth of a planet in a single crystal, but all it means is that in your own inimitable way you care about money just as much as the rest of them. You're frightfully sorry about Tnoe, of course, but money comes first. Well, I won't allow it, do you understand? Whatever happens, Tnoe is going to be all right. If I have to get her out of there myself."

[142]

"Why don't you?" asked Caleth, quietly.

Derec walked across the room to where there should have been a window but wasn't. He imagined looking for Tnoe among a huddle of grey tents, all exactly alike, while faceless figures sprang out at him spitting green fire. "Take him alive," said the cold voice of Varagin Karel, as he went down with his legs full of holes. He saw himself wired up to a hideous machine, with goggling eyes which flashed on and off whenever he told a lie. Electronic tentacles were twisted round his arms and legs. In the background, Tnoe was struggling in the grip of a monstrous gorilla, probably Borogoyn. "I am not a violent man," said Varagin suavely, "but I am afraid this is absolutely necessary. Now talk. Or I will have to ask Caleth . . ."

Derec turned from his contemplation of the wall. In Caleth's face, he saw understanding and even pity. He hated both.

"We'll have to make a deal," he said.

For the moment, Caleth did not argue. He would not save one life at the potential cost of so many others. He knew that, and Derec knew it. The message had come in earlier that morning: "Do nothing, and Tnoe will not be harmed." Instructions to follow. But if silence and inaction were to be the price, then they could not pay. There was too much at risk. The spacelink was in the enemy camp, and somehow they had to get a message to the Planetary League. Caleth surveyed the outdated computer with a sigh. "It's a pity this does not work," he said. "We could have used it to lock into the Inter-Planetary Exchange. What went wrong with it, Pzyche? Do you know?"

Pzyche was sitting in the shadows, at the back of the room. "No," she said, almost in a whisper. "I know nothing about computers."

Caleth examined the machine more closely. "It looks almost as if it has been vandalized," he murmured.

"I will make some greentea," Pzyche said flatly. "Everyone should have greentea, first thing in the morning. You can't just get up."

[143]

"We haven't been to bed," Derec said shortly, adding in what was meant to be an undertone: "That girl talks as if she's mentally deficient." He shook Tirril, who had fallen asleep. "You're opting out. Tnoe is your client: it is your legal responsibility to try and keep her alive. Wake up."

"Poor Tirril," said Caleth. "Democracy is very tiring. Greentea is a good idea, Pzyche. Then we should all try and get some sleep."

When Pzyche came back, they were arguing again. She wondered if Derec and Caleth would come to blows. If they did, she hoped Derec would get the worst of it. "I am no use here," she thought, shocked by her own bitterness. "I cannot help Tnoe, and the others just think I am stupid. I might as well be dead."

She put the mugs on the table. Caleth said: "Thank you" but Derec merely swallowed a mouthful and went on arguing. Pzyche wished she could bring herself to like him. She knew it would please Tnoe. But she did not think she liked any of them very much. Except Professor Galbrenzil, who reminded her a little of her father. Not just because he was an academic. Perhaps it was the way he used to talk to himself. Doctor Corazin had certainly talked to himself far more than he ever talked to his daughter. She had not loved him, but she had grown accustomed to having him around, and there were so few things to which Pzyche was accustomed. When her father died, she had not minded very much. But she would have minded about Professor Galbrenzil, if she had ever learnt how to mind.

"Of course I don't want Tnoe to die," Tirril was saying, miserably. "I don't want anybody to die. I don't particularly want to die myself."

"You're a useless coward," said Derec.

No one spoke to Pzyche. No one noticed when she went out. At the foot of the stairs was the local communicator, installed on the orders of Borogoyn. Pzyche considered it for a moment, thinking her own thoughts. In the other room, the shouting grew louder. She closed the door, very softly, and went back to the communicator.

She pressed out Borogoyn's personal code.

13

Tnoe recovered consciousness in the Scrambler. She knew it must be a Scrambler because the floor was bouncing up and down, throwing her head from side to side. There was a violent ache in her left temple. She tried to put her hand up to her face, but her hands were tied. Afterwards, she realized she must have groaned.

When she came round again the ground was quite still. This time, she decided, they had hit her on the right side of her face. She could not remember the blow, but her whole head throbbed. She tried to make out where she was but her sense of perspective was distorted, and for a moment, terrified, she felt as small as an insect, with an enormous cliff leaning over her, pressed against her cheek. She tried to roll away and the world rearranged itself. The cliff shrank into a windowless wall, topped with towers. The ground reached out towards a distant plateau under a low sky. There was nobody about. Tentatively, Tnoe sat up. Her head swam but she was all in one piece; nothing had fallen off. She was sitting on the back doorstep at Castle Kray. She was alive. She was (evidently) free. Her ordeal was over. She thumped on the door.

At Castle Kray, the doors were made to close and stay closed. Borogoyn must have known he would have trouble forcing an entry. The lock rattled feebly. The thumps went through her head.

Tnoe took her boot off and banged it against the panel. She really could not face getting up and walking round the front. She wanted to be *carried*. "Why the *back* door?" she wondered, annoyed with Borogoyn for all the wrong reasons. Then the door opened and Derec was there, carrying her inside to order while she wept a little and the pain in her head became for a few moments miraculously unimportant. Caleth brought her some kaffine, liberally laced with spirits. Everyone asked everyone else what had happened. "You ought to get some sleep," said Derec, dabbing at her temples with a wet cloth. "Tomorrow morning you're going to have a lovely pair of black eyes."

"I don't want to sleep." said Tnoe. "Why is it people are always trying to make me go to sleep? Last night it was Varagin with some perfectly disgusting soup (I knew it was drugged, too) and this morning Borogoyn with his big fists. And now you. I've had enough of going to sleep." She thought of yesterday's make-up, still clinging tenuously to her eyelashes. "I want a bath. And then food. Lots and lots of food. And I don't want to cook it myself."

"I'll cook," said Caleth tranquilly. "Go and have your bath."

Derec carried her upstairs and deposited her in the bathroom. Tnoe threw her clothes on the floor, adjusted the temperature to maximum, and added nearly half a bottle of foaming oils and three-quarters of bath scent. Pink bubbles piled up around her as the water streamed in, overflowing the sides of the bath-tub. She scrubbed, thankfully, at the remnants of her make-up. Wet hair trickled down her back. Her bruises smarted and then eased in the warm water. It was, she decided, the loveliest bath she had ever had. Life (she thought) was a series of historic baths. She recalled a seaside holiday when she was four or less, sitting in a basin no bigger than a large casserole. (It was one of her earliest memories.) Or at eighteen, when she had stayed out all night for League Week and fallen into the harbour at Seaport Camarest wearing her best silk tunic, and some people in a watercruiser had fished her out and put her in a bath inlaid with blue taupe, with brushes of mermaid's hair and soap bubbles all colours of the rainbow. And when the heating system at Castle

[147]

Kray had finally been mended, and she and Pzyche had taken their first bath for over a week . . .

She had reached her left foot and was just about to insert the bath brush between her toes. "Pzyche," she said. "Pzyche?"

Suddenly, Tnoe panicked. She did not stop to think; it wasn't necessary. Her left foot was forgotten. She scrambled out of the tub and reached for a bath-wrap, scattering bubbles in every direction. Water dripped after her down the stairs. In the kitchen, Caleth looked up from his cooking. There was a strange and exciting smell creeping out of the neutron oven, but Tnoe did not notice. "Pzyche," she said.

Back upstairs she ran from room to room, slipping on her wet feet. She found empty corridors, unmoving shadows, spaces that stretched from wall to wall. Her fear grew with the opening of every door.

"Damn the girl," said Derec. "Where has she gone?"

The local communicator was switched off. Tnoe switched it on and pressed out Borogoyn's personal code. "Not at home," said a recorded message. "Please leave your name and number." On the in-channel, a blank.

"She hasn't even left me a message," said Tnoe. "Nothing." She was shivering in her bath-wrap and a small puddle of water was accumulating on the floor at her feet.

"I'm afraid it's my fault," said Caleth. "I should have known what was in her mind. I am sorry I never tried to find out."

"You mean," said Derec, blankly, "she has gone to Borogoyn? Of her own accord?"

"Instead of me," said Tnoe. "Instead of *me*."

"What else?" said Caleth.

"Of all the *stupid*—"

"Stupid?" Tnoe rounded on Derec, incredulous. "It was a brave thing to do. It was the bravest thing I've ever heard of. *I* haven't got that kind of courage. Don't you understand? Borogoyn didn't want me; he never wanted me. I was just a hostage. But he wants Pzyche. He had a mistress—I forget her

[148]

name: something long, with lots of syllables—but she's gone. He wants Pzyche and now he's got her. And she can't even bear to be touched . . ."

"He may be a hired thug," said Derec, looking at Tnoe's bruises, "but you can't seriously think he would harm her. He can hardly hold her safety over our heads one moment and then rape her the next. It's totally inconsistent."

Caleth said: "I don't know," but Tnoe's hands clenched on the communicator. It was a gesture which was not at all habitual to her.

"Borogoyn doesn't *think*," she said. "He's not exactly a thinking person. He drinks too much."

"What about Varagin Karel?" Derec said to Caleth. "Your non-violent friend. Or doesn't he count rape?"

"You don't understand," said Tnoe. "Varagin won't like it. But the men work for Borogoyn. Perhaps they wouldn't stand for a killing, but they'll probably approve of rape. It's a natural, healthy, virile thing to do. Privateers are supposed to go around raping and pillaging and having a good time. In books, I used to think it sounded fun. But not for Pzyche." Her face twisted. "Not Pzyche . . ."

There was a silence in which Tirril thought about saying the wrong thing but refrained.

"Well," said Tnoe, turning expectantly to the men, "what are we going to do?"

"Ask Caleth," said Derec. "He's the man of action. He had several plans for rescuing you. Which shall it be, Caleth? Plan C? Plan D? Why don't you tell her?"

Caleth leant against the stairway, his face in shadow. He was not angry with Derec. The sour, sarcastic words passed him by almost as if they had not been spoken. He knew what he had to do. It was a question of priorities, that was all. Derec was young, opinionated, over-emotional, probably deeply shocked by his first contact with violent death. Caleth was sorry for his resentment, even as he was sorry for Pzyche, but it made no

[149]

difference. He had lived too long and seen too much not to recognize his responsibilities, even if he did not particularly like them. "There is nothing we can do," he said, wearily. "Don't let it trouble you: the decision is mine. I am the one who will have to sleep with it."

To Derec's surprise, Tnoe did not seem to be angry. She looked into Caleth's face, a tired, ugly face, twisted by the old scar into that patronizing facsimile of a smile which always irritated Derec so intensely. From the very first, something about that face had inspired Tnoe with absolute confidence. It was the face of someone who has lived by certain standards, no matter how difficult or painful, who has done what he thought right, and paid the price. Certain people have the gift of inspiring confidence. (Derec resented him all the more because he was not used to having confidence in anyone but himself.) Tnoe looked into Caleth's face, and saw that he had made up his mind. She said, pleadingly: "There must be *something* . . ."

"Anything I could do, I would," said Caleth. "You know that."

Tnoe said: "I can't bear it."

"Your sister must be a very special person," Caleth said gently, "you love her so much. I am sorry I never got to know her better."

"Don't," said Tnoe. "Don't talk as if she's dead already. She's never really been alive. I know it sounds horrid, but my father deserved everything he got. It was all his fault. All her life, she's had nothing, and now she never will have anything. By the time Borogoyn's finished with her, she'll never want anyone to touch her again. And she's so *beautiful*. Sometimes, I even thought she was beginning to love me . . ."

Derec put his arms round her, but she shook him off. "You ought to get dressed," he said. "It won't help anyone if you catch pneumonia."

"I never catch anything," Tnoe said inaccurately. But she went upstairs.

[150]

"For the future," said Caleth, "we ought to set a watch. I don't want to be taken unawares. But it won't be necessary tonight."

Later, they had supper. Caleth had re-programmed the austracisor for Mnowan spinach and edible fern, and had made a sauce with red sugars which few mastercooks could rival. But nobody was very hungry. "You're a good cook," said Derec sourly. "Whatever made you take up archaeology?"

"Why can't you shut up?" Tnoe burst out, unexpectedly. "What's the point of hating each other, or even *blaming* each other? It doesn't do any good. I wish I'd said something to her, that's all. I don't know what. Just something. This place seems so *empty* without her."

"Nonsense," said Derec. "She never said anything. She had no personality. You might as well say a haunted castle feels empty without the ghost."

"In a way," said Tnoe, "she *was* rather like a ghost. She belonged here. We don't belong. We're just strangers, passing through."

"I suppose," Tirril said tentatively, "you are quite sure she's gone? I mean, she was always very quiet. And there's that locked room upstairs."

"Idiot," said Derec.

"I meant to ask you," Caleth turned to Tnoe, "what's in there?"

"It's the library," Tnoe explained, too quickly. "Doctor Corazin—my father—had the largest collection of brainprints in the world. Pzyche locked it up when Borogoyn's men came. She was afraid it would get damaged."

"Have you the key?" asked Caleth.

"Pzyche had it," said Tnoe. "I think she gave it to Varagin."

For a moment, she thought they would not notice. Then:

"Varagin?" Caleth said quietly.

"*Varagin?*" Derec, sharp.

"Varagin?" Tirril, astonished.

[151]

Guilt was written all over Tnoe's disastrously expressive face. "He came here," she said, hurriedly. "It wasn't important. He came yesterday, when you were all out. I didn't want to worry you."

"What did he come for?" asked Caleth, still gentle.

"And why the hell didn't you tell us?" Derec added furiously.

"It wasn't important," Tnoe repeated, wishing she was a better liar. "He wanted to see the library, that was all. Pzyche unlocked it to show him, and—and then she gave him the key."

"Shut up," Caleth said to Derec, rather less gently. "Tnoe, you must tell us what happened. I'm afraid we have to know. What is really in that locked room?"

"I told you," said Tnoe. "The library. Brainprints. The recorder."

"A recorder?" queried Caleth.

"For experiments," said Tnoe. "The Doctor—my father— was a psychospecialist. He used it for experiments." Unfortunately, she felt impelled to continue. "Pzyche showed me how it worked, once, but I wasn't really paying attention. She is better with machines than I am."

"For example," said Caleth, "the computer?"

"Yes," said Tnoe, suspiciously, "Pzyche used the computer. But it's broken."

"It has been vandalized," said Caleth. "Pzyche told me she knew nothing about computers. There appear to be some unpredictable gaps in her ignorance. Tnoe, I must have the truth. You can't expect us to deal with problems if we don't know what they are. What is all this about?"

"Please," said Tnoe. "Don't make me tell you. Please."

Pzyche thought about leaving a message but there did not seem to be any point. She told herself that what she was doing was courageous and necessary and the only thing to be done, but she did not feel either brave or frightened, only a sort of cold unhappy detachment. It was as if she was driving the Ita Spear with her eyes shut towards an unseen cliff edge, but as long as she did not open her eyes she would not see the drop or feel herself being killed. There was a horrible inevitability about her actions, as though she was a robot, long programmed, responding to a key which had been there since she was made. At the back of her mind she knew it was not so. She could put on the brakes, if she would only stop to think; but she did not think.

Borogoyn came to the back, as she had told him. She knew the others would not hear. She was waiting by the door with Tirril's denominator, which he had left in the hall the previous night. It was loaded. (She had done it herself.) "Tell the men to carry her over here," she ordered. "If she is all right, I will come out to you."

"How do I know you will keep your promise?" said Borogoyn.

His voice sounded contemptuous but she could not see his expression. He had gone out of focus and all she saw was the distant skyline, a thin hard rim round the edge of her world. She searched for the correct phrase. "You have my word," she said.

Borogoyn laughed. It was not a pleasant laugh. Once, long ago, he had kept his word, when a man in gaol had asked him to take care of his wife. Released early owing to a typing error, the man came home and broke Vinya's jaw and three of his ribs. He was very young then, but he learnt from the experience. He had no intention of being limited by a misguided integrity; his sense of self-preservation was too strong. But he still believed other people were stupid enough to be trusted.

Pzyche did not move. Borogoyn nodded, briefly, and one of the men lifted Tnoe out of the back of the Scrambler and carried her to the door. When he moved away, Pzyche bent over her sister, still holding the denominator. Tnoe's breathing was even and the pulse in her neck regular. Pzyche did not look at her face; she had an idea it would be better not to. She stepped over the body and walked across to the landmovile.

"Give me that," said Borogoyn, holding his hand out for the denominator.

Pzyche said nothing. Suddenly, she was beginning to realize what she had done. Borogoyn was only a yard from her and she thought she could see the very pores in his skin, excreting mucus, the grime lodged in tiny wrinkles round his eyes, the sharp hairs growing on his chin. He smelt like a man. Pzyche had never smelt man before. (Forn had washed and shaved before every visit.) She thought: If he touches me, I shall die of horror. But supposing she didn't . . .

With a sudden quick movement, she threw the gun as hard as she could. One of the men made a move, as if to go and fetch it, but Borogoyn detained him. "Get in," he said. He did not want a fight, not now. "Let's go." Pzyche thought about crying out but it was too dangerous, or too late. Vinya dragged her into the Scrambler and someone started the engine. They drove off. The sound had died away before Tnoe began to come round.

At the camp, Varagin had returned from his survey. The results confirmed what he had already come to suspect, and he was not at all happy. Immediate action was obviously essential. Borogoyn, he knew, would want to move out as quickly as possible. He thought of the wealth of mammonite yet to be mined, and decided they still had a little time. In the camp, he was met by a stranger. "There's a message for you," he was told. "Courier from Teuxis. Confidential." Varagin opened Krater's instructions in private. Suddenly, he found himself smiling. He had been given authority for a purchase price of up to ten million tela, and for what? The imminence of danger made even a weathercloth tent look like comfort. Varagin liked the feeling of danger. It gave an illusion of depth and meaning to an existence which he found generally superficial. He laughed rarely, but when he was afraid, he liked being able to laugh. He destroyed the message over the firepot and went to see Tnoe.

She wasn't there. "What does this mean?" he demanded of the guard, who was looking uncomfortable. "If anything has happened to her—" Sateleptra, he thought, was the sort of girl who inevitably got murdered. But Tnoe was not.

"Vin's back," someone called. Varagin went outside.

The Scrambler had pulled up in the middle of the camp. Pzyche was sitting in the front, high up. The men had already got out and she was quite alone. Her hands were buried in her lap, clasped or clenched, and she was staring straight in front of her with a steady vacant gaze. A little wind came from nowhere in particular and lifted the hair back from her face. Presently, Varagin saw Borogoyn open the door and order her to get down. He took her arm, and although she hardly moved Varagin thought he sensed her instinctive recoil. He was very angry. He was so angry, he almost forgot the unwisdom of acting in anger. He had learnt: when you are angry, think of infinity. Count the stars. He found himself studying Borogoyn like an assassin with an immediate contract, looking for weak points. Vinya was taller than he, much heavier, solid with muscle. He thought little. He lost his temper. But he would expect an easy victory; he did not know about the training of Nepeth. It might be an interesting fight, thought Varagin, if no one else joined in. Already, he had himself under control. He walked towards the Scrambler.

"We did an exchange," said Borogoyn, evidently annoyed at having to explain himself. "She offered herself in her sister's place."

"Very noble," sneered Varagin.

Borogoyn shrugged, off-handedly. "This one's more docile. We had a little trouble with the sister."

"It didn't occur to you," said Varagin, "to consult me first?"

"No," said Borogoyn. "It didn't. You may be Krater's special delegate, but these are *my* men and *I* give the orders. I'm sick of your interference. If you're killed Krater won't weep for you; he'll just replace you. He's got no time for people who can't

[155]

look after their own skins. I'm in charge here and I ordered the exchange. What are you going to do about it, Karel?"

Imperceptibly, the men closed in around him, forming a half-circle. But Varagin was not going to lose his temper now. "Wait," he said, with a faint, ambiguous smile. "In time, folly catches up with fools. You forget, Vinya, you are talking to an intelligent life-form. I know this must be very new to you."

As he turned away, he found himself face to face with Pzyche. For a moment they looked at each other, expressionless. Then:

"We must accelerate the work on Level 3," said Varagin. "The detectors indicate possible deposits further along the edge of the plateau. It would be the height of stupidity to kill each other, when we might be making money."

"Don't press me, Karel," said Borogoyn.

"Don't bore me, Vinya," said Varagin.

14

They put Pzyche in the tent which Sateleptra had occupied and left her alone. "You'll want to change your clothes," said Borogoyn. "There are lots of things here. Take what you like."

"I think I'd rather stay as I am," said Pzyche, doubtfully. "Thank you."

Borogoyn said: "Get changed," and went away.

At the back of the tent, there was a whole partition full of clothes. Pzyche had never seen such colours, or imagined that tunics could come in so many different shapes and styles. Tnoe had brought few of her best things to Krake, and in any case, neither she nor Tnar would ever have worn the fashions favoured by Sateleptra. Pzyche held up a long blue tunic which seemed to consist entirely of a complex system of drapes, trying to work out how to put it on, and failed. In the mirror, she was shocked to see how different she looked, with the colour against her skin. She had never worn colour in her life. She tried to put the tunic back, but the material clung to her arms and when she pulled herself away it slipped to the floor. She left it there.

Beside the bed there was a closet, containing bottles of scent and lotion, make-up sticks, assorted trivia. Pzyche tried the scent but she did not like it much. Since Derec came, Tnoe had taken to using scent, something with a sweet silvery sort of smell which reminded Pzyche a little of Borogoyn's winter roses. But this scent was like nothing Pzyche had ever smelt. It was hot and spicy and very strong. When she replaced the cap on the bottle, she found some of it had come off on her hands. Tnoe's scent was a clear liquid, almost like water, but this was a viscous yellow oil, very sticky, and she could not get rid of it. When she rubbed her fingers on her tunic it left a dark stain.

For a while nothing happened and no one came. She could hear few of the sounds of the camp. Presently, she went to the entrance, and peered out. A guard rose up before her, much too close.

"I'm thirsty," said Pzyche. "I'd like some kaffine."

The guard passed on her order without comment. The kaffine was still hot when it arrived and Pzyche barely noticed the flavour. She remembered Tnoe telling her that kaffine was good for shock. She wondered about Tnoe, and what the others were all thinking, but it did not make her feel any happier. Some time later, Varagin came in.

He had not intended to come. After the confrontation with Borogoyn, he had gone to the spacestage. There was a freight-ship waiting, loaded with mammonite. (Krater and Varagin had agreed it would be best to hold the stock on Krake until the conditions of sale were finalized). Beside it stood the space-craft in which Borogoyn and the first of the men had arrived. It was a small, ugly machine, saucer-shaped like the old-fashioned Explorer modules, squatting clumsily on its retract-able legs. From close to, the silver shield looked scarred and discoloured as though from too many belly-flops into too many polluted atmospheres. Krater had said that once the project was under way it could be scrapped. Varagin went inside, checked the fuel, the pressure, the life-support systems. It was unnecessary, but he felt cautious. By the time he re-emerged, Borogoyn had gone down to the mine. Varagin did not want to go and see Pzyche. He knew it would be better not to. But he went.

She was sitting on the bed when he came in, cupping her cold kaffine between her hands. It was rather dark in the tent, and when she looked up, her eyes were full of shadows. Varagin sat down beside her. In any case, there was nowhere else to sit. There was nothing he particularly wished to say to her. He had been so angry, at first. He had wanted to shake her, to slap her, to beat her head against reality until her mouth came open and her hair fell over her face, until she looked dishevelled and human and in pain. But now she was there, he could not even put his arm round her. He had done it before, without thinking, but this time he had stopped to think, and it was too late. She looked shrunken and cold, like a small naked creature enduring grimly through a black frost. Bones showed in her neck and wrists. But he did not feel any pity. Pity was for the blind, the maimed and helpless. Pzyche was a healthy and potentially normal individual, just like any other. There was no need for pity. "Well," he said presently, "what are you doing here?" When she did not answer he continued, caustically: "I must be very obtuse, but I fail to see in what way it helps your friends, or your sister, or anyone else."

"It seemed like a good idea," said Pzyche, "at the time."

"They said that about splitting the atom," Varagin retorted. "What sort of a good idea? You must have known I would not let any harm come to Tnoe, unless it was unavoidable."

"*I* knew," said Pzyche.

"And the others?"

"They didn't ask me. They just argued. I think Caleth wants to trust you, but he doesn't. You are not very trustworthy, you know."

"Yes," said Varagin, "I know. So what did they say?"

"Caleth talked a lot," said Pzyche. "He always does when he is trying to be persuasive. He won't compromise, not even if you kill me. He isn't that kind of person."

"And—Derec?"

Pzyche said savagely: "Derec thinks I am not right in the head."

"I see."

"You always *see*," said Pzyche, without gratitude.

[159]

"You're jealous, aren't you? Inglorious common-or-garden jealousy. As described in Vard: *The Average Mind*, volume 30, page 1025. Before Derec came, you must have had all your sister's attention. Now, of course, she doesn't notice you so much. How does it feel, Pzyche, to have such a standard emotion? What does jealousy look like, on the recorder? Five green lights in a circle, isn't it?"

"I was no use to them," Pzyche said, tightly. "It didn't seem to matter. . . ."

"You were jealous," said Varagin. "You thought you would offer yourself in Tnoe's place to hurt her, to hurt Derec. You wanted their whole life to be poisoned by your magnanimity. Perhaps she would blame him for what you had done, even hate him; she loves you, after all. Perhaps he would blame himself. You behaved like a child in a tantrum. "I'll kill myself. Then they'll be sorry." Poor little fool. People don't think like that, Pzyche. They just murmur: How sad, and get on with their own lives. Nobody wastes time carrying around a burden of guilt unless they really want it."

"Like you?" said Pzyche.

For a moment, Varagin was taken aback. "We aren't discussing me."

"No," said Pzyche. "We never do. You like telling other people the truth about themselves, but not the other way round. If I get hurt, it's good for me. If you get hurt, it just hurts. That's right, isn't it?"

"At least you admit it *was* the truth," said Varagin, sharply.

"I suppose so," said Pzyche. "Only it didn't sound quite so selfish, inside my head."

This time, Varagin put his arm round her. She started to draw away but evidently thought better of it. "We deceive ourselves," he said. Unexpectedly, it sounded like rather a comfortable sentiment. "As you say, I do it too. I have no particular right to criticize you."

Presently, she asked: "Will Borogoyn—hurt me?"

"You know that," he said. Suddenly, he wondered if she did.

"I learned about copulation," said Pzyche, "when I was twelve. It came under biology. But I still don't understand why people should want to do it."

Looking down at her, Varagin was conscious of a desire to explain. A very lengthy explanation, with a great deal of unnecessary detail. To his annoyance, he realized the desire had been skulking at the back of his thoughts, unrecognized, since he first saw her. (Perhaps even before.) He was not an optimist. But he thought, given time, he could make her understand.

There was no time. Abruptly, she said: "I hoped, when he touches me, perhaps I might die. But . . ."

"You won't," said Varagin. "People don't usually die of disgust, I'm afraid. It'll happen and you'll have to live with yourself afterwards." He added: "Anyway, it's your own fault."

"Would *you* kill me?" asked Pzyche, glancing up at him with a sort of vivid desperation. "Now, quickly. Before Borogoyn comes. I trust you. You could do it without hurting too much. You could, couldn't you?"

Varagin was aware of an indescribable confusion of emotions, eluding any attempt at self-control. A cold sweat broke out on his temples in spite of his training. His pulse accelerated. "I could," he said, in the pale dry voice of someone whose vocal chords have become temporarily unreliable, "but I won't. It would be—wrong."

Outside, a tuneless electronic tone announced the change of shift.

"Why?" asked Pzyche.

"You took the decision," said Varagin. "You must take the consequences. Anyway, it is possible to keep your self-respect through almost any form of humiliation, if you are strong enough. Prisoners from a hundred dungeons and interrogation chambers have proved that. It's a question of coming to terms with your own limitations. I could not possibly deprive you of the chance to find out how strong you are."

[161]

"I am not very strong, I think," said Pzyche, missing or ignoring the implicit sarcasm. "But you are right: it is my responsibility. I beg your pardon for asking."

There was a brief silence. Varagin knew he ought to go; now the shifts had changed, Borogoyn would be back any minute. He said: "This is an incredible conversation."

"I find all conversation incredible," said Pzyche. "Particularly if I'm in it."

Varagin said: "It's a useful thing, conversation. Try it with Borogoyn. He hasn't heard of it either. You can experience a new sensation together." He wanted to get away. He wanted nothing to do with Pzyche, or emotion, or uncontrol. He had almost forgotten the far greater problem hanging over his head. "Stop fishing for pity," he went on, savagely. "Indulge in a little self-pity if it makes you feel better. But don't expect any from me. I keep my pity for people who really need it. You're an adult who made a stupid mistake, something adults have been doing all over the galaxy ever since the big bang, and, like them, you've got to learn to survive the results. That's evolution. Learning to grin and bear it. In the event, there are worse things than rape. Much worse." He got up. "I have to go," he said, feeling horribly dissatisfied. "Good luck."

He meant it unkindly, but Pzyche did not mind. After he had gone, she felt very desolate. She supposed she would have to put on some of the clothes. Soon, Borogoyn would come back. "Let me help you," he would say, standing right up close. Pzyche went over to the partition and tried to find a tunic she understood.

At supper, there was little conversation. Borogoyn drank persistently but not to excess, like someone who is determined to have a good time but wants to remember it afterwards. Pzyche came in late, under guard. She was wearing one of Sateleptra's tunics, something not too silky and loose about the chest. In colour, it was a bright hard green. Her arms were bare. She

[162]

looked, thought Varagin, like a child dressed up in her mother's clothes, graceful without style, awkward and overthin, wearing the sash too tight and tangling her feet in the hem. The tunic was not really too long; it was just that Pzyche had never worn a long tunic. She did not look at Varagin. She sat down and began to pick at her food.

"You're not eating enough," said Borogoyn.

"I'm not hungry."

Borogoyn dumped another spoonful of vegetable matter on her plate. "Eat," he said. "You'd better have a drink, too. It'll make you feel more solid."

Pzyche did not particularly want to feel solid. The vegetable matter made its way down to the pit of her stomach and stayed there, in a hard lump. Borogoyn put a mug of ptermix in front of her. "Drink it," he ordered. Pzyche peered into the mug. There was a yellowish froth on the top, like scum. Below, she could see her reflection in the dark liquid, bending to and fro. It smelt (she thought) like an unopened room, where a pile of old cabbage leaves was slowly deteriorating. "Drink it," said Borogoyn.

Tentatively, Pzyche drank. Varagin restrained an impulse to take part in the scene. He could feel the nerves prickling all over his body. But he knew, if he defended her, it would only make matters worse.

"All of it," said Borogoyn. "It's alcohol. Does you good. It'll help you to relax."

Pzyche drank. Afterwards, the taste would not go away. She could feel the roof of her mouth wrinkling in disgust. She imagined little black toadstools growing inside her throat.

Borogoyn sat watching her hands, resting uncomfortably on top of the table. Her fingers were curled and not very long, like the fingers of a child. Her nails were short and unpolished. Borogoyn imagined those hands moving across his chest; the butterfly touch of her fingertips. Of course she would struggle, at first. Under the hard green material her limbs looked fragile

[163]

and insecure. Her flesh would be soft and cold, holding the hot red marks of his fingers for days afterwards. There would be a moment of futile resistance, of stretching, of pain. Then she would be right under him, wriggling, squirming, like a little white tadpole ... (As a boy, he had enjoyed collecting tadpoles. But they always died.) Suddenly, he realized he had allowed his imagination to impede his appetite. Borogoyn's imagination was a faculty he used, under normal circumstances, about as much as his appendix. He looked down at his plate, and found himself thinking the slivers of meat substitute resembled undersized tadpoles, swimming in the thin gravy. He went on eating.

Varagin left a little while later. Vinya was drinking more slowly now, like a man with a purpose. It was pointless for him to stay. He went out without looking at Pzyche. The last thing he heard was Borogoyn, ordering sweets for her.

Outside, the air felt cold but not fresh. It was a night without stars. Varagin wandered round the perimeters of the camp, trying not to think. They had a proper guard now. It was too late to do anything constructive, even if he had felt the inclination. Tomorrow, he would go to her, hold her (if she would let him), tell her she was alive and sane and relatively uninjured, and that was what survival was all about. Tomorrow, unless the world ended, Pzyche would still be there ...

Much later he saw Borogoyn, going into his tent. She was with him. The guards, dismissed, went off to get drunk. Varagin stood in the shadows, waiting. Tomorrow had no reality any more. He was waiting, in the present; the past was a matter of fruitless regret, the future, fruitless speculation. He wanted to walk away, to lie down on his narrow bed and dream about cornfields, full of thriving weeds. But he stayed, growing colder, waiting, endlessly, to hear her scream.

Pzyche had not enjoyed the sweets. She had been brought up on a strictly functional diet, and she found the coating of red stickiness and the filling of green stickiness equally nauseating. Borogoyn did not eat any. Sweets, in his view, were for women

[164]

and children. He would never have believed Pzyche did not like them.

After Varagin had gone, nothing seemed quite real. She could not imagine continuing to exist beyond the next few minutes. She could not imagine waking up in the morning, a broken, altered creature, different beyond measure. Perhaps she would go mad. Perhaps she would slide easily over the brink into a world of half-lights and shadows, forever outside reality, insensible to her fate. "No use," Borogoyn would say, and she would be let loose in the wastelands, to wander at will. Pzyche remembered Forn. It would be poetic justice. But she did not really want to go mad. She had a feeling that as a plan of action Varagin would not think much of it. "Come with me," said Borogoyn. Outside, she noticed idly that it was going to rain. Rain was rare on Krake. She had no plans any more. She had never had any plans. Somehow, she could not imagine seeing the dawn break tomorrow out of the same pair of eyes.

Borogoyn's tent was a little bigger than Sateleptra's and smelt of man. (Pzyche was getting to know that smell.) As they came in, he kicked an assortment of unwashed clothing under the bed. There was a low table on which stood a bottle, a mug of cold kaffine and a half-eaten sandwich. There were no chairs. Pzyche did not particularly want to sit on the bed. Not that it would make any difference, in the long run. But she did not want to. She stood, uncertainly, just inside the entrance. Borogoyn adjusted the overhead lamp and turned to look at her. Her bare arms felt horribly exposed but not cold (she was a little surprised, not to feel cold). Outside, the heavy sky pressed down against the camp, blacker than the inside of a wolf's belly. Varagin saw the glimmer of light through the thick weathercloth shrinking in upon itself as though the dark was taking over. Presently, only a faint greenish glow showed that the tent was still alive.

Her flesh was cold and soft, as Borogoyn had imagined. Under the tunic he could feel all the curves and hollows, the

[165]

moulding of her ribs. He wanted to be gentle. He wanted her to struggle, but not too much. He wanted to inflict only a very little pain. She sat, motionless, while his hands moved inside her clothes. She did not think she would be able to move even if there had been any point. Her heart beat violently inside her throat. Presently, she felt his mouth against her face. She imagined great red weals springing out on her skin from the touch of his lips. His mouth felt like toadstools, only softer. She stared straight ahead with unfocusing eyes, through him, through the walls of the tent, into infinity . . .

When the scream came it was not, somehow, what Varagin had expected. For a moment, for all his training, his heart stopped. But it was all wrong. It should have been a scream of intolerable anguish, of violation and terror. Instead, it sounded more like a howl. A deep-throated masculine howl of unspeakable fury. Varagin warded off the guards with a brief gesture and went into the tent.

Pzyche was crouching on the edge of the bed, still covered largely by the hideous green tunic. Her head was bent and her hair hung forward so Varagin could not see her face. Borogoyn stood over her, cursing.

"Having trouble?" said Varagin, with sadistic relish. "I could have told you it was a little unwise to give her all that food. Let alone the drink."

At the crucial moment Pzyche had evidently managed to be sick, mostly on the floor and partly on Borogoyn. He was so angry, he hardly knew Varagin was there. In any case, he would have thought it did not matter. Varagin, for all his faults, was a man like other men. Men did not fall out over something as trivial as the mistreatment of a mere female. He had been bewitched by her coldness, her untouchable innocence. He had fantasized about tadpoles and gentleness and emotional susceptibility. In short, he had made a fool of himself. Varagin watched in a sort of fascinated horror as Vinya tore off his belt, kicked his fetid skins across the floor. Something bright and

[166]

sharp fell softly at Varagin's feet. He noticed, irrelevantly, that Borogoyn was bow-legged. His calves bristled with hair and muscle. Pzyche did not even try to move. He caught her by the hair, slapping her head to and fro. His hands squeezed her throat, her arms, her thighs. Great gashes appeared in the green tunic, showing flesh. He felt between her legs, fingering, crushing, tearing. Her arms flailed aimlessly, like the arms of a rag doll. Her legs went sideways, out of control. Varagin did not know when he picked up the knife. The hilt fitted into his hand as though it belonged there. He drew nearer, sick with disgust. (Afterwards, he always said it was disgust.) On the bed, Pzyche screamed.

Borogoyn saw the gleam of the knife even as he turned. But it was too late.

15

Rain was rare on Krake, particularly in the Cold Season. Moisture evaporated from the artesian reservoirs in ubiquitous mists and fell to the earth again as dew. Disembodied H_2O meandered about the atmosphere like a questionable visitant whose presence can be felt but never seen. There had not been a real downpour for over five years. But that night it rained. Not just a few drops, but a violent, torrential rain such as Krake itself could barely remember. The dry earth was pock-marked with the onset of the storm. Then the earth turned to mud and the horizon vanished and in Borogoyn's camp the tents began to leak. Hollows filled up with water which had never filled up with water before. Streaming curtains swept across the plain, obliterating the landscape. At Doctor Corazin's grave the flowers were beaten into the dirt. In the castle, Tnoe stood listening. She could not hear the drumming of the rain against the walls; they were too thick. But there were distant gurgling noises, as if the water was making its own gutters along the gutterless roofs, and from the upstairs windows she could see the castle lights gleaming on raindrops as long as spears.

She was thinking about Derec. He hadn't understood, of course. "This passion of yours for helping people who ought to be able to help themselves," he had said scornfully, many times before. Pzyche, he evidently considered, must be mentally disturbed, a not uncommon result of prolonged solitary confinement (that was how he described her upbringing) followed by too much excitement. After all, this man Forn, what had he *really* done to upset her? He touched her, said Tnoe, unable to explain. He *touched* her. She had not looked at Derec then, in case she saw what he was thinking. She had not looked at anyone. She was picturing Pzyche, in the camp of the enemy, and the ungentle hands of Vinya Borogoyn ... She loved Derec very much. She always would. He was so strong, so confident, so self-sufficient. He had not the faintest suspicion of how much he needed her. But she acknowledged with rare maturity that no relationship is ever quite perfect. Perfection is something to work for, something special and unattainable that looks at its best from a great distance. Anyone who got there (she thought) would die of boredom. Who was it had said: "True harmony is the marriage of two identical clones"? She had to accept that Derec would never love or understand Pzyche as she did. And, if she was absolutely honest, she knew that deep down inside she did not mind as she might have done, because Tnoe was essentially female, and Pzyche was a beautiful girl. But she did not want to look deep down inside, not just now. She ought to rejoin the others, downstairs, but still she stood by the window, staring out at the rain. She could not see the big rock, or the ridge, or anything any more. Only the rain, falling, ceaselessly, within the short range of the castle lights, and beyond, the dark.

Borogoyn lay on his back, staring up at the roof of the tent with a surprised look on his face. It would stay there, now, until the face itself disintegrated. Varagin went down on one knee beside the body. But he was quite sure Vinya was dead. There had been a sickening moment when the knife met resistance, gristle or bone, a second that seemed like an hour, pulling at the knife, the body, pulling, the warm wet gush as the wound opened and the blade came free. The next time, Varagin had struck home. The knife was broad-bladed and clumsy, unlike the N'pethic scalpel, but he knew where it should go. He thought his reactions were slow, dangerously, agonizingly slow, but Borogoyn did not seem to move at all. He gave a kind of grunt, pain or surprise, that was all. Then he was lying on his back, staring upwards. The blood, which had been forming a little pool at his side, gradually stopped. Varagin felt shaken and faintly sick. He had killed very few people. And the horror of firing a gun or dropping a bomb cannot compare with the immediate proximity of death. Varagin tried to close the eyes but they opened again. The corpse looked startled and curiously alert.

Pzyche said: "There is blood on your hands." He had not seen her move but she was crouching beside him. There was a bruise high up on her cheekbone, very dark red.

Varagin nodded and stood up, slowly. This was the time when self-control was important, when it was necessary to think fast and act faster. *Afterwards.* His brain, obstinately, refused to function . . .

Pzyche's eyes followed him across the tent. He picked up a cloth (he thought it was one of Vinya's shirts) and tried to clean his hands. It was not very effective. He looked round, but there was no water. Presently, Pzyche spoke again.

"It's raining," she said.

He could hear the rain, beating against the weathercloth. In one corner, a droplet found its way in and trickled down towards the floor. Then another. And another. Varagin felt protected by the rain, hidden, shut in. The tent walls shuddered and moved under the onslaught of the raindrops. He listened, thankfully, to the ceaseless tattoo. "We must get out of here," he said.

Pzyche came and stood in front of him. A torn strip of cloth fell away from her shoulder, exposing her breast. "Put this on," said Varagin, thrusting a shirt at her. "Hurry." Suddenly, he was aware of time.

She was lost in it. The ends hung down almost to her knees and the sleeves drooped over her hands like a clown's. "Roll them up," said Varagin. At least she was covered. He picked up Borogoyn's jacket and threw it round her.

"I'm not cold," said Pzyche.

Varagin said: "You will be."

Outside, the rain hit them with the force of a physical blow.

[170]

Varagin wanted to take a Scrambler but the landmoviles were under cover and there would be people about; he dared not arouse suspicion. Between the tents, there was nothing but the rain. Light came from the main tent, some way distant, but no sound reached them. At the edge of the camp, Varagin distracted the guard while Pzyche slipped past. It was not difficult to become invisible, in the pitch dark with the water getting in your eyes and blinding you. Afterwards, he said something to the guard which neither of them heard and walked off into the rain. He found Pzyche on the edge of the bomb-site, trying to shelter in the lee of a wall. Already, her hair was black with water and slicked down against her head. Her eyes looked up at him with a sort of calculated trust, as though she had considered the various options and decided he was the best. (It was the calculation he liked, not the trust.) "What now?" she asked.

"We walk," said Varagin.

The uneven road was dangerous in the dark, but Varagin did not want to use a handlamp, not till they had passed the ridge. He did not think they could be seen from the camp unless someone was looking. In any case, it would be many hours, perhaps not till morning, before anyone ventured to enter Borogoyn's tent. When Pzyche stumbled, he took her arm.

As they passed the rubbish dump, he saw the rain was eroding the loose matter on the top. There was something white sticking out which he thought might be Sateleptra's foot. Pzyche was wearing her sandals. They were a little too big for her and they slipped in the wet as she walked. Already, she was muddied over the ankle.

"Are we going to walk all the way?" she asked him, once.

"Have you any other suggestions?"

Beyond the ridge, he switched on the handlamp. (He had picked it up in Borogoyn's tent, before they left.) In the dark, it was difficult to be sure of their direction. The rain had already almost obliterated the track made by the passage of various

[171]

landmoviles. "This way," said Varagin, with no particular confidence. Pzyche followed him.

The scant soil had turned into a thin mud which sucked at her sandals. Once, they had been silver, but you could not see that any more. Out on the open plain there was a strange, wild wind, galloping round in circles. Borogoyn's big jacket buffeted to and fro. Underneath, little trickles of water found their way into the secret places of her body. Wet hair slapped against her face. Soon, she was shivering.

"Walk faster," said Varagin, barely audible over the howl of wind and rain.

Pzyche stumbled after him.

It rained all night. At Castle Kray, Tnoe was playing cards. "It will distract you," said Caleth. But the four suits seemed to run into each other and half the time she scarcely knew what she held in her hand. Tirril, who had come to the conclusion he was a good card-player, got interested in the game and then felt guilty about it. Derec, like Tnoe, did not seem able to concentrate. Caleth shuffled and reshuffled, deftly, but there was a very serious expression on his face. The expression had been there ever since he learned the truth about Pzyche.

"She is obviously not responsible for her actions," Derec had said.

"No," said Caleth. "Everyone is responsible for their actions. Pzyche is not mad, although perhaps it would be better if she were. If she was intelligent enough to do what she did, then she will be intelligent enough to accept her responsibility."

"What are you thinking?" Tnoe asked him, much later.

"Of wastefulness," Caleth answered, slowly. "The waste of a human soul, alone in a desert like this. A human soul warped and misdirected by the horrible errors of those who mean well. Someone should write a book about it, a book about the failures, the madnesses, the endless casualties which result from the noble efforts of people who think they know best. 'Those Who

[172]

Mean Well'. It would make a good title. The book should be compulsory reading for all sociologists, psychiatrists, philanthropists and would-be Utopians everywhere. What will Pzyche do, in the wide world? She has destroyed in innocence, unknowing. What will she feel, when she has come to *know*? And yet she gave herself for you, Tnoe, in a gesture that might perhaps be called beautiful and even generous . . ."

"What do you mean," said Tnoe, "*perhaps?*"

"We cannot know," said Caleth, "what went on in her mind."

Tirril won the first game; Derec, in a brief fit of concentration, the second. In the third or fourth, Tnoe lost track of the play altogether. Shortly before dawn, she sat up abruptly with an ache in her neck. She must have fallen asleep. She had fallen asleep and her head had slipped sideways: that was why her neck ached. They had forgotten to switch off the firepot and the fuel was running out; the flame had sunken to a faint glowing ring. Beside her, Derec sat with his chin dropped on his chest. He was frowning horribly as though at some disapprovable dream. On her other side, Tirril lay back with his eyes closed and his mouth open, breathing regularly. Caleth was not there.

"Caleth?" She spoke in a whisper, but he came in.

"It's still raining," he said. "This weather is very strange. Unfortunately, I know little of Kraken meteorology." He glanced at the other two. "Let them sleep."

"Did you see anything?" Tnoe asked.

Caleth shook his head. "Nothing," he said. "Only a light, maybe, out across the plain. Moving. It was difficult to be sure. It may have been a will-o'-the-wisp, or some freakish effect of atmospheric electricity. It may have been imagination. I do not see Borogoyn making an attack, not in this weather. If he did, the advantage would be all on our side. This is a defensible house."

Tnoe looked relieved. They sat for a while in silence so as not to wake the others, feeling the kind of hopeless serenity that

[173]

you feel when you have run through all your emotions several times over and now have nothing left. After a while, Caleth said: "I think I'll take another look." He was halfway up the stairs when they heard the banging on the door.

Afterwards, Tnoe always said she *knew*. She did not pause or think. Even before Caleth had reached the foot of the stairs she was at the door, wrenching at the old-fashioned bolts, pressing out the code on the key panel with feverish fingers. The others were awake now, spilling, sleepily, into the corridor.

"Tnoe—"

But she had already opened the door.

It was Varagin. His black hair was plastered down against his skull and his eyes glittered, unnaturally, between tired eyelids. His glance flickered past Tnoe, touched Caleth, rejected the others. He was breathing very steadily, as though with a conscious effort.

Pzyche had collapsed against the wall outside. Varagin caught her wrist and pulled her into view, roughly, because he was tired: a limp, bedraggled creature dressed inexplicably in a monstrous travesty of a jacket; wet ragged hair; bare legs. Her face was quite colourless with fatigue.

"I thought," he said, "I ought to bring her home ..."

It was Tnoe who took her inside, hugging her, tightly, regardless of territorial violation. Pzyche's legs would scarcely support her and she clung round her sister's neck, her cold cheek pressed inadvertently against Tnoe's. Derec said: " Put her in a chair. Later, I'll give her a check up. But not now. She's totally exhausted." He stared at her curiously.

In the corridor, Varagin and Caleth stood face to face.

"I used to wonder," said Caleth, "if you had a better nature." He remembered the cold intelligence and vengeful temper of the boy he had known. But they had grown up together, after a fashion. Even in the commune there was a bond.

"I haven't," said Varagin. "Surely you remember? You were the one with the better nature. I never liked you, you know."

[174]

Caleth smiled with gentle mockery. "How very distressing," he murmured.

It might have been the sudden transition into a warm interior, but he thought, for a moment, a little touch of colour came into Varagin's pale face.

Next door, Tnoe was chafing Pzyche's hands. "She's icy cold," she said. "Someone get my fur coat. I think it's upstairs. And ask Caleth for some spirits."

"Whatever is she wearing?" asked Tirril.

"Never mind that," said Tnoe impatiently. But as Varagin came in she looked up at him with an anxious query in her face.

Varagin managed a shadow of his old unpleasant smile. "She's all right," he said. He was very weary. "You needn't worry."

"There's a bruise on her face," Derec said suspiciously.

Varagin threw him a brief, hostile glance and said nothing at all.

About half an hour later Pzyche, enveloped in a bath-wrap and Tnoe's fur coat, was curled up in serviceable armchair obediently sipping spirits. Varagin sat opposite her, wearing Derec's skins and a shirt which had once belonged to Professor Galbrenzil. (Derec was not very pleased with this arrangement, but Tirril's skins were too tight and Caleth's too short.) Wet clothes hung over the convector, steaming.

"Are you sure he didn't hurt you." Tnoe asked her sister, for the third or fourth time.

"I don't think so," Pzyche said, sleepily. "I didn't notice."

"Interesting," commented Derec. "She seems to have blocked her mind off from the whole experience. Even if anything had happened she would scarcely have been aware of it. God—or Vard—knows what it could have done to her subconscious. Some psychospecialist is going to have a lovely time with her, if and when we get back to Fingstar."

"Nobody is going to have a 'lovely time' with my sister," Tnoe declared sweepingly.

[175]

"It might be of use," said Derec. "I wouldn't know. Thank the gods it isn't my job. I'm only concerned with tangible things: blood vessels, and bacteria, and the spleen." He added, thoughtfully: "It's odd to think all that used to constitute the main interest in my life. Now, I have other worries. But I'm afraid I haven't Caleth's thirst for adventure. I should rather like to see a spleen again."

Pzyche put down her glass. "I don't think I ought to drink any more of this," she said carefully. "It might make me unwell."

"You can't be sick again," said Varagin. "It isn't necessary." Exhaustion made him brusque to the point of rudeness. "Put her to bed, Caleth. And get rid of the others. I want to talk to you."

In the end, it was Derec who carried Pzyche upstairs. Tnoe, consciously tactful, did not comment. Pzyche was asleep even before she got to bed. Tirril took first watch. Out over the plain the clouds were breaking up, and a bilious dawn came creeping through the gaps. Ingellan gleamed briefly, low over the horizon, and then went out. Tirril built card-houses to keep himself awake, but they always fell down. In his office in Camarest, a world away now, he had often passed the time building houses with the index cards from the filing system. With practice, he had grown quite skilful. But this time his houses would not stay standing. Eventually, he decided the planet itself had the shivers.

Downstairs, Caleth told Varagin: "You ought to get some sleep, too. You look done in."

Varagin ignored him. "We must talk," he said.

"Are you going to tell me why you did it?" asked Caleth.

Varagin shrugged. "Does it matter?"

Caleth said gently: "Only to you."

Perhaps exhaustion had weakened Varagin's usual façade. "Call it a sudden impulse," he said. "I didn't like Borogoyn. I didn't like being manipulated. I suppose—I didn't like myself

[176]

very much. You wouldn't understand. Your smug self-satisfied morality must have kept you comfortable for years. Anyway, it *doesn't* matter. That's why I had to talk to you. As far as this planet is concerned, nothing matters very much any more. Not even archaeology. We'll have to cut our losses, if we get the chance. It may already be too late."

"What do you mean?"

"According to my researches," said Varagin, "this entire planet is about to blow up. I give it a week at the outset. Shall we get some sleep?"

PART IV

16

Dawn, in Sunset City, came long before anyone got up. Even
the tourists stayed in bed. Owing to a peculiar imbalance of
atmospheric pollution, there were almost no colours : it was like
a dawn among the stars, a slow growth of white light spreading
into a blue-black sky. Two or three moth-eaten moons faded
gradually into daylight. When the sun was well over the distant
mountains there was a moment as swift as the blinking of a
camera eye, and suddenly the whole sky turned to azure. Movement filtered through the empty streets; sound trickled into the
silence. There were six hours till sunset. The city came to life.

Krater had been up a long time. He had had a window made
in the side of the Sunrock, its shutters camouflaged against the
rock-face: a forbidden window that looked towards the dawn.
He slept badly, perhaps owing to the various aches and pains
which gnawed at his joints. He took too many sleeping pills,
and now none of them worked any more. Alcohol rotted his liver
and hennebuhl riddled his lungs. His doctors grew steadily
richer. He woke early, always irritable, and sat in his chair by
the unlawful window (it was the only one of his crimes for
which he did not have a licence). Down in the city, grey streets
interlocked with grey streets. There was a glimmer of dead
windows, a stretching of shadows. Morning stole softly past
faceless buildings. It gave him a sense of power, looking out
over the world where he reigned like a spider. He had only to
pull a thread, and the buildings would disintegrate, the streets
trickle away into dust. Sometimes he was tempted to pull that
thread, just to pass the time. He was so painfully bored. He was

bored with the food he ate, the wine he drank, the status sym-
bols which surrounded him. He was bored with his doctors, his
illnesses, his hypochondria. The very beauty bored him; he had
seen too much beauty. Power, the exercise of power, gave him
a momentary stimulation. But then the boredom would creep
back, deadly, implacable, rotting his very soul. Evil is boredom.
Hell is infinite boredom. Occasionally, he told himself that if
the fates had endowed him with imagination or academic ability
he might have dealt differently with his life. But since, most of
the time, he was not unduly dishonest with himself, he knew
that he must have chosen to be bored, somewhere long, long
ago, frightened by the commitment of emotion or pain. His
mind festered between narrow walls, laughing. Laughter was
his substitute for joy, the savage laughter of one who takes a
twisted pleasure in a twisted joke. Sometimes, he wondered if
Sateleptra was dead yet. He knew Vinya's temper from experience. They should be getting along well by now, Karel and
Borogoyn, barely speaking, the resentment of each acting as a
curb on the other. His judgement was never wrong. It was difficult, manipulating someone as subtle and complex as Varagin
Karel, someone with so few weaknesses to take hold of. But his
very fastidiousness would be his undoing. There was only one
thing troubling Krater, a small, niggling thing that came back
in the mornings to disturb his ennui with the dawn. The
actress's daughter ... A detail that was trivial but unplanned,
a loose thread in his steel web. If she was still alive, the deal
should have gone through by now. (If she was still alive.) But
she was only female after all. Krater thought little of sex, particularly with women. As for love, that was something he had
read about, long ago, before books and poetry were swallowed
up in the interminable boredom of everything else ...

While Krater was looking out at the dawn, Pzyche was asleep.
She had not enjoyed being carried upstairs by Derec, but she
did not protest, partly because of Tnoe, partly out of sheer ex-

haustion. The grip of his hands on her body was tight and dry. Too many people had touched her lately, pleasant and unpleasant: Tnoe with her warm soft cheek; Derec, lifting her, cautiously, into his arms; Vinya's hands, seeking, clutching, his knee in her thigh, his thrusting fingers . . . In her sleep, Pzyche dreamed she was a child again, learning about reproduction. On the computer screen there was an incomprehensible diagram of a section through the male genitalia. Pzyche knew that was what it was because the computer said so, but it did not look like anything she had imagined or seen in pictures. Suddenly, the diagram disappeared and there was a slow-motion film of apes engaged in courtship display. One of them began to rush towards her, out of the picture. It wasn't an ape: it was Borogoyn, running, bow-legged, with his arms above his head and his paws outstretched as though to clutch her. But he could not get out of the picture. Already the screen was shrinking, smaller, smaller, until the ape Borogoyn was no bigger than an insect. Someone was turning the knob, turning him off. His simian grunts faded to a cricket-like chittering. Presently, he was so small he did not seem to be moving at all.

"Switch it off," said Varagin.

Pzyche pressed the button. Emergency Cancel. The screen vanished.

Varagin was standing beside her. For no particular reason, they were in the library. She wondered why he was not wearing any clothes. It did not bother her very much; she was merely curious. He looked like a painting she had seen once, she thought it was called "Beastbirth", with a strange, unnatural light, torches or firelight, playing on his muscles. Of course, she thought vaguely, halfway to waking, he had to take his clothes off, they were all wet . . .

Pzyche emerged from her dream feeling inexplicably comfortable. In retrospect it seemed faintly amusing, although she could not think why. Her experience of humour was so limited. Even the ape Borogoyn appeared comical rather than frightening, with his bare leathery bottom and prehensile feet. She had only been frightened just for a moment. She wondered what had woken her. The room was filled with a cold gloom and through a crack between the shutters filtered a single ray of morning. She did not think she had slept very long. No sound penetrated from below stairs but the plumbing, which was rather old-fashioned, hummed faintly as the water circulated from the hydrant. She sat up. Something must have woken her, movement or sound, a shudder in the ground from a footstep on the plain. She had been too tired to wake of her own accord. Everything was very still and quiet. But she had the strange impression that just before she opened her eyes the whole room had twitched, as though shaking off a fly.

She got up and went to the window. Daylight came in as she opened the shutters, a cold, disheartened daylight. The rain had darkened the earth and at intervals there was a faint grey gleam where the water had not yet drained away. Clouds still trailed across the sky, no longer heavy but thinned and frayed like a bundle of streaming rags. The sun, white-faced, peered out briefly and then withdrew. Low over the horizon there was a moon left over, Wormwood, like a twist of old rind. Suddenly, Pzyche found herself thinking it looked like home. She had never thought about home before. Perhaps it came to her now because she knew very soon she would have to go away, to escape, out into the wide world where the sunrise was pink (or white, or yellow) and territorial violation occurred every time someone passed you in the street. Last night, the wide world in all its natural brutality had come very close. Pzyche was not at all sure she was brave enough to face it, alone, knowing none of the rules. Perhaps Borogoyn's men would go away. Perhaps archaeologists would come, impractical, self-absorbed intellectuals who would talk without listening and dig holes in the ground and ignore her. But she knew really it would never happen. She could feel the walls of the castle, very strong and solid, going down into the earth like roots. She felt very safe, with those walls all around her. It would take a lot of explosive to get in. Five hundred years ago, when mines were shallower and equipment less sophisticated, when there were no college degrees in subterranean engineering, no home leave, and no bathrooms, the castle had been built by a mine-owner who wanted to keep an eye on his investment. In those days, the miners were a half-starved rabble, unwashed, uneducated, exploited by their masters and deprived of sex for long periods. But the castle had stood five hundred years and looked as if it would stand another five hundred. For a moment, Pzyche thought she would never have the courage to leave.

She got dressed, slowly, and went downstairs. Even before she had reached the ground floor she could hear Derec's voice, sharp with unbelief. "How can you be sure? It might just be a resurgence of old volcanic activity. We could be safe twenty miles away."

"Such things have happened before." Varagin this time, sounding tired or bored, as though he had been explaining the same thing over and over again. Pzyche entered unobtrusively. "Stick to your spleens, doctor. I am a geospecialist: it is my job to know about rocks. There should not *be* any volcanic activity on Krake. The planetface is old and cold. The plate movement, such as it was, has virtually stopped; the rocks will hardly shift one hundredth of a span in a whole millennium. When the original accident occurred, my instruments were jarred by seismic vibrations which should not have been there. I did not know—I did not *want* to know—what was the true cause. But I returned with more accurate instrumentation. Disbelieve me if you like. You are welcome to stay behind."

"B—but I don't understand," stammered Tirril. "How on earth can a whole planet just blow up?"

Pzyche, who had been paying careful attention, sat down rather suddenly.

"In planetary terms," said Varagin, "there is no such place as 'on earth'. We are in space. You are aware, I trust, that not only

[185]

your planet of origin but this planet as well is not actually flat?"
Tirril, who was not yet used to Varagin, went very red. "How
intelligent. We progress. At the heart of the planet is the molten
core, which, in the case of Krake, contains a very high level of
radioactive matter. Over millions of years this matter has been
gradually disintegrating in the process known as atomic fission.
You may perhaps have heard of it. Intense heat and nuclear
energy are given off. While the planetface has been cooling, at
the heart of the planet the temperature has increased. In the
end, the build-up of pressure has become too much. The planet
is at breaking point. Already, I suspect, there are places where
the crust has begun to disintegrate. According to my instruments, we go next."

Caleth said with repressed frustration: "We are living in an
age of high technology. Radiation levels at the planet core could
have been monitored. We should have *known* . . ."

"Unfortunately," said Varagin, "the trouble started rather a
long time ago. When the planet was created, to be precise.
There was no one around to give it a check up before they put
on the crust. And this is the Outmost System: modern technology went out of fashion here even before it came in. I doubt
if this planet has had an electrocardiogram in its life."

"Can you tell," asked Derec, "exactly when it's going to
happen?"

"Soon," said Varagin, with a brief smile. "Very soon. There
have been indications ever since I came back: the unusual
warmth, the increased rate of evaporation, last night's rain-
storm. I doubt if Scharm's 'routine' helped very much. We are
sitting on an old fault, running, at a guess, along the edge of the
plateau. It has not caused any trouble for a million years or so,
but there is still a weakness in the rock. Here, the crust will
break first. You will be glad to know Dragoncrake is right on
top of the faultline. The ridge may even be part of an old
volcanic cone. I would not want to be underground, when the
fault starts to give way."

"So," said Caleth, "we have found it after all. The Dragon of Dragoncrake. I wonder if the Professor guessed?"

"You mean the city was *inside* a volcano?" said Tnoe.

"The volcano must have been long dormant when they built the city," Caleth said thoughtfully. "There was, perhaps, a narrow chasm, barring the gateway. From time to time, I imagine, there was a flicker of fire in the gap. But as the centuries passed the fires sank, and the chasm closed. The god of the city—the dragon-god—had gone away. Perhaps the people, too, went away. Only a shallow step remained, where the lips of the rock had met, unevenly, like a wound that heals awry. Water trickled in behind doors that were shut forever. Until Man came back . . ."

"So it was all for nothing," said Tnoe. "The raid, and the Professor's death, and everything. Even the crystal never really mattered." She found it all rather difficult to take in. The ground under her feet looked so solid.

"We risked everything," said Derec, "for nothing. I always said it was ridiculous."

"If you wanted to know about the crystal," said Varagin, "you should have asked Pzyche. She recognized it from the start."

"*Pzyche?*" Caleth said sharply. The others looked blank.

"She told me," said Varagin, tenderly, "she thought you weren't interested."

"But she *can't* have—"

Pzyche whispered, palely: "It's true. I knew what it was. I didn't think—"

Caleth said, almost savagely: "Why didn't you tell us?"

But Pzyche knew the answer to that. "You never asked," she said.

Suddenly, she began to laugh, a queer, distorted laugh that sounded almost like hysteria. For a horrible moment, Tnoe thought her sister did not look like herself at all. There was a note of sophistication in her laughter, an element of evil mockery, as though some malign influence had touched her in her very innocence. She could not stop laughing.

It was Varagin who slapped her face. Not hard, but sharply. She fell silent at once. "Pzyche," he said very quietly, but there was an edge even to his quietness, "listen to me. You thought it was clever, didn't you? They believed you were stupid, so you decided to pay them back by pretending to *be* stupid. You were turning inward upon yourself, gloating over your own secret cleverness. Perhaps you thought it was funny. You haven't had much to laugh at, so far. Perhaps it was an unconscious reaction, an instinctive withdrawal from responsibility. But responsibility belongs to all of us. If you want to grow, you must accept that, and learn to look outward. If you turn inward, eventually you will find there is nothing there. Condition X. You will become mentally deformed, warped by the pull of the vacuum, growing in upon yourself. In the end, you will go mad. Do you understand me?"

Pzyche nodded, very pale. "*You* thought it was funny," she whispered.

"At thirty-three," said Varagin sharply, "I'm irreclaimable."

Pzyche murmured in a carefully toneless voice: "I see," and for a moment he thought she smiled almost naturally.

Derec started to say something but Caleth interrupted him. "It's over and done with," he said. "Leave it. We have to decide on a course of action. The obvious thing is to try and arrange a truce with Borogoyn's men. They have the transport. Perhaps whoever takes over will be more amenable to parley. Unfortunately, we have very little alternative."

"What will you offer them?" said Varagin. "My blood?"

Derec said, unforgiveably: "Why not?"

"Supposing they just go away and leave us here?" Tnoe interjected hurriedly.

"Precisely," said Varagin. "The one advantage we have is that I did not discuss what I discovered with anyone. Not even my late colleague. You were planning, if I guess correctly, an

[188]

attempt on the spacelink, or perhaps a further foray into the mines. Stick to your plans. That is what they will expect. Meanwhile, there is a Novamark C module—what is usually called a spacetray—on the spacestage. I checked it yesterday and all systems are fully operational. I know how to handle the controls. I imagine Caleth does too. It's our only chance."

"*Steal* a spaceship?" said Tirril, forgetting to stay silent.

"Are you having moral scruples?" asked Varagin.

"It might work," said Caleth. "I've never flown a spacetray but I was co-pilot for a while on the old Astromark Explorer. It would mean dividing our forces. Two at least to stage the diversion; the rest to take over the ship."

"It's a brilliant idea," said Derec. "Who's going to stay behind?"

"You have a better plan?"

"I hope," said Tnoe, "that is, this is a very difficult thing to say, but if the whole planet is going to blow up" (she still could not believe it) "surely it's better for two of us to stay behind, than—than all of us—"

"Nobody is going to stay behind," Caleth said flatly. "We'll work something out. We have to."

There was, Tnoe decided, very little point in panicking. The danger hanging over them was too huge to be frightening. You couldn't run anywhere; there was nowhere to run to. Two months ago, she would have become hysterical. But she had lived with fear for too long now, in one form or another, and though she would never grow accustomed to it she knew it would be quite useless to lose her self-control. Gradually, the horrible sinking feeling in her stomach went away. She tried to behave normally, not to think too much, above all not to let herself start shaking. "It won't happen," she told herself. "We have *time* . . ." What was it they used to say? Stop the planet; I want to get off. She wondered what congenital idiot had thought up the laws of gravity.

[189]

"I can't imagine it happening," said Pzyche, unconsciously picking up the direction of Tnoe's mind. "In one minute, or in three, we might be dead. But I can't imagine it. Do you know," she added, "when Borogoyn wanted to make love to me, I couldn't imagine that, either? I knew it was going to happen, but I couldn't imagine it. So in the end, it didn't happen. Perhaps, when you can't imagine something, it *doesn't* happen."

"Can you imagine getting away?" asked Tnoe.

"No," Pzyche said.

The girls made breakfast; the men made plans. Nobody felt much like eating anything. "I'll go on watch," said Caleth. "We move tonight. Our chances are better in the dark. Meanwhile, we must try and get some rest. Fortunately, Borogoyn's men should be fully occupied with the murder."

"But shouldn't we go *now*?" said Tirril. "I thought—"

"This planet has been here a long time," said Varagin. "It'll hold a little longer. I hope."

"I'll never get any sleep," Tirril said.

17

In the camp of the enemy, Scharm, he of the routine, had taken over. "They probably won't move until dark," he said. "We have time to prepare."

It was nearly midday before they had found Borogoyn. "He's enjoying himself," the men had said, some grinning, some indifferent. If that was how his taste ran, they did not mind. Most of them thought Pyzche too skinny to be interesting. They all hated Borogoyn, of course, but it was a cordial hatred, the kind of hatred you feel for someone you have known a long time whose bad points have become agreeably familiar. Borogoyn was loud, violent, colourful. When they worked for other, more civilized overseers, they would boast of his drinking proclivities, his brutal temper, his total lack of redeeming features. He was as strong as a bull and as quick as a pile-driver. He would kill you as soon as look at you. They were all very proud of him. No one particularly wanted to go into that tent and tell him he ought to get up.

It was Scharm who missed Varagin. Someone said he must have gone off in a Scrambler, to do another external survey, but the Scramblers were all in camp. Who cares? said an engineer who had never been to college and deplored Varagin's professional superciliousness. Nobody liked Varagin. He was a stranger, aloof, sarcastic, suspiciously intelligent. He had no vices, which was unnatural. His insistence on safety precautions they had imputed to self-interest or some other ulterior motive, probably sinister. If he had disappeared, so much the better. Perhaps he had fallen down a crevasse. Perhaps Vinya (the old bastard) had murdered him. It had almost come to a fight only yesterday. "Perhaps," said Scharm. An hour later, when nothing had happened, he went into Borogoyn's tent.

They carried the body out on a board, under an old sheet. Scharm uncovered the face, briefly, and looked down at it without interest. In death, the eyes seemed to have sunken in, the eye-pouches sagged further down the cheeks. When he closed the lids they did not open again.

"Karel will learn his mistake," he said, "when it's too late."

"How many of them are there now," asked one of the men, "holed up in that castle?"

"Too many," said Scharm, who did not know.

"We've got the explosives; can't we clean them out?"

"The building is too solid. We'd have to get in close—too close. If we wait, they'll come to us. They must: it's their creed. Moral responsibility." Something which might have been contempt flickered across Scharm's bland face. "They'll be after the spacelink. Take them alive. They ought to be questioned."

"And Varagin Karel?" someone asked.

"He isn't important now. Kill him. That's an order."

The men did not particularly relish this assumption of authority, but no one objected. They were a little afraid of Scharm. He was a man of few words and fewer ideas, with the physique of an android and the cool, calculating intelligence of a one-track computer. He had trained in the Assassination Corps of an obsolete imperialist army, and his sole ambition in life was to dispose of the maximum number of human beings as quickly and as efficiently as possible. He did not like blood: it was too messy. He did not like screams. He liked darkness and silence, and the stillness of an unmarked grave. He liked little heaps of dust, and weapons that reduced people to little heaps of dust. Perhaps he had been brainwashed, sometime in the long-forgotten years of his training, but if so he would never be able to call back the memories that had gone down in the dark. He did not dream. Krater knew him for what he was and used him

[192]

accordingly, but always with circumspection. There is a legendary button at the heart of the universe which, it is said, triggers the final, unimaginable implosion that will reduce all the worlds to a single point, no bigger than a pinhead and so heavy that the void itself would be warped around it. Scharm, he knew, was the kind of man who would push that button. He was a believer in death for death's sake. His spirit was so empty he did not even know when he was bored.

"Varagin knows the layout of the camp," he went on, "so we'll change it. Move the spacelink from the minehead to the spacestage. That will confuse them. And—"

"*Move* the spacelink?" said someone. "It's a hell of a job."

"Do it," said Scharm, uninterested. "And see it's well guarded. Constantly."

"There's the old Novamark—the spacetray—"

"That can be scrapped. Get it out of the way. When we clear out, we'll go by freight. The Novamark isn't spaceworthy any more."

"Should we empty the fuel tanks?"

"Are they full?" Scharm looked faintly surprised. "Do it if you have time. You're going to be busy. Get moving."

Sitting around waiting for something terrible to happen is always much worse than when you actually start to move. During the afternoon, Tnoe lay in bed trying not to listen for the first distant rumble of doom, and every second seemed to stretch into eternity. Somehow, she must have slept, briefly, because when Caleth came in she sat up with a start to find it was growing dark. She put on a thick jacket and left her coat. "It'll slow you down," said Caleth. It was a good coat and Tnoe did not abandon it without a certain sentimental reluctance. But she knew what Derec would say. "It won't keep you warm when you're dead. Nothing warms the dead." Whatever fear he might feel, she thought with pride, he controlled it very well. He was practical and intolerant and almost the same as ever. Only

[193]

sometimes there was an edge in his voice which should not have been there. Fear, real fear, was a relatively new experience for Derec Rolt, and he did not like it.

Downstairs, Tnoe found herself thinking how different the others looked, under stress. Tirril seemed to have acquired a certain hopeless resolution, as though, faced with the uselessness of terror, he had realized there was nothing to do but be brave. His young, shapeless face looked haggard and almost interesting. Varagin smiled more, a swift feline smile unlike his usual restrained lip movement. Caleth was always calm and self-contained, but underneath Tnoe thought she sensed a kind of glitter, as though in the moment of danger he felt very vividly the pleasure of being alive. "Like Varagin," Tnoe thought, surprised. "They are the same kind of people, in a way. Only Caleth must have lived by his principles, while Varagin probably didn't think it was worthwhile having principles at all. I wonder how well they *really* know each other?" But it was Pzyche who shocked her. In the last day or two, her face seemed to have come alive. There was expression in her eyes, shadow and sparkle, and a feverish colour came and went in her cheeks. Sometimes, Tnoe was reminded of her mother. "If we get away," she thought, "none of us will ever be the same." But it was difficult to believe in getting away.

In the early evening, they were ready. Caleth and Derec carried denominators; Varagin declined. Presumably he had a weapon of his own. Tirril was secretly relieved to be told he was too incompetent. Pzyche had retrieved the third denominator and hidden it in her jacket without telling anyone. She was a little unsure about using it but it made her feel solid, having it there. When everything else had become so unstable, she needed to feel solid. "She's beginning to look almost animated," Derec told Tnoe. "It must be the excitement." "It's death," said Tnoe, with a peculiar shudder, terror or anticipation. "When it comes very close, that's when you know you're alive. Look at Varagin." Pzyche herself thought she was as quiet as

[194]

ever. Whatever doubts and insecurities she might feel were carefully concealed, buried deep in what she hoped was her subconscious. She concentrated very hard on behaving just as usual.

For the last time in its life, the Ita Spear wouldn't start. Caleth tapped the engine here and there, like a doctor with an asthmatic patient. Presently, it emitted a familiar half-hearted cough. Pzyche knew the same strange pang she had felt earlier. *Home.* Clouds had reassembled on the horizon, rimmed with the last glare of the sunset. The sky was like a huge lightless bubble. Over the plain, vision was deceptive. Rock and stump merged into the background, grey and shadowless. When they drove off, taking a wide detour to avoid the usual route, Pzyche did not look back. She had a feeling that if she did she would see the solid walls of the castle trembling like something under the sea, until presently they collapsed in upon themselves and were dispelled into a mist. Beyond, the horizon would rear up like a tidal wave . . . She must not look back. She must look forward, always forward, and the world ahead would remain as she had known it, though the world behind disintegrated into chaos. If she turned round, then the chaos would overtake her, and she would perish. She must look ahead, beyond Krake, beyond the sparse familiar stars at the edge of the galaxy, into new worlds and cluttered constellations, into the future (if there was one), without hesitation, without regret, without fear. But she wanted very much to turn round. She held onto something, tight, tight, and kept her eyes in front of her.

Tnoe felt the grip of cold fingers on her arm, pinching her flesh. But she did not say anything.

They left the Ita Spear at a distance from the camp and approached cautiously. It was quite dark now. Varagin had the grenades (smokespinners, they were called). Caleth had brought them, thinking they might be useful, along with the denominators, the pack of cards, antiseptic lotion, spidercord, wine. By this time, Tnoe would not have been particularly surprised if

[195]

he had produced a pair of seven-league boots. On the edge of the bomb-site, they separated. Derec was to go with Varagin. Caleth had to manage the spacetray and Tirril lacked the necessary nerve: there was no other choice. "Don't kill each other," said Caleth, with what might have been a smile.

Varagin's eyes glittered strangely. "Give us ten minutes," he said. "Then move."

"I don't trust him," thought Tnoe, with a sudden impulse of panic. "Supposing it's a trap . . ."

But Caleth had already offered Varagin his hand. "Good luck," he said.

Varagin accepted the handclasp as if he did not know what to do with it. "If we don't get back quickly," he said, "don't bother to wait."

"We'll wait," said Caleth.

No one said goodbye. Derec's face, in the dark, looked horribly grim, as though all the muscles in his jaw were clenched. He did not say anything; perhaps he was afraid his voice would give him away. In the face of his silence, Tnoe did not say anything either. Afterwards, she thought that in all the months she had known him she could never have imagined such a parting. But it was over before she had time to think. "Come on," said Varagin, and they vanished into the darkness. Nearby there was the sound of a stone, displaced, resettling itself in a hollow. They retreated into the shadow of a wall and crouched there, waiting. Caleth took out his timewatch and they could see the seconds, faintly luminous, ticking past.

"Supposing it's a trap?" Tnoe whispered, and then wished she hadn't. "Do you trust him?"

"Not much," said Caleth without comfort.

Somehow, the ten minutes passed very slowly and were over too soon. "Now," Caleth whispered. Beyond the wall, night had deepened. The clouds were pale against a starless sky. There was no moon. They picked their way round the edge of the bomb-site towards the spacestage. Every so often there was the faint chink of loose rock, the sound of some tiny pebble, rolling, wantonly, an unguessable distance into the dark. Once, Tirril clutched at Tnoe's arm, perhaps to steady himself, releasing her after a moment with a mouthed apology. (She thought it was an apology.) "Surely," she said to herself, "they should have set off the grenades by now . . ." Pzyche was a little way ahead of her. In the dark, she seemed to glide along, as noiseless and insubstantial as a shadow. Suddenly, Tnoe saw her stumble and put out her hand. Caleth turned to help her, but it was not necessary. She had already straightened up and was standing looking down at her feet. But there was something about her pose, an unnatural rigidity . . . Tnoe hung back, curiously reluctant. She saw Caleth bending over something on the ground.

The rain had made heavy inroads into the rubbish dump, washing the body of Sateleptra down towards the track. Her outflung hand had caught at Pzyche's foot. When she touched it, Pzyche knew what it was. The flesh felt limp and cold, not like flesh at all. On the inside of the arm there were shapeless, discoloured patches, decay or other stains. Pzyche looked away, hurriedly, and found herself staring at a mass of matted dark stuff, mossy and yet not like moss, spilling from under a pile of filth. Hair. The face (fortunately) was buried. "Borogoyn's handiwork," said Caleth. A smell was borne towards them out of the darkness, a many-coloured, many-headed smell. Pzyche said to Tnoe: "Don't look." She wished she could wash her hands.

On the far side of the camp, there was a dull explosion. The grenades.

"Run!" cried Caleth. Sateleptra was forgotten. They stumbled over the body and ran.

The camp seethed like a wasps' nest in the process of fumigation. Men blundered and shouted. One of the tents caved in, whether by accident or design nobody knew. A guard with psychopathic tendencies shot himself in the foot. Smoke rolled towards the bomb-site with incredible speed, swallowing up

[197]

direction, vision, form. Scharm, who rarely swore, swore.

"We've done it!" said Derec, with a touch of exhilaration.

"Not yet," said Varagin.

He switched on the electronic pathfinder, and they plunged into the smoke.

At the spacestage, Caleth had come to an abrupt halt. The freightship was there, a vast hulk bellying through the darkness. There was a light in the control cabin, shuttered. Caleth hesitated, then switched on his handlamp, sweeping the perimeters of the launch-pad. "Come *on*!" said Tnoe. "We must get to the ship." And then: "What's wrong?"

"The Novamark," Caleth said slowly. "It isn't there . . ."

As though at a signal, lights came on all around them: stark, white lights, brighter than magnesium. The spacestage was imprisoned in light. Guards sprang up in front of them: two, four, five. Tnoe screamed. She was losing her head, she knew she was losing her head, but she could not control herself any more. They were going straight into the trap. She saw guards, everywhere, leaping out of the ground like warriors from dragon's teeth. She must get away, run, find Derec . . . Caleth tried to stop her but it was too late. She was gone into the darkness, running, towards the camp. Tirril (he never knew why) went after her. Three guards followed. Two set on Caleth. One fired, wildly, but Caleth was on top of the other, rolling over and over on the ground. Then the three of them were all entangled in a shapeless heap, spewing legs and arms, grunting, gasping. Pzyche watched, motionless. She felt small and exposed in the middle of the empty spacestage, trapped in the naked light. She knew she ought to join in, but she could not think where to start. She drew nearer, and a random kick landed somewhere in the vicinity of her knee, almost knocking her off her feet. Suddenly, she remembered the denominator. She pulled it out and pointed it, aimlessly, in the direction of the struggle. Under her finger the trigger felt loose, yielding. Pzyche calculated the odds. Two to one . . . Her face was as white as the lights. She hesitated, horribly, clenching her nerves. On the ground, one of the figures went still. A guard. Caleth and the second stood up, pulling away from each other. Caleth's hands hung limply at his sides. The guard swung his fist. Again. Again. Caleth's body began to buckle, reluctantly, as though it were made of some substance more durable than flesh. Pzyche felt as noticeable as a mouse on an empty floor and equally unimportant. The guard seemed totally unaware of her. His fist went to and fro like a machine. Pzyche tried to aim, carefully, but her sense of perspective seemed to have failed. She thought: "I can't do it . . ." The gun spoke.

Somehow, she was still on her feet. The guard had fallen and Caleth was at her elbow, saying something, between coughs, something comfortable and encouraging. Under the breathlessness and the pain his voice was as gentle as ever.

"It's all right," Pzyche said, not very coherently. She meant: I'm all right. She thought they ought to move but she did not feel she could say so. She did not want to stay there, looking at the fallen guard.

"We'd better go and find the others," said Caleth, without his usual air of decision. "If we can." They had lost, anyway. The Novamark had gone, if indeed it had ever been there. They might as well try and die together. (Particularly Varagin.) "Keep close to me," he said.

The smoke was beginning to creep round the spacestage, blurring the lights. A grey shadow passed across Pzyche's face. Caleth switched on his pathfinder, already tuned in to Varagin's, and followed the flickering red light into the camp.

Tnoe had not gone very far before she realized she was completely lost. A tent loomed up in front of her through the smoke, its sides swelling and shrinking as though in some supernatural wind. There was no wind. She did not know if she had passed one tent or many. She called: "Derec! Derec!" regardless of danger, but all around there were voices calling, though she could not tell how close they were or what they said. Suddenly, there seemed to be people everywhere. Someone snatched at her hair but perhaps he misjudged the distance or perhaps she moved too fast; the fingers seemed to slip through her hair like vapour. A gap opened before her and she plunged through it, running, blindly, until she thought she was alone. Her eyes were sore and she remembered too late to cup her hands over her nose and mouth. She stood still for a moment, her eyes creased, trying to get her breath. She had no idea which way to go. Something came up behind her, moving sideways, warily, like a clumsy long-legged crab. There was an awkward collision. "Tirril!" said Tnoe.

"We'd better keep together," said Tirril, with a firmness he did not feel. "Hold on to me." He gripped her arm, tightly, just to make sure.

A billow of smoke blew over their heads, thick and then thin. In a sudden gap they saw the pithead tower, black against a tumbled sky. "Quick!" cried Tnoe. "This way!" Tirril could see no good reason for heading towards the mines, but he did not stop to argue. They made their way between the tents, passing right through a crowd (it might have been a crowd) who recognized them too late. When Tnoe bumped into somebody, she said stupidly: "Excuse me!" They had no time to lose their way. Towards the perimeters of the camp, the fumes were already beginning to disperse. Beyond the main tent (Tnoe guessed it was the main tent) they came to a place where the smoke was as thin as whey. Ahead, they saw someone approaching. Two men. They looked tall and terrible in the dimness. Tnoe and Tirril turned to double back, but their pursuers had drawn too close. Two more figures, unidentifiable, appeared out of the darkness. Lights crossed overhead and passed on. Tnoe clutched at Tirril and buried her face in his chest. She did not care what happened now, as long as it was quick, and she did not have to look . . .

And then, incredibly, they were all together. There were

[200]

hands on her shoulders, Derec's hands. She heard Caleth's voice, quiet and deadly; Varagin, acid. She was shaking with relief. Opening her eyes, she saw Pzyche, looking pale and oddly wild.

Caleth said softly: "Treachery?"

"Don't be a fool," snapped Varagin.

There was no time for argument. Close by, someone shouted an order, and figures materialized swiftly through the thinning smoke. What followed, Tnoe thought, was like a fatalistic dream. Everywhere they turned, pursuers sprang out at them. Guns spat and missed. One shot singed Tnoe's hair; another scorched Derec's arm. Two or three of the enemy fell, perhaps killed. "We're going the wrong way!" cried Tirril, with a sudden realization of danger.

"We have no choice," said Varagin.

They tumbled through the opening, falling over each other's feet, and the doors closed with a soft mechanical snick. They were in absolute darkness. Then the floor lurched and plummeted beneath them as the lift began to descend.

"I thought," said Tnoe, into the ensuing silence, "this was the last place we wished to go."

"You thought right," said Varagin.

Presently, he enquired: "What went wrong?"

"The spacestage was crawling with guards," said Caleth. "Someone had mislaid the spaceship."

"So you decided I had betrayed you?"

"What would you have thought," asked Caleth, "in my place?" Somehow, now he was there, no one doubted Varagin any more. It had all been a horrible accident, a malignant quirk of fate. Fate, Tnoe thought, was always portrayed as malignant. Now she knew why.

"The same." From his voice, Varagin shrugged. "Why speculate? It wasn't you I betrayed."

"I know," said Caleth. "If you get off this planet, you're a dead man."

In the dark, only Pzyche sensed Varagin smile.

The lift jarred horribly as it hit the bottom. Perhaps something had jolted the mechanism. Varagin pressed the emergency button to hold it there. "That gives us about twenty minutes," he said. "We may as well have some light." They heard him groping for the switch. Presently, the nitron lamps came on along the passageway. "Let's move."

Beyond the great Door, the pit yawned blackly. There was only a faint gleam of water crawling in its depths. The trail of lights round the edge looked frighteningly diminished by the enormous darkness pressing in from every side. For a minute they halted, hearing each other breathe. The image of the dragon watched them, starkly, out of a single acid-blue eye. "Get us out of this one," Derec said to Caleth, without satisfaction.

"Perhaps the passage we used before—"

"I'm afraid not," said Varagin. "I had it blocked up."

Derec said: "You would."

After a while, Tnoe suggested: "There must be other passages." She sounded hopeful rather than convinced.

"If we could hide in the city till daybreak," Caleth said thoughtfully, "we might have a chance." He turned to Tnoe. "You said, I think, that light filters in by day. If light can get in, maybe we can get out. But we'll have to wait for the dawn."

They started to move along the lip of the pit towards the ledge. Nobody had any other suggestions. "What if the planet blows up?" asked Tirril, unnecessarily.

"What do you want?" said Varagin, "a parachute?"

By the time Scharm had sorted the pursuit into some kind of order the ledge was empty. The men gathered in the doorway, rattling their weapons, and only their own echoes came back to them out of the dark. They had seen the city in the grey light of day, the columns and archways, holes and hollows where an army might lie hid. A single chain of lamps had been set up, beyond the first great stalactites, and the tentative reach of the light served only to multiply the shadows, making the darkness look many-cloaked and potentially alive. "If we had gas," Scharm said thoughtfully, "we could use it to flush them out. As it is, we'll have to wait. It would be foolhardy to penetrate the city in the dark."

Someone said: "Slow-burners?"

"They don't last long enough. We'll wait. Ten of you stay here on guard; the rest go and get some sleep. Changeover in three hours. Move."

"What will *they* do?" asked a very young tough with as yet undeveloped mental capacities.

"Whatever we do," said Scharm, showing his teeth, which were broken, in a mirthless attempt at a smile. "They have no choice. If we go and play hide-and-seek in the dark they could pick us off one by one and slip past to the exit. As long as we stay here, they are trapped. We wait till daybreak. So must they."

"Till daybreak," said Caleth. They had taken refuge in one of the huge stalactites, hollowed out with a succession of chambers turning upon the spiral like the inside of a nautilus. In one such chamber a hole or window looked towards the Door. They waited in utter darkness. Beyond the pit they could see men moving about in the circle of the nitron lamps. Gradually, all movement stopped. "A pity," said Caleth. "I half hoped they might follow us. We could have taken them singly, probably without using denominators."

"Yes," said Varagin indifferently. He did not particularly want to kill again, but he knew, if it was necessary, he would do it.

"They are too patient," Caleth went on. "There is someone out there who thinks."

Varagin said shortly: "Scharm."

"There are only about a dozen of them," Derec said, after a while. "The rest seem to have gone. Surely we could manage

[203]

some sort of a surprise attack." He did not like the thought of the long hours till dawn, waiting, inactive, in the belly of a potential volcano.

Varagin raised an eyebrow, a gesture that was quite wasted in the dark. "To take them by surprise," he said, "we would have to crawl across the bottom of the pit on our stomachs, hoping they wouldn't look down, and then climb out quickly up a ten-span step when their backs were turned. After you."

"I'm afraid," Caleth concluded, "we have a long wait. Tirril, take first watch. If any of you go into the chambers facing away from the door, you can use a light. But keep it shielded." Somehow, he produced a small flask, and they all had a drink. Caleth was the sort of person who always had a small flask, in an emergency. Even Varagin did not decline. The alcohol tasted warm and sweet and sharp as a tooth.

"It's funny," remarked Tnoe, "I have this terrible craving for pink sugarfruit. I can't think of anything else."

After that, no one said anything for a long time.

18

In the dark, thought Tirril, it was very difficult to tell who was there and who wasn't. Derec and Tnoe had moved away some time ago; he was not sure about Varagin. Beside him, there was a stillness which might have been Pzyche. Opposite, he could see Caleth's shoulder, silhouetted against the lighter blackness beyond the opening. He was beginning to be very sleepy. He did not say to himself: This is the last night of my life; but the thought was there, in his subconscious, popping up every now and then like a malignant gremlin. He did not think he would be able to sleep at all. The city seemed to be pressing in on him, thick with shadows. "It's creepy," Tnoe had said, when she was there. But it was a strange kind of creepiness, frightening only in its strangeness. Gradually, as he grew accustomed to it, Tirril began to feel comfortable in the dark. Daylight and danger slid away from him and he fell into a tangled dream which he could never remember afterwards. When he awoke, very suddenly, he was expecting to hear music. For a moment, he thought he was in his own bed, on Fingstar. Then realization came to him. He blinked, looking for Caleth's shoulder, but it had gone. Beyond the pit, the heel of a boot struck the rock with a sharp metallic note which carried easily across the echoing space of the cavern. Tirril sat up quickly. "They are going," said Caleth's voice, right beside him. "A change of guard. Others will replace them."

"I'm afraid I fell asleep," Tirril said guiltily.

He did not hear Caleth move away but presently his shoulder

reappeared, against the opening. "It doesn't matter," he said. "Sleep if you can. I am not tired."

Tirril thought he sounded oddly defeated. The thought frightened him, just for a minute; it was so unusual for Caleth to sound defeated. He faced every difficulty with a sort of calculated optimism, a resilient faith in his own ability to win through. Tirril, like the others, felt he was someone who had never given up, never surrendered, always survived, somehow, to fight and stumble and stand fast again. It was something in his face, that battered, careworn, careless face: the ruthlessness of principle, the weakness of humankind. "I am glad," Tirril had thought once, looking at Caleth, "that I am just a lawyer, and I don't have to have any principles. It must be terrible having to live up to them." But this time there was a note of despair in Caleth's voice which Tirril had never heard before. He had a feeling that if he could see him he would be sitting there, hunched up like a kobold, wrapped in some remote, bleak mood of bitterness and loss. Caleth never had moods. Tirril knew he ought to do something, say something, but his mind was empty. He was filled with a kind of horrified concern.

"It's funny," he remarked awkwardly, after a pause, "but I feel almost safe in the dark."

"Yes," said Caleth. "This is a good place."

"I wonder what the people were like," Tirril continued vaguely, "the people who lived here?"

"Who knows?" said Caleth. "Ghosts do not necessarily have hands and feet. Perhaps they were not like people at all." To his relief, Tirril saw he was talking again, like he used to, talking himself out of that imagined mood of blackness and despair. Maybe it had never been there, except in Tirril's mind. "There is something here stronger than memory, something which has been preserved a long time in the loneliness and the dark. I have often wondered if air and light dispel atmosphere, even as pictures fade in the sun. And people bring their own atmosphere with them. If you visit the castles of fallen kings, on planets

[206]

where great empires, old in barbarism, crumbled only centuries
ago, you will find there is nothing there. Only walls, and broken
stone. Too many sightseers have passed and stared, and the
high seats are empty. Only in the desolate places where Man
never comes, such things linger on. The feeling is very strong
here. All the ghosts have come out, like rats leaving a sinking
ship, and they throng the shadows." Tirril shivered, suddenly
nervous of the terrible unseen all around him. He imagined the
movement producing ripples in the darkness, so that Caleth felt
it. "They are not interested in us," he said. "Perhaps they do
not even know that we are here, or different from them. All
such phantoms are blind. The spiritualists of Mism believe that
is all we come to, after death: a thought lingering in a familiar
place, gradually eroded by time, and oblivion, and life. Perhaps,
tomorrow morning, we shall be able to prove them wrong. Have
you ever thought about life after death, Tirril?"

"No," said Tirril. "Well—no. It didn't seem to be necessary."

"Good," said Caleth. "It isn't necessary now."

No one had noticed when Pzyche went away. She felt her
way along the wall with the tips of her fingers; through the next
chamber, and the next. Presently, she came to an opening
through which she glimpsed a shielded light. She could hear
Derec and Tnoe, talking softly. She crept back very quietly the
way she had come. Caleth and Tirril must still be there: Tirril
was breathing audibly, as though he had fallen asleep, and there
was an irregular outline against the window-space which might
have been Caleth. Pzyche crossed the chamber, noiselessly, but
she thought perhaps he heard, although the outline did not
move. Beyond, there was only darkness. The floor sloped upwards and the rooms were smaller. She counted two doorways.
Her eyes were stretched for any glint of light.

"I am here," said a voice, very close to her.

Pzyche sat down, carefully, without touching him. Her heart
was beating very fast and even in the dark Varagin knew her

[207]

face was vivid and strange. When she spoke, her voice sounded quick-breathing and uneven.

"They are all so *calm*," she said, "so acquiescent. Even Tirril does not seem to be really afraid any more. He just sleeps. Derec and Tnoe were talking, but I could not hear what they said. It was all secrets and whispers. If you sit in the darkness for a long time it seems to get inside you, so you think you are invisible. But when the daylight gets in we will still be here, and the men will still be here, and we will all be able to see each other just the same. I think—I am *afraid*. I know it would be stupid to panic. But I can't bear waiting and doing nothing. I don't feel invisible and safe. I feel—I feel alive. I don't think I ever felt so much alive in my life . . ."

"What do you want me to say to you?" said Varagin. "That you are not in the dark, there is no pretence of safety? You know that." He switched on the lamp, cupping his hands over the source, so she saw the light shining redly through his fingers. The hardness in his voice sounded curiously intense after the silences and the whispers of the others. Without asking, she knew he too was afraid. He said: "It would be *very* stupid to panic."

"You have so much control," Pzyche said disparagingly.

He covered the light with his jacket. For a moment she saw his face, dimly, and the glitter of his eyes. Then he stretched out on his back, staring into the darkness. She had an idea he had been like that when she came in.

She said, violently: "I can't *sleep*." Varagin did not answer. "Were you asleep?"

"No."

"Where were you?"

"In a cornfield," said Varagin.

"I have seen a picture of a cornfield," Pzyche remarked, "on the computer. Was it a dream?"

"No," said Varagin. "A mental exercise. I was building a wall, stone by stone." Perhaps because he could barely see her, he thought he was talking to the darkness, to himself. She had gone very quiet. "Beyond the wall, they razed the corn to the ground, and built a city. Behind it, I lay hidden, looking up through the corn-stems. I think I was looking at the sky."

Pzyche asked, after a pause: "Shall I go away?"

Varagin turned towards her. "No," he said. "There is no cornfield. There is only you, and me, and the light. Very probably that is all there ever will be. Tomorrow, we will put out the light. There will be dusk for a little space, and then neither darkness nor light, forever and ever. Stay if you like."

Pzyche drew a little nearer to the light, so he could see the line of her nose, and a single strand of hair, gleaming like a spider's thread. "I used to have two moons, and a green sunrise. But I wanted the sunrise to be pink. So now I have only a little light, for always. Perhaps it is a punishment."

"Sometimes," said Varagin, "you talk nonsense."

"So do you," said Pzyche.

Presently, she asked him, like a child: "What happens when you die?"

"I don't know," said Varagin. "I have no experience." After a moment, he continued: "I was taught that death is final. But we live in a finite universe, and there may be other realms beyond finality which our laws of time and science cannot compass. In mortal terms, I believe death is the end. We leave our memories behind us. However, I may be wrong. It is a favourite delusion of humanity that the eternal continuum must be devoid of sorrow, pettiness, and sex. In the event, we have yet to prove that eternity exists at all."

"Yes," said Pzyche, "but what do you *really* believe? Now—today—tomorrow?"

"Nothing," said Varagin. "There is now, today, tomorrow. That is all. After that, you and I will effectively cease to be. If not before. Our only immortality is with those who remember us. Personally, I hope I shall be very, very mortal."

[209]

"No one will remember me," said Pzyche. "There isn't anyone."

"In that case," said Varagin, "you have nothing of which to feel ashamed."

There was a short silence, broken only by a faint ringing sound, metal on rock, from the far side of the cavern. Then Pzyche said: "I killed someone today." After what Varagin had said, the memory left her with a horrible sense of power and finality.

"Yesterday," remarked Varagin, "so did I. Or had you forgotten?"

"It is a terrible responsibility," Pzyche said, rather inadequately, "killing people."

"There are so many shades of responsibility," said Varagin. (She wondered if he was thinking of the bomb.) "I am afraid you will have to live with it, at least for a few hours. Responsibility develops character, it makes you think before you act. If you survived, it might be good for you. Or it might not. I have lived with my responsibilities a long time."

"Are you still feeling guilty," asked Pzyche, "about that girl?"

"I never feel guilty," snapped Varagin. "Remorse is only another form of self-indulgence. You are what you are. Without violence, you would never learn discipline. It is pointless to regret. If you live to be old, and die in your bed, life is still too short to be wasted."

"It is difficult," said Pzyche, "not to regret things."

"Life is difficult," said Varagin. "No one, really, ever lives by what they believe. We can only try."

After a while, he moved the light. Pzyche lay down beside him on her stomach. She had taken off her jacket and rolled it into a bundle, like a bolster, but it was not very comfortable. The atmosphere in the chamber was tense and airless, so that when she did not talk her breathing became constricted from thinking of it. Sometimes, she imagined the rock felt warm.

[210]

Presently, Varagin grew tired of listening to her restless movements. "Put your head on my shoulder," he said. Her face was turned towards him; he could not see her expression. The light filtered through her hair. She seemed to be considering him, warily, like an animal sensing a trap. But the bait, if there was one, was unidentifiable. She cradled her head in the hollow of his shoulder, crushing her ear against his chest. His hand lay on her hair so lightly she hardly felt it. But she was very conscious that it was there. He waited, interminably, until she began to relax. Then he drew her a little closer. She could hear his heart, hammering against her eardrum. It sounded loud and very rapid. She imagined a great dark red bulb glowing and throbbing just under the mantle of muscle and bone. The air around her seemed to press closer, vibrating like a harp-string. She remembered vaguely reading somewhere that when you laid your head against someone's chest the pulse you heard was your own, pumping the blood through the arteries of your ear. Suddenly, she was aware that the great red monster was inside *her*, pounding violently, faster, faster, bursting against her ribs. The blood raced round her body like water in a circulator. She gasped : "I can't breathe."

Varagin put both arms round her, pressing her face into his neck. For a moment, he held her so tightly she was really frightened. "Now can you breathe?" he said. No, she mouthed, suffocating. Her nose was flattened against her face and the muscles in her chest tightened like a clamp. When he released her, she thought he was smiling.

"Don't think about it," he said. "Thinking makes anything difficult. By tomorrow, your problem should be solved. Permanently."

She was breathing unsteadily and her pulse seemed to have been crushed out of existence. Presently, she felt better. "I'm sorry," she said. "I think I must have panicked." She liked it when he talked about death in that matter-of-fact, slightly flippant way, as though it were a mere triviality, a disagreeable commonplace, like a late breakfast or an injection. It was not that she was any the less frightened. But if she could smile and pretend to be brave, she found, in the end, it made her *feel* braver. This time, when she laid her head on his shoulder, she concentrated on the warmth that came through his thin shirt, and the movement of his ribs against her own. After a while her mind emptied, and she drifted, idly, on the borders of sleep. She felt a faint touch, like a fingertip, moving through her hair, but her perceptions were drowsy and the sensation became confused, in a dreamlike way, with a wild wind on an unfamiliar planet, combing out each separate strand against a rose-coloured sky. She found it so difficult to imagine pink. She had grown up in a world where the colours were drab and few: grey rocks, brown earth, grey-brown shadows. She had seen the flame on a firepot grow from blue to violet, from violet to gold. She had seen ashes glowing red. And on the computer, there had been pictures in cheap technicolour, thin and garish like paintings on tin. But when she did not look at it directly, she could *feel* the pinkness, in her dream, feather-soft, cloud-soft, pressed against her cheek. She was sleeping on clouds, somewhere high up, with the sunrise far below struggling to break through. Above her, the pinkness faded into infinite space, cool and fearless. Stars winked like eyes. Neither the sunrise nor the clouds disturbed her territory. She was a part of them, a wisp of air, floating, mindlessly, in an immeasurable gulf of sky. Her dream clouded over with pinkness, and she closed her eyes against it, so it would not go away, and abandoned herself to sensation.

Varagin stroked her, very gently, like a kitten, feeling her curling round him in her sleep; the touch of her breath, her cheek, her thigh. His hands were unhurried but his mind moved, restlessly, in the circle of the darkness. He had pulled his jacket over the light so there was only a faint glow in the chamber, insufficient to reach the walls. In her dream, he wanted Pzyche to feel the presence of light, and be comforted. But he did not want her to wake and see the bitterness in his

[212]

eyes. He had waited on the edge of death before, watching life sliding away from him, vivid and perilous, afraid (only a fool is never afraid) but without conscious regret. Only now, when death was as certain as the opening of a door, he knew what he would have given for just a little more time. Another day, another night; a season; a year. Pzyche lay very close to him, but he wanted her closer, closer than touch, closer than need. He wanted to possess her, physically and mentally. He knew that whatever he did she would grow separate from him, uncontrollable as a weed, hurting him, always; but it did not seem to matter. Being in love is wanting without fulfilment, an eternal hiatus between what you must have and what you cannot have. Even the commune could not take that away from him. He had grown up without tenderness, and he knew he would never be tender. He had used Livadya and the memory of her love to seal himself off from emotional commitment, out in the cold: the easy option. He could never love lightly; it would always hurt too much. But Pzyche was very different from Livadya. Sometimes, in her strange, cold moods, he saw something of his own implacable withdrawal. Understanding had come to him, unwanted, and now it was too late. He could feel her breast, pressed against his side, but he could not even kiss her, in case she drew away. He touched her, very lightly, so she would scarcely feel it. He knew bitterness edged with pleasure, pleasure edged with bitterness. "What would you do with her," he asked himself, "even if you had time? She knows nothing." Neither reason nor impulse answered him. It was not necessary. He did not even know if she loved him, or if she felt anything for him at all. Now, he would never find out. He thought of waking her, making her talk; but her sleep seemed too tenuous to be lightly broken. Perhaps he was afraid of what she might say. The night drew on. He lay, unresting, wishing he had the ability, or the desire, to hold on to this moment of time forever.

Perhaps, thought Tnoe, the night will go on indefinitely. When

[213]

you are waiting for something, something vital or terrible, it is impossible to imagine that the waiting will ever end. She thought she had slept quite a long time, but it was still utterly dark. Derec had put out the light hours ago. They had talked for a while, carefully, trying not to speculate on a nonexistent future. "It's my fault," Tnoe had said, with all the luxury of self-blame. "I thought it was so important, not having any money. It's nothing now." Later, she had cried a little. "If only you hadn't come."

"Rubbish," said Derec. "Do you wish *you* hadn't come?"

"No," Tnoe whispered. "No, I suppose I don't. I was *meant* to come. It was what my mother wanted."

"If your mother had known about all this," said Derec, "I'm damn sure she would have preferred you to stay at home."

He held her for a while, very tightly, until she stopped crying. Presently, she remarked: "I wish I believed in God. It would be much more comfortable."

"Gods thrive on trouble," Derec said drily. "Atheism is the only rational attitude to religion; anything else is pure hypocrisy. Science has proved conclusively that faith is a behavioural syndrome."

"Are you sure?" asked Tnoe.

"No," said Derec. "Not really. But that's probably because I'm a coward."

She could not remember falling asleep. But she was wide awake now, staring into the darkness. Close by, Derec was lying, turned away from her; she could hear the faint rasp of his breathing. He had a slight tendency to asthma which had evidently been aggravated by the atmosphere in the cavern. She pressed herself against his back, thankful just because he was there. It was a nice back, a broad, solid, reliable back. She could feel his shoulder-blades straining against his shirt, the bumps of his vertebrae. The heat from his body seemed to flow into her. She realized with a queer pang of terror how warm the chamber had become. The first time she had visited the city,

[214]

with Pzyche, she remembered shivering in Udulf's leathertype ... "Pzyche," she thought, with a sudden impulse of conscience. "I ought to be with her. She might need me." She did not want to leave the comfort of Derec's back. She would have to crawl away, soundlessly, feeling her way along the walls. She lay for a little while, thinking about moving. But she had a feeling, based on she knew not what, that Pzyche did not need her just now.

19

Up on the planetface, dawn was not far off. A pall of cloud hung over the horizon, so low that cloud and land almost met. Beyond, there was a livid strip of sky. In the camp, lights showed here and there and then went out. Tousled figures, sleepy and sleepless, began to congregate at the minehead. Some were less enthusiastic than others. "They've got a secret weapon," said a man who had never seen a denominator. Someone else expressed morose contempt. There was another interminable period of waiting, and then gradually the chink of sky seemed to widen, like the lifting of an eyelid, and the topmost rim of the sun peered over the horizon, shooting a single cold green glance across the plain. In the cavern, Caleth and Tirril saw the guard doubled and trebled. Men were moving about, checking their weapons. There was a sound of voices, hushed and mute like whispers and then suddenly loud, where the wayward echoes of the cavern caught a slight inflection and distorted it out of all proportion. "They've got a flask of kaffine," said Tirril.

Caleth did not comment.

"I know it's very trivial," Tirril remarked, "but I wish we had some kaffine."

"Trivial things are the most important," said Caleth. "Or so it feels."

When the others came back, he passed round the last of the spirits. No one talked much. Tnoe swallowed awkwardly and felt vaguely sick; she told herself she was not used to alcohol for breakfast. When everyone had had a mouthful there was still a little left. "We'll leave it to our luck," said Caleth.

More waiting. The darkness did not seem to get any lighter. It must be like this, Tnoe thought, before an execution. She remembered hearing an eccentric great uncle, many years ago, arguing in favour of capital punishment. At the time, she had been rather shocked to find she agreed with him. Her mother's moral and political views, like those of most Ifingens for the past two or three thousand years, were vaguely and ineffectually liberal. "I wouldn't wish this on anyone," Tnoe thought with sudden passion. "No matter what they'd done."

A long time later, she realized she could see shapes in the darkness, the outlines of huge columns or stalactites. There was a queer, hunched up stone a little way away, like a sentinel. In the chamber, it was still utterly black. Beside her, Derec moved restlessly. His arm was very sore where he had not been able to treat the burn and he found the pain intensely irritating. It was so unimportant. The atmosphere was warmer than ever and a trickle of sweat teased its way down the back of his neck.

"It won't get much lighter." Varagin.

Across the pit, almost all the men were on their feet. There was no more talking. The sharp click of a safety lock carried distinctively in the silence. Presently, one of them came and stood right on the edge; even at that distance they could feel his cold unblinking stare.

"Will he ask us to surrender?" whispered Tnoe.

"No," said Varagin.

More waiting. It was like the moment at the end of a space-flight, thought Tnoe, when you think the ship will never land. Ages later, or so it seemed, Caleth said: "We'd better move."

No one was particularly relieved. Outside, Tnoe realized she had left her jacket behind, but it was too late now. The darkness had turned from black to grey and they could see each other's faces, pale and featureless, and the movement of their eyes. Derec was carrying his denominator but he dared not touch the

[217]

trigger; his fingers were slippery with sweat. In the range of the lamps, they could see the men moving in single file along the ledge. Two or three others slipped over the edge of the pit and vanished in the shadows. They were wearing night-visors, useless in the pitch dark but dangerously effective now the dregs of the morning had leaked in.

"They are coming," said Caleth.

Then it happened. For an instant, it was as if everything blinked: the light, the darkness, the shadows. The rock itself seemed to twitch, imperceptibly, like an animal twitching in its sleep. There was a moment after when none of them were quite sure of what they had seen. Then Tnoe knew a sensation of claustrophobia so violent and terrifying she thought she was going to faint. She was in an elevator, falling. The air above seemed to be coming down on her like an avalanche. She tried to scream, but no sound came out. On the ledge, one of the men had lost his footing and fell several spans. There was a curse and a shout. "Move!" ordered Scharm. If his instinct gave him any warning, he did not listen. He was totally preoccupied with the business of extermination.

There was a shock as if the very fabric of the planet was being torn apart, and the chasm opened. A column of flame leapt a hundred spans into the air and hissed against the cavern roof. A scarlet glare dimmed the daylight; red shadows danced in the city. Scharm was standing on the very edge of the pit. His face turned red, and then black. His eyeballs withered. For a second his body seemed to hang, impossibly, over the gap, borne on the updraught of heat. Then he was gone. On the ledge, the men clung to the rock as though paralysed, their cries lost in the noise of rending stone. Tnoe stuffed her fingers in her ears and closed her eyes. She felt as if the impact of air and sound was crushing her very skull out of shape. Presently, she realized someone was gripping her shoulders, shaking her, tugging her. When she opened her eyes, she saw that it was Pzyche.

And then the world went mad. The ground heaved and split.

[218]

They were thrown sideways, tumbling, helplessly, down a rocking see-saw of stone. Huge stalagmites leaned like trees in a gale. Right above them, a vast column cracked like an eggshell, the outer wall peeling off in a single shard many feet thick and crashing towards them. Shadow stretched across the light. Pzyche felt a weight on her back, pressing her down against the rock. Varagin. For an instant, she thought she heard his voice, cool and quiet amidst the chaos. "Shut your eyes." There was a moment of impact which seemed to loosen every joint in her body. Then stillness. Something wet trickled down her cheek. Blood. Not her own. She looked up. Miraculously, the rock was suspended just above them, shielding them from the tumult of breaking stone. Enormous splinters fell like leaves. Beyond, the light had changed.

"Come on!" Caleth's voice, hoarse with dust. They scrambled out, awkwardly, onto a pile of rubble. Somehow, they were still alive. There was a cut on Varagin's temple and Tnoe could not use her left hand. Only Pzyche noticed she was crying. The earthquake paused, as though holding its breath. All around them teetering masses of stone seemed to be balanced on a needlepoint, leaning at fantastic angles half a degree from destruction. The red glare had diminished and the desolation was filled with a pale cold light. Dust hovered over cracks and crevices. Beyond the pit, the ledge had gone. For a moment, when they hesitated, there was no other movement in the whole of the city.

"The light," Pzyche said, bewildered, "where is it coming from?"

"*There*," said Caleth.

Far above, the earth had opened. The cliffs were scarred white where they had been torn apart. Beyond, remote and impossibly beautiful, there was a tiny patch of sky.

"This way," Caleth said, and they followed him, without thought or plan. The floor of the city was broken into huge jigsaw-pieces of stone which tilted perilously at the touch of a foot. Ahead of them loomed a giant stalactite, blasted as though by a thunderbolt; its outer wall had so nearly crushed them only moments before. Now, only the skeleton remained, a twisted fretwork jutting towards the riven cliffs like a fragment of some ancient limb. As they drew nearer they saw it might once have been a stair.

There was no time for either hope or fear. Tnoe glanced up once and saw the precarious spiral winding dizzily above them until it was lost to view among the shadows of the cavern roof. She could not see if it ended or if it reached the rift and the distant glimpse of sky. I can't do it, she thought automatically, looking at the terrible climb and the gap-toothed grin of the nearest bend where two or three steps were missing altogether. But the very distance seemed unreal. Caleth took the lead, followed by Tirril and the girls; Derec and Varagin brought up the rear. They could only go in single file. When they came to the first gap, Tnoe took her sister's hand and did not look down; there was no time to hesitate. Soon, she was gasping for breath and a violent stitch was stabbing at her side. She found herself wishing she had attended her dance class more regularly or joined a gymnastics club as her mother had suggested. Ahead of her Pzyche, too, appeared to be flagging, but when Tirril faltered Tnoe saw her thrust her hand savagely into the small of his back. It was a violation of his territory, but the imminence of danger seemed to have broken down the last barriers of her conditioning. Once, Tnoe stumbled, and Pzyche caught her arm and pulled her to her feet almost brutally. Come on, she mouthed, but she had no breath to spare for speech. Her face was so white and fierce it looked hardly human any more.

When Tnoe looked up again she was surprised to see how close they were to the roof. The cliffs were drawing in on either side and the thread of sky had widened: it looked dazzlingly bright against the darkness of the cavern but she could not make out what colour it was. The feeling was returning, painfully, to her left hand and she wondered if and when she was going to get her second wind. In the end, she decided there was no such thing as a second wind anyway. Behind her, Derec was breathing hoarsely. No one looked back. They could all hear the subdued grumble of unsettling rubble, the hiss of hot gases escaping from widening cracks. The sound grew and then seemed to die away into a murmur, deceptively gentle, which shuddered through the rock like a sigh. Tnoe thought: It's going to go quiet again. She was horribly afraid of the quiet. A second wind, she discovered, is merely the impulse of energy that you get from returning fear. Suddenly, they all found they could move a little faster.

Round the next bend the cliffs closed in, and Tnoe was able to press herself briefly against the security of a solid wall. Far below, the silence was broken. Derec, glancing down, saw a cloud of boiling vapour rushing towards them and beyond, a tumult of liquid fire which heaved and bubbled like the contents of a monstrous cauldron. The sudden draught of heat stifled what little breath they had left. Noise filled them. Tnoe felt Derec pushing her from behind and somehow she managed to go on. She had stuffed her fingers in her ears but it did not seem to make any difference and she needed both hands to climb. Then the angry yellow light was cut off as they plunged into the depths of the cliff and for a few horrible moments she struggled on in the noise and the dark, feeling the rock shake beneath her. Gradually it grew quieter. Ahead, she heard Caleth, calling out something unintelligible. She had just time to think it sounded vaguely encouraging before she found herself stumbling out of the heat and the darkness and into the open air. Behind, the ridge was torn by the earthquake; mustard-coloured fumes were pouring through the gap. A flurry of fine rain blew in her face, cool and sweet on the tongue. She staggered to a halt, purposeless, blissfully thankful for air and light. She would not have cared if the world ended, if only she could get her breath back first.

In the camp of the enemy, the last of Scharm's men were running to and fro in panic. The tents were flattened and the pithead tower had gone. A mottled web of cloud was stretched across the sky. But above where the shaft had been the cloud seemed to be sucked earthwards, drawn into a thickening column of ochreous vapour. Curling flakes of ash floated on the wind. The column grew denser every second. Scarlet lightnings licked about the base.

"Caleth!" called Varagin. His voice was sharp and imperative. "The Novamark!"

To their left, they saw three black figures, running as though with a purpose. Beyond, there was a squat saucer-shaped object, perched at a precarious angle on crooked legs. The spacetray. In that moment, Tnoe knew they were going to make it. They *had* to make it. No one could get this far, and then fail. Already, Caleth and Varagin were racing to intercept the men. "Derec!" she cried, her voice cracking. He sprinted after them. Tirril and the girls, still exhausted and breathless, followed as fast as they could. The first man was too far ahead and they saw Caleth stop and draw his denominator. He took aim, carefully, and then fired. Once only. The second man rounded on Varagin, weapon in hand. He moved too slowly; perhaps he thought his opponent was unarmed. From somewhere, Varagin produced a long knife, so thin it was scarcely more than a needle-gleam in the daylight. The man crumpled up as if he was falling asleep. Only Caleth recognized the art of Nepeth, as sweet and painless as a release. He ran back, but it was not necessary. Derec took the third man, hitting him, clumsily, with the butt of his denominator.

"You're supposed to pull the trigger," remarked Varagin, unsmiling.

They scrambled through the hatch into the spaceship. There was no time to let down the steps. Inside, they found themselves in a single chamber, shaped like a soup tureen and almost equally cramped. Padded seats were built into the curve of the walls. Tnoe sat down, rather quickly, and felt for the safety belt,

[222]

but when she pulled it came away in her hand. Derec pressed a switch. "At least the lights work," he said. In the middle, there was a hexagonal computer complex, glittering with innumerable controls. It all looked completely incomprehensible. Caleth scanned the main panel and pressed a button. Tirril slipped through the hatch even as it closed.

The next few seconds were almost unendurable. Tnoe gripped the arms of her seat, digging her nails into the fabric; afterwards, she found she had peeled it right off. The computer began a countdown. Ten, nine, eight . . . "Never mind that," said Varagin. "Just go."

He pressed Emergency Take-off.

The ship lurched and seemed to rear up on its side. The antigravity thrust must have failed and they were thrown one on top of another across the tilting floor. Outside, there was a grinding crack, as though the ground beneath them was splitting open. The engines pounded, uselessly. The walls shook. "This is it," thought Tnoe. "We're going to be killed after all . . ." And then they were airborne.

Varagin crawled across the floor and managed to adjust the faulty mechanism. They scrambled back to their seats. "Fifteen seconds to atmospheric exit," said Caleth, fortuitously identifying the correct gauge. "Flightspeed two one. Four one. Six one . . ."

"I hope the ship can stand it," remarked Varagin.

The pressure stabilizers were working overtime and Tnoe felt herself being squashed against her seat. She could not get her breath. She wondered if she would go mad with claustrophobia first or merely be horribly space-sick. It was much too hot. Beside her, Pzyche's face had gone bright pink. Some strange distortion of the air made everything look fluid and unstable; any moment, she thought, the controls would begin to detach themselves from the computer and swim away. The ship seemed to have grown to enormous size while she was shrunken into a corner, as small as a cricket. The walls glowed.

[223]

Three seconds, said Caleth, but his voice was lost in the whine of overcharged systems.

Exit . . .

It was all over in a moment. The pressure decreased and the interior of the ship seemed to crystallize into its normal shape. The silence of deep space was all around them.

Caleth set a course for Fingstar. "Flightspeed eleven one," he said. "Increasing. How fast do you think she'll go?"

"I have no idea," said Varagin. "I daresay we'll find out when the shield starts to split. Personally, I think we should remove ourselves from the vicinity of Krake as rapidly as possible."

Caleth said: "Let's take a look," and pressed a button. The shutters slid back from the lower windows. Behind them, the receding planetface towered like a wall. At that distance the contours of the land were lost and they could see nothing but a grey featureless mass. Pale swathes of cloud drifted across it. Pzyche tried to visualize the small circle of her life, lost in those nameless wastes; but her mind shrank. She had always thought of Krake as the castle, the ridge, the empty plain. That was something she could understand. But it became meaningless amidst the desolation of that vast cold world. She thought, blindly: "I didn't even know my own planet . . ."

Suddenly, there was something else. A tiny flicker which grew and widened, spreading across the planetface with horrifying speed. Now, it was a glittering crack, hundreds of miles long. The planet crust seemed to be peeling away from it like skin around a burn. And then it was as if the ship itelf had begun to go backwards and the planet was rushing towards them, a dense eruption of matter bursting through the atmosphere and spewing into outer space. The pale light of O fell on curdled billows, solid as dough.

"Fourteen one," read Caleth. "How's the pressure?"

"Unhealthy. Try fifteen."

"Can't we go into timespeed?" asked Tirril.

[224]

Varagin did not trouble to answer.

Gradually, the planet slid away from them. Stars lifted over the rim. About the equator, cloudy masses broke and re-formed, drawn into a vortex which shrank, spinning, down the vast maw of space. Fossil appeared to their left, pockmarked with shadows; Wormwood was hidden. Far below, Ingellan gleamed, briefly, against a darkness without spark or star.

Caleth steadied their speed, rechecked the inertial navigation.

Varagin said: "Pressure substandard."

Behind them, the dark globe of Krake diminished, slowly, until it fitted into a single window. Now, even Fossil was swallowed up in its outline. There was a long period when the planet did not seem to be getting smaller at all. As so often happens with space travel at normal speeds, it looked as if the ship was hardly moving. Pzyche felt a queer kind of panic. Krake was left behind her forever and her whole universe was reduced to a tiny module, suspended in space. The galaxy stretched ahead of her, vast beyond comprehension, a glittering soup of suns and stars, asteroids and nebula, white dwarfs and black holes. On a thousand different planets a thousand different civilizations went about the business of evolution, reproducing and regressing, making war and peace, dying and being born under the auspices of nonexistent gods. Somewhere in a primaeval ocean a few intelligent atoms were creating a molecular revolution. Pzyche knew it was real because she had learnt all about it, theory and practice, legend and history, from the infallible teachings of the computer. But she had never had any proof. Computers were made by people, and people told lies. Deep inside her, she did not really believe there was anything out there at all.

Beyond the window, the shape of Krake suddenly changed. The sphere seemed to stretch and warp as though it were made of plasticine. One side bulged outwards, impossibly, like an exploding pear, dragging the planet from its axis. And then everything was swallowed up in an appalling brightness which

[225]

seemed to burst against the very walls of space. Caleth felt for the switch to close the shutters, but it was too late. A light filled the ship which took the lids from their eyes. "Now," Pzyche thought, "there is nothing left at all ..." But the thought dwindled and was lost in the searing radiance that burned into her brain.

20

It was one o'clock in the morning when they arrived on Fing-star. "This is ridiculous," said Pzyche, bewildered. "Time lag," Tnoe explained. They made a rough landing on the emergency spacestage which was kept for such occasions and almost never used. One of the engines caught fire but the three firemen had gone to a literary dinner and a mechanic doused the flames with a manual extinguisher. There was an ambulance but no doctors. Fortunately, no one was hurt. Caleth dealt tactfully with the forces of bureaucracy, represented by a tired-looking man in a dressing-gown roused from somewhere on the premises. Derec lost his temper. Tnoe took the opportunity to retreat into the facility room and have a wash. "Tomorrow," she said through gritted teeth, "*nothing* is going to interfere with my bath."

Pzyche had followed her. In the mirror, her face glistened with sweat and dirt. There were huge drawn shadows under her eyes. She had lost all her earlier sparkle and her voice sounded flat and dull. "We're still alive," she said.

"I know," said Tnoe, "but it hasn't hit me yet."

I ought to be excited, Pzyche was thinking. I am on another planet. I am going to see all the things I have only seen in pictures. What is the matter with me? She felt like a saucepan which had just been taken off the boil.

Outside, Caleth had obtained the loan of a landmovile. They drove out of the spaceport through Camarest. Beyond the side-screens, Pzyche glimpsed dark cluttered buildings, random lights. She did not want to peer out. She told herself she was too tired. On the edge of University Complex there was a stretch of water, dappled with moonlight; sallowiles trailed their membrous branches in the stream. As they crossed the bridge she saw a solitary leaf floating on a ripple, sharp-edged against the image of the moon. It was a detail so vivid, so utterly unlike anything she had ever known, that suddenly her eyes hurt her, and she could not look. And for the rest of her life, if ever she saw sallowiles growing by a stream, she would feel the pricking of unfamiliar tears.

At Caleth's flat, they had supper. "It must be suppertime," Tnoe said, "somewhere." Caleth produced several bottles of a heavy red wine which made Pzyche sleepy and Tirril garrulous. Tnoe reflected idly on the recent fluctuations in her financial position. "I suppose," she said, "now the planet's gone, I must be destitute again. If only we'd picked up a few pieces of mammonite when we were in the cavern. But I never thought of it . . ."

"A few pieces," said Varagin, "would bring you nothing but trouble. The market is very—sensitive. As it is, you now own sixty per cent of an unexplored asteroid belt . . ." Tnoe laughed. "Unless, of course, you choose to sell."

"Sell?" queried Derec, sharply. "But—"

"I gather," Caleth said, "that Varagin has something in mind."

"I have an authorization to buy those shares from Tnoe for the sum of ten million tela," said Varagin, "to be paid immediately through a finance company in Camarest. All it requires is her signature—and mine."

"Ten million tela!" Tnoe murmured faintly. "But I've only just got used to being poor again!"

"No finance company will pay out that kind of money for shares in something that doesn't exist any more," Derec said scornfully.

"I said the deal was going *through* a finance company," said Varagin. "It isn't their money. And it isn't for them to ask questions. If the freightship had not been destroyed, the shares

[228]

would still be extremely valuable. The company does not know the details of the situation and, being Ifingen, will not presume to speculate. They will merely honour their side of the bargain. All we have to do is sign."

"How much," asked Derec, suspiciously, "does your signature cost?"

"I was thinking of a split," said Varagin. "For example—seventy-five : twenty-five."

"You want twenty-five per cent?" Derec was indignant.

"I want seventy-five per cent."

In the end, they agreed to fifty : fifty. Caleth, amused, felt quite sure that was what Varagin had intended all along. Tirril drew up the agreement.

"Who is the lucky buyer?" asked Derec. "Are we allowed to know?"

"I doubt it," said Caleth.

"All that matters," said Varagin, "is that I am the one who will be held responsible. Which is why I should like my share, immediately, in the form of a bond which I can exchange on any planet in the League. I shall be leaving on the first flight tomorrow morning."

"First flight where?" asked Tnoe.

"Wherever it goes," said Varagin.

The girls slept in Caleth's bed; the men in the living room. Caleth and Varagin talked late. The lights were turned down and Tnoe, exhilarated by drink and deliverance, had turned the picture to the wall. "I'll buy you a nicer one," she said. "Not one of those horrid natural food pictures. Something cheerful . . ."

Around five o'clock, Tirril woke up and decided to go home. He found it curiously difficult to walk straight. Arriving nearly an hour later in the street where his mother lived, he went into the house and loudly announced his return. Unfortunately, it was the wrong house. Owing to an administrative error typical of Ifingen bureaucracy, all the front doors in the street had the same key code. By the time Tirril had located his own entrance hall, large numbers of irate people had been rudely awoken at least two hours earlier than was their custom. Tirril, who was hungry again, requested breakfast. His mother, three sisters, and an aging great-aunt came fluttering down the stairs, wearing assorted expressions of shock and disapproval.

"The planet blew up," Tirril explained, "so I had to come home."

"Darling," said his mother, "it's six o'clock in the morning. Don't you feel you're being a little bit thoughtless?"

"But I might have been killed!" said Tirril.

"I will mention it to your uncle," promised his mother, "tomorrow."

In Caleth's bedroom, Tnoe told her sister: "You can have half my share, of course."

"I don't know anything about money," said Pzyche.

After a while, she asked: "Where shall I go?"

"You'll stay with me," Tnoe said. "You'd like to, wouldn't you?" They had turned the light out and she could not see Pzyche's face at all.

"I thought you were going to marry Derec."

"Yes, of course," Tnoe responded. "But it won't make any difference."

"You love him, don't you?" Pzyche said, an odd note in her voice. "What is it like, being in love?"

"It's difficult to explain," said Tnoe. She tried a few muddled sentences which petered out in confusion. "It's difficult," she repeated. "It creeps up on you without your noticing, and suddenly the whole world seems to turn upside-down. It's like the kind of stomach ache that you get from looking at ice cream when you're desperately hungry. Or like standing on a cliff edge, and looking down, and not being able to see the bottom . . ."

"Does it make you happy?" Pzyche asked.

[230]

"N—no," said Tnoe. "Not always. Sometimes, not ever. Some people seem to fall in love just to make themselves miserable. I'll try to explain. When I first met Derec, we argued all the time. In a way, it was exhilarating. I'd never met anyone who disagreed with so many attitudes which I'd been brought up to hold sacred. Life and art and things. He used to say that I didn't *really* believe the things I'd been taught: it was just laziness, or insularity, or the habit of acceptance. And suddenly I found myself wondering if he might be right. I loved Mummy very much but theatrical people live in a totally artificial world. I didn't belong. Being the daughter of an actress isn't like being an actress: people like you, or tolerate you, for your mother's sake, but you don't really matter in yourself. Derec seemed to understand all that. It was wonderful, having someone who understood. Even when we argued, it was wonderful. He was so utterly different and exciting and *real*." Unexpectedly, she continued: "When Mummy died, I should have married him. I told myself I couldn't because of the money: he was a student, you see, and too poor to support me. But I think perhaps I was deceiving myself. We'd have managed somehow. *I* was the one who couldn't face not having any money. So I ran away ... I'm glad I did it now, though. I'm glad I met you. Even last night in the cave, I didn't regret it."

"What if you'd been killed?" Pzyche asked.

"I'd have been dead, I suppose," said Tnoe. "So I still wouldn't have been able to regret."

"How do you know?" Pzyche said.

But Tnoe was not listening. "Anyway," she went on, yawning sleepily, "everything has worked out beautifully now. I shall marry Derec, and have lots of money, and you must take your share, and not argue, because it's just as much yours as mine ..."

"I shan't need it," Pzyche whispered. But Tnoe was asleep.

Pzyche wondered if she should ask her for a ring, or something to keep. Tnoe wore two or three rings. But a ring was just a cold band of metal which had nothing in particular to do with its owner. In the dark, Pzyche could not see her sister at all, but she imagined her face as she had seen it so often before, closed up with sleep: the limp mouth, the crumpled hair, the spidery shadow of her lashes lying on her cheek. When she shut her eyes, she could see Tnoe quite clearly. So she knew everything would be all right.

The next morning, Pzyche found Varagin in the living room, alone. He was wearing his black leathertype and blowing savagely on a mug of kaffine. "You're going," she said.

"Yes," said Varagin.

"What time is the first flight?"

"I've missed it."

"Why?" Pzyche asked.

Varagin said cryptically: "I overslept."

"I'm glad you haven't gone," Pzyche said with constraint. Suddenly, conversation seemed not merely difficult but impossible. She continued, rather breathlessly: "I wanted to—to see you. I don't think I ever said thank you."

"You have nothing for which to thank me," snapped Varagin. "Everything I did was entirely in my own interest. Otherwise I wouldn't have done it."

Pzyche murmured: "Even killing Borogoyn?"

"Especially killing Borogoyn," said Varagin. "He was very trying to work with."

He took a mouthful of kaffine and found to his annoyance he had scalded his throat. Pzyche waited, politely, for him to catch his breath. "Where are you going?" she asked.

Varagin attempted a shrug. "Anywhere," he said. "The Ark, the Distaff, the Wheel. I am going to see cities, and trees. I might even manage a pink sunrise, if I don't oversleep." Suddenly, she knew he was smiling. "Have you anything to pack?"

"No," Pzyche whispered.

[232]

"Then let's go."

"Do you think," asked Tnoe, "she will be happy with him?" She and Caleth were sitting on the balcony lingering over a late breakfast. Pzyche and Varagin had left over an hour ago and Derec had gone into University Complex to collect some books on the evolution of the spleen. Life, Tnoe thought, was very nearly back to normal.

"Does it matter?" said Caleth.

"Of course it matters! I am going to marry Derec and be passionately happy and I wanted so much for Pzyche to be happy too."

"You talk as if happiness is something you can have to order," said Caleth. "That's nonsense. Happiness is a rare, magical moment that comes before death, or before birth, or the first time you look out at the stars. You cannot say: 'I *will* be happy.' Content is another matter. But it isn't really very good for you to be contented all the time. People who are too contented grow fat and comfortable; it is suffering and misfortune which shape the soul. Look at yourself, Tnoe. Because of what you have been through, you are a stronger, more complete personality. Pzyche is young and unformed; she will grow faster in bad weather. You and I should not presume to wish her anything but courage and the ability to hope."

"If only Varagin will take care of her!" Tnoe said without much confidence.

"She must learn to take care of herself," said Caleth. "He knows that."

Presently, Tnoe asked him: "Do you think *I* will get fat and comfortable?" She sounded rather attracted by the idea.

"No," said Caleth. "You will have problems like everyone else. Derec will work too hard and be frustrated when people refuse to accept his ideas. Old friends of your mother will insist on coming to your wedding. The economic situation, as usual, will deteriorate. Your neighbours will demand your sympathy and your children will reject it. One day, you will pluck a grey hair from your left temple. I foresee a life of unending misery and discomfort. But you will never be bored."

Tnoe laughed and then cried a little, though she did not know why. "Will you be here?" she asked him, dabbing at her eyes with a crumpled disposable which might once have been Sateleptra's.

"Yes," said Caleth. "I'll be here."

Tnoe poured herself some more greentea. It was cold. "Do you think," she said, "I will ever see Pzyche again?"

"Maybe," said Caleth. "Who knows? I cannot promise you anything. But I think perhaps we will all meet again, someday. Even the Professor . . ."

Tnoe said, surprised: "You sound almost religious."

Caleth smiled. "Religion is like fungus or middle-aged spread: it grows on you with time. In the old days, they used to talk about the music of the spheres. Now, we call it physics, and the Theory of Universal Probability. But the music is still there, for those who want to hear. Go down to the beach and pick up a shell, one of those white trumpet-shells with wrinkled lips. If you put it to your ear, you will hear the sound of every sea in the universe breaking on every shore, until the world ends. I need no other token of immortality."

"Yes," said Tnoe, "but when is Someday?"

"That," said Caleth, "is the question."

In the flat, they heard the shutting of a door and a familiar hasty step. Tnoe looked at Caleth; but he only smiled. She left him alone in the sunlight, and went inside to propose to Derec.

Owing to the complexities of interstellar time zones, Krater was at dinner when they brought him the news. At the far end of the table, the representatives of various questionable governments sat in their assorted costumes eating with their assorted table manners. The delicacies of seven systems were spread out in front of them and a bizarre selection of cutlery waited at every elbow. One man was spearing small white peas on the point of a very thin knife. Another was using his fingers to roll a mixture of nutmeal and minced vegetable in a purple lettuce leaf. The representative of the most questionable government was not eating at all. Despite the formal dress and careful courtesy of his guests Krater, as usual, lounged in his chair, with his shirt open to the waist. There were old wine stains on his sleeve. It was as though he fed his jaded ego by showing contempt for these illicit ambassadors of young and greedy powers. In the bluish light his large immobile face was the colour of watered clay. He could not remember when he had last sat in the sun.

A servant brought him the communication. It was brief and to the point. As Krater read, a certain stillness descended over the table. His face did not change; the plastic surgeons had seen to that. Only the loose skin round his eyes moved and twitched like the skin round the eyes of a lizard. Then the unheard of happened. He stood up.

The representatives murmured and shifted in their chairs. Krater towered over the table, his huge hand crumpling, uselessly, at the scrap of paper. An odd little sound, silent as a hiss, came from the crack between his lips. Under the yellowed skin of his chest, they saw all the muscles flinch as though from a blow. Then he pitched forward onto the table and lay still.

They felt for his pulse, but his wrist was too thick. Gradually he grew colder, and a spittle of sauce congealed on his face. Presently, the doctor came and confirmed that he was dead.

In half an hour it was all over the Undercity.

[235]